I0452554

THE PERFECT
ANGEL

A *LANCE PRIEST* NOVEL

CHRISTOPHER
METCALF

TT Tree Tunnel Publishing

Published by
Tree Tunnel Publishing, LLC
Tulsa, Oklahoma

Cover photo courtesy Wikimedia Commons: Artist Vassil
Sépulcre Arc-en-Barrois 111008 12.jpg. Back cover artwork
courtesy Wikimedia Commons (public domain).

ISBN: 978-0-9837447-9-5

www.treetunnelpublishing.com

For angels mine

The world is flat.
Don't believe it?
Ask someone who fell off the edge.
— Anonymous

ACKNOWLEDGMENTS

Too many to thank. It all starts with Diana, my Marta, my everything. Kids keep growing and changing and inspiring their dad. Need to thank many for feedback and encouragement, including Jim, Jay, John, Susan, Josh and Rick. Cathy did another excellent job correcting and improving my words. Want to thank all who contact the author and provide reviews and thoughts. Writing is a lonely endeavor. And again, I must extend appreciation to Google Maps[®] for allowing a domesticated, land-locked writer to travel the world.

CIA Mission Statement

We are the nation's first line of defense. We accomplish what others cannot accomplish and go where others cannot go. We carry out our mission by:

- Collecting information that reveals the plans, intentions and capabilities of our adversaries and provides the basis for decision and action.
- Producing timely analysis that provides insight, warning and opportunity to the President and decision makers charged with protecting and advancing America's interests.
- Conducting covert action at the direction of the President to preempt threats or achieve US policy objectives.

Message 1 - 11:49 p.m. March17... (*Russian, translated*)
"Hello baby, darling. My love... I know.
"Did you see the moon earlier? So big, so bright...
"It was Vienna... and that night at the top of that mountain in Colorado.
"Do you remember?"

Message 2 - 9:07 p.m. May 11... (*English*)
"Is this it? (indistinguishable noise)
"Is this where I say goodbye? How I'm supposed to do it?
"I tried. Just yesterday I tried again."

Message 3 - 7:12 p.m. July 28... (*Russian children's song, translated*)
"Once there was a grandma who had two merry geese."
"One was grey and the other was white. Two very merry geese."
"One was grey and the other was white. Two very merry geese."

Message 4 - 5:28 p.m. October 11... (*Russian, translated*)
"I'm sorry. I just...
"It was never supposed to be this way. Me here, you gone. Never.
"Can I... can I tell you how I am, where I am? Can you tell me? (indistinguishable noise) "I'm sorry. I miss you..."

Message 5 - 4:02 a.m. April 17 ... (*Turkish, translated*)
"I love you. I need you. Get ready. Call the doctor, now. Be prepared."

Prologue

Relentless was the killer.

Endless was his energy. Limitless was the extent to which he was willing to push, to exceed. He championed a lost cause, a lost love. This made him dangerous, deadly. It also made him perfect. But alas, perfection is a curse.

For once perfection is achieved, it can never be so again. And once perfection is lost, it can never be repaired, never be perfect again.

Something had to be done.

The leaks started four years ago. Someone without Seibel's unique view of the world, his world, would have missed them. The leaking of vital information affiliated with his Special Activities Division unit within the CIA didn't show up in any evidence admissible in court. It was subtle.

The first was an echo of sorts. He detected fragments of precise information about top-secret activities in Baghdad in

1991 relayed by FSB (formerly the KGB) field agents in Istanbul. It was nothing more than rumor.

A second round of leaks discovered in documents found in a mob safe house in Moscow contained details about his two deepest of deep-cover operatives. Only four people on the planet possessed knowledge tying the two of them together.

The final compilation of aggregated data assembled from various sources detailed ultra specific elements that again, only four humans, knew.

Something had to be done.

The leaks were indications of a deadly infection. He could not allow it to fester, to spread to other organs. The Master knew what he had to do.

The price for playing this game would be loss. He would lose at least one of his confidants -- his key field agent, his brilliant psychologist or his unsurpassed information gatherer. One of them had betrayed him.

When the third Black Angel list appeared 14 months ago, he knew the stars had aligned. Seibel unleashed hell and suffering and pain and misery. Lance and Marta, his most dangerous weapons, would be the collateral damage in this violent game of hide and seek.

Take a deep breath.

Chapter 1

Sarajevo, Former Yugoslavia, June 17...
Blazing, flying, hurtling he came. The Black Angel.

Death lay in his wake. Moving, ever moving. To stop was to consider the previous moment and that led to consideration of prior minutes, hours, days, months. Instead, he hunted. He killed. Slaughtered perhaps a more appropriate word. Yes, slaughter. That described his actions.

Down from the mountainside he drifted, danced, dealt death. And then more death. The Black Angel was more than myth. He was real, too real for many.

But there was no time to reflect on the name, the myth. He ran. His breathing almost silent. His footfall eerily quiet as he approached them. The small troupe was on their way back up the mountain after inflicting pain and misery and rape and shame, so much shame on the unfortunate residents of Sarajevo. His approach brought him to within feet of the soldier on point. A blade sliced through black night into a waiting throat. One killer down, four to go. He stepped sideways to bring the blood-covered blade into the chest of the next in line. The young man gasped and began to scream. That meant the three remaining in the five-man squad would die within moments. And they did.

A silenced Sig Sauer handgun ignited in the black. Six shots, six violent whispers. Six holes in three heads. Five down. Five more killers dead. The Serb forces sent out dozens, hundreds of five-man squads to attack and kill and then run.

The Black Angel turned away and burst into a sprint, through trees on the rock-strewn hillside. "Killside is more like it," he whispered between breaths. The words exhaled in Russian. He'd not spoken English in weeks, or was it months now? He ran on. To stop was to allow thought, and thinking led to pondering and pondering never led to anything good. Not anymore. He wanted only black and the mission. The list.

Every action, each and every movement, was strategic. He tracked down, followed, investigated and then intervened in the lives of those on the memorized list of nine. Some lived; others didn't.

He came to a ravine and dipped down into it then up the other side. The night's chill had settled in, but did not settle on him. His action, constant, rhythmic and deadly, created heat. It burned up the store of fuel inside. And that fuel was hatred.

He stopped for just a moment. Calculation of step-count told him he'd covered four miles. But since a good bit of it was vertical, he'd only come two and a half miles into this steep valley. He listened. They were just ahead. It was a larger group. He ran toward them. No hesitation. No fear, for what was fear? "What is fear?" he whispered to no one. "Fear is wanting. Fear is only found in those with hope." The words whispered as he slowed to a silent jog. The troupe was 70 meters ahead and below. He stepped left, uphill several paces. And stopped only long enough to place the gun in his gloved hand against a tree. He focused on what he knew he'd find. It was the glow of several cigarettes. Knowing when to fire was easy. The Black Angel just had to wait for the glow to be brought up to a mouth where the pinpoint of orange brightened as smoke from the cancer stick was sucked into lungs.

He fired seven shots at three glowing ends of cigarettes. He slid to the right, moving down the incline. The remaining members of the squad fired in the general direction of where he'd been a few moments earlier. But he was gone. Three members of the troupe would not make it home. The Black Angel raced on, moving down deeper into the valley. He could tell he was near the bottom. How could he tell? Because he had memorized the topography of this small mountain range. Satellite imagery and maps combined in his head to create a 3-D map that he could see anytime, anywhere.

He reached the valley floor and jumped across the gentle babbling of a brook. No time to stop and enjoy this most peaceful sound. He kept on. Moving, running through black and night. He didn't look behind him, seldom did anymore. He corrected his course and moved up a hillside. He counted step number 8,000 since starting this excursion 58 minutes ago. If he were running on a flat surface, 1,500 steps equaled a mile. On these rough slopes, 2,000 or even 2,500 steps were required for each mile. On he ran. He was tired this night. Sleep had escaped him yesterday. He'd waited up for her. She never came.

Black Angel ducked under a branch, sidestepped a dead pine tree and stumbled over another rock. It was not Mr. Smooth tonight. Nope. It was clumsy killer. He chuckled as he began to strain from the ascent up the steep terrain. But up he went. The indiscriminate firing from the troupe of Serbian soldiers behind him ended. Quite a racket. Up he climbed; breathing with mouth open. Lungs nearing max capacity and output, pulse above 170.

He turned to the left to follow a line that provided a slightly easier route.

It was a little over a half mile to the tiny village perched atop the crest of a mountaintop. Between him and the village there was another group of soldiers. He did not know if this squad had been down into the city yesterday to do their dirty ethnic cleansing business. He would find out shortly. He pressed on, up the hill toward them. Undoubtedly, they were on alert after the shots fired by the small band of killers he had left 10 minutes ago. On he went. Forward. Heart pounding out a rhythm he tried to match on a four-beat quickstep.

He listened to the thumping of his heart, super aware of the sensations occurring inside. He focused on his internal anatomy and physiological processes consuming huge amounts of calories. He felt muscles. He sensed the adrenaline secreting and now pulsing through his bloodstream. Nerves twitched at the ends of his gloved fingers and the ends of his toes. He slowed his climb and turned his head. He closed his eyes.

In only three weeks, the Black Angel had become a skilled mountain tracker. He was already a killer, but he'd elevated his game there as well. He breathed in the smells of the forest, the moss, the leaves, the decay. He heard movement. Behind him, maybe 60 meters. Black Angel rolled to the left. He came back up on his feet a few paces from where he had been. He squatted on his haunches and peered into the dark below. Footsteps. Moving quickly, but not toward him. They were progressing sideways on the hill below. Sounded like three sets of footsteps. Why had they separated from the others? That was easy. They were converging on the area. Good. Perhaps one of these soldiers would have the information he needed. Maybe they knew where his target, where number five on his list of nine was hiding.

Black Angel burst down the hill diagonally. He made no attempt to silence his approach. The three men who had passed moments earlier stopped. They heard the noise, the pounding of feet on rocks and dirt and grass. They each spun toward the sound of approach. Too late. He was on them with slashing blade and driving elbows and knees. Two fell before they could lever the triggers of their AK-47s. A neck broken; another neck nearly severed. Two down meant a third cornered, scared. The third soldier ran from death behind him. He sprinted down the hill in uncontrolled steps. Gravity hastened his descent. The runner screamed. His words blurted out in Serbian, his dialect from the north. He pleaded for help, for mercy. Above on the hillside, other soldiers fired down into the black that shrouded everything in the lower depths of the valley.

Like a lion hunting, stalking, Black Angel separated his prey from others in the herd. The frightened man ran like a bat out of hell, tripping and falling often. He continued down the hillside screaming back over his shoulder. Then, the soldier stopped and ducked behind a tree where he turned and fired his AK-47 into the darkness behind him. He screamed as he fired in a scatter pattern. "Die you bastard. Go back to hell!"

Black Angel watched from below as the man shot without aiming up the hill. The Angel had raced even and then ahead of the lone soldier soon after the chase began. He stepped behind a tree and whispered in Serbian, "You will soon enjoy the comforts of hell my friend." The soldier, still heaving in deep breaths, turned toward the whisper and fired the remaining rounds in his gun. The Angel laughed quietly in the darkness. It was a disturbing sound of pure joy. And it unnerved the Serb soldier even more. The poor fellow relieved his bladder into his pants and took off laterally along the hillside. His legs too weak to carry him back up.

Between rasping breaths, he shouted out to the surrounding trees, "Help me. For god's sake, help me." After just over four minutes, the Serb turned to descend the hill again. In the distance, the glimmer of lights could be seen through the smothering trees. A farmhouse maybe. Salvation potentially.

He raced down the hill and then out into the gentle sweeping slope of a meadow. The farmhouse now only a quarter of a mile ahead, the soldier picked up his pace. He was going to make it.

But alas, salvation is not so easily achieved. The Black Angel had anticipated this move nine minutes ago when this chase began. He guessed the soldier would not choose to climb the hill to the mountaintop village. The lone farmhouse was the next obvious destination. It was situated in a beautiful meadow on the east side of the valley with a delightful stream flowing on the west side.

The soldier thought he could make it to the structure and put a closed door between himself and the angel of death haunting him. It was a natural assumption. It was what a human would do – seek safety within four walls and the barricade of a door.

Just 250 meters from the house, the man tripped over something in the tall grass. He sprawled out, tumbled and rolled to a stop, heaving, crying. He was so close, but far from safety. He had tripped over a foot stretched out before him. The foot was attached to the leg and body of the Black Angel, who had lain in wait a whole 30 seconds for the man; adjusting his position a few feet to the right to be sure he was in the soldier's path. He stepped over to the man, looked down on him. The moon, obscured by a blanket of clouds, provided only the faintest glow. If the moon could send its reflected sunlight down upon this meadow, the pale light would show the Serb soldier that his tormentor, his killer, was no demon. Just a man. A man with black, lifeless eyes.

"Get up," Black Angel switched to Russian. "Move." He kicked the crying, sputtering soldier.

"No. Leave me demon. Go to hell."

"I will, undoubtedly," Black Angel replied. "Hopefully not too long from now. Maybe tonight. Get up; move."

He pulled the man to his feet and delivered a painful blow to the soldier's kidney area. Then he kicked him in the rear and shoved him forward. On they went; away from the farmhouse, into the trees. He drove the soldier on, up hills, down into ravines. Kicking him when he fell. Poking him in the center of his back with the point of his bloody knife blade.

They continued on like this for two hours. Up and down hills. Hearts pumping, lungs heaving. The pace tortuous. The soldier gave up pleading after an hour. He held a glimmer of hope that maybe he would survive this. Live to tell about his brush with death. "Where are we going?" He pleaded for the hundredth time but got no reply. "How much longer?" Nothing.

On and on they went. They came near several villages, but not close enough for the soldier to attempt escape. When they neared a squad of Serb soldiers, the angel increased the pressure of the knife in the man's back to keep him moving, and keep him silent.

And then they stopped. They were there. Creeping morning light was inching into the eastern sky above the mountains. The soldier looked around. It was a clearing. A hundred meters to the south, a huge manmade pile of earth stood. A hole beside the pile waited. Realization came to the Serb soldier. He shook his head and then dropped to his knees. He wasn't going to survive after all. This was not a welcoming clearing, a place of peace. This was a graveyard. The man had not been here before, but had heard of it, of them. Mass graves. Fields like this where holes were being dug and corpses dumped into them. Hundreds, thousands of corpses.

"Please." He pleaded from his knees.

"Don't beg. Be a man in your last moments," was the reply he received.

"Why me?"

"Why them?" The Black Angel waived to the area beside the open hole. The ground was smooth, too smooth. The blade of a bulldozer had graded it. It was a filled hole. Humans lay underneath. The war had already reached levels of cruelty not seen on this continent for 50 years. "Why her?" The angel whispered.

The minutes that followed were not pleasant. The soldier, no innocent youth, relieved himself of the burden he carried. He admitted to the atrocities he had committed. He spoke of the leaders who ordered him to commit said atrocities. He provided names, locations and then, after 13 minutes, he said the name the Black Angel waited for.

"And that is where the Russians joined us. Their leader was given command of our company for the operation."

"How many Russians?"

"A dozen. Maybe more."

"Special operations?"

"Yes. Very special."

"What was this operation?"

"We surrounded an apartment building. Inside were Muslims, but not local. They were from Afghanistan. They were real fighters; Mujahedeen. They would not surrender." The soldier looked down as he spoke, the diffused morning light illuminated his face. "The Russians were there to see that no survivors escaped."

"Were they successful?"

"Yes. When we could not take the building with men and guns. They called in an airstrike. The building was demolished."

"That seems a little extreme. Many civilians could have been killed."

"Many were. " The soldier shook his head.

The Black Angel stayed behind the man as he spoke. "I need the name of the Russian leader. You know this, yes?"

"Yes. It is Colonel Kryzgolov. I heard him called that by several of them."

Done. Number six on his list.

Black Angel kicked the soldier in the head, knocking him to the ground. And he was pleased the soldier did not beg. Not yet, at least. He bent and pulled the man's wallet from his pocket and examined its contents.

"Novar. You have beautiful children. Your wife seems lovely."

"Yes. They are my life." The Serb whimpered, his face in the dirt.

"No. Death, rape, torture is your life. You can say, like others, that you are doing all this for your family, to protect your Serbian family and heritage. But that is a lie. You know it." The angel bent down to place a knee in Novar's back and whisper into his ear. "I see from your I.D. card, you live in a town north of Belgrade. I look forward to my visit there in the days ahead. Your family will not be tortured. Your wife will not be raped, but she will suffer. Goodbye."

Black Angel disappeared. In the creeping morning light, he left the Serb soldier beside the huge dirt pile and empty hole. He was alive for one reason; he had not seen the Black Angel's face. The Serb soldier had one purpose now. He was to spread the myth, the story, the legend. Death is among us.

Heroin is an opiate drug that is synthesized from morphine, a naturally occurring substance extracted from the seed pod of the Asian opium poppy plant. Heroin usually appears as a white or brown powder or as a black sticky substance, known as "black tar heroin."

Chapter 2

Lance Priest is dead.

He wouldn't use those exact words. No, Geoffrey Seibel would be more delicate, more eloquent. Seated opposite Janet Loomis and her husband Rich, Seibel projected the image of remorse; his head bowed at the appropriate angle, his eyes smiling, yet glistening with sorrow for their loss.

He had been here before, in this very room two years earlier. Seibel lied to these two people before, one a mother, the other a stepfather. He sat here and spoke with them about their son's great achievements as a soldier in Kuwait. Their son Lance had earned distinction and honor in Iraq. He was injured, but would be fine. He was a fighter. Seibel left out the part about Lance being in Baghdad with a team of CIA operatives and Delta Force specialists to intercept nuclear weapons and try to assassinate Saddam. And he neglected to tell Lance's mother that her son was a spy, a spook, a CIA operative trained to hunt, destroy and kill. And he was the best Seibel had ever seen.

Then, as now, he wore the uniform of a major in the U.S. Army. The uniform was only a partial lie. Seibel was, at one point in his distant past, a distinguished officer in the nation's armed forces. It was a long time ago. Wearing the uniform now was a cover he assumed several times a year. He used the uniform like he did most everything else in life. It was there to help him achieve a goal. A prop. Nothing more.

He traveled to Tulsa, Oklahoma this time to personally deliver terrible news to the parents of one of the country's brave soldiers. He could tell by the way they sat holding hands on the sofa across the coffee table from him that they knew he had not come for pleasantries. So he got right to it.

"You both know how proud of Lance the Army and our government are," Seibel nodded his head as he said the words.

"Yes, we all our," Rich spoke for both of them.

"And you know that because of his impressive work in Iraq and other assignments, Lance had been given additional responsibilities." Seibel looked each of them in the eye.

"We don't really know what Lance has been doing the last couple years. He told us it was a special assignment that required him to travel a lot," Rich squeezed Janet's hand. She sighed; it was painful for Seibel to watch.

"Major Seibel, do you have something to tell us? We are pleased to see you, but why are you here?" Lance's mother had the gift of directness. Seibel liked that.

The CIA legend nodded and leaned forward to rest his forearms on his thighs. The uniform was a little snugger than it had been the last time he was here two years ago, right after Desert Storm. "Yes Mrs. Loomis, I have something to tell you, to tell you both. For the last two years, Lance was assigned to an anti-terrorism taskforce operated jointly with the FBI. He was tracking several terrorist cells. His gift with foreign languages, especially Arabic, was extremely useful." And with that, he let it slip, gently. He used "was" instead of "is." The past tense of the word had a physical effect on the mother. She inhaled sharply but kept her eyes on Seibel.

"Lance was working with the team tracking the cell responsible for the World Trade Center bombing last week." Seibel paused.

"Go on sir," Rich urged him on and put a reassuring hand on his wife's shoulder.

"Lance was very close, extremely close. He was there, in the building. He was in the parking garage where the explosion took place." Seibel looked down at the hat in his hands. He didn't need to say more. They knew why he was here.

Janet dropped her head and put a closed fist to her mouth. "Is he gone?" She whispered the words.

"Yes ma'am. He was killed in the explosion, along with several others. He served his country well, a hero." Seibel raised his eyes to meet Rich's. Janet could only look at the floor. She had just learned her eldest son was dead. She shook her head slightly as a tear began its journey down her cheek.

"Did you bring him home? Did you bring his body?"

"Yes. I escorted his remains and casket." Seibel nodded. And with that, Janet broke down. Rich took her into his arms. She buried her face in his shoulder. She sobbed. The two men let her.

Minutes later, Janet and Rich stood to thank Major Seibel for coming in person to deliver the news. Rich shook the Major's hand. Janet gave a wet hug. Seibel stood outside the home signaling a white van parked down the street to pull up to the curb. There were plans to make, a funeral to arrange for a fallen hero. Lance had always expressed his desire to be cremated.

Seibel stood beside the van as four uniformed Army personnel stepped out of the vehicle and stood at attention. He turned back to look at the house. He knew a woman stood behind the closed front door. Maybe she had fallen to the floor. Such a terrible blow. To have your child die before you.

Seibel knew that pain as well. But he didn't think about that standing there in front of the grieving home. His face showed nothing but remorse and sorrow. Behind his eyes there were other feelings. Like always.

Light and dark blurred. Time fell in on itself. Movement, jarring movement, bookended by endless immobilization. Pain was measured in degrees, but not really. There wasn't really any feeling. Not really. There was always something insulating. Something smothering everything else. One thing kept it all from collapsing into blackness. It was Neil Sedaka.

Chapter 3

Moscow, USSR November 23...

Two folded sheets of paper were inserted in the closed door. Someone had been here.

Deep-cover CIA specialist Geoffrey Seibel suddenly stopped seven feet from the door and spun around with handgun drawn in the darkened Moscow hallway. Seeing no one, he turned back to the door and pulled out the sheets of paper. He couldn't help but look around again. No one was stirring in the apartment building at 3 a.m.

He unfolded the papers and took a few steps to the one working light bulb in the hallway. The first sheet held a handwritten list of nine names, some with additional names beside them. Written below the list were three simple statements, "These people are lost, no longer yours. Their allegiance has turned. Destroy this information immediately, but do with it what you will."

Seibel looked down the hall again. No one was there. He reviewed the names a second time. He knew three of the nine.

Each person listed was a deep-cover operative like himself, working for the CIA in the Soviet Union.

He pulled the second sheet of paper in front of the first. An outline of a person was sketched in the top right corner. The image was smeared somewhat. The words written in Russian across the page were done so in a very formal manner, almost like calligraphy.

Seibel whispered the words as he read.

"As the night brought blackness, he was born. He crept from city to smaller towns.

Ancient debts were owed. He was their collector. Legends tell of his brutality, his cunning.

No man was safe in the night. No man has lived who has seen his face.

The Black Angel knew only the mercy that death brings to the cursed, the damned."

Six words were written across the bottom of the crumpled sheet -- *The Black Angel returns. Destroy this.*

Seibel folded the sheets, stuffed them in his pocket and turned from the doorway. He walked down the hall, bounded down the stairs to the building's tiny lobby and burst out the door into the cool Russian night. He raced from streetlights into a dark alley. He was spooked, but didn't know why.

Eight minutes later, he stood over a metal barrel. The flickering flame of his lighter lit the words on the pages again. He memorized their contents, then touched the flame to the corner of the pages. The flame consumed paper, cast shadows that merged with the blackness of the alley and illuminated the face of the Black Angel.

A legend was born.

Chapter 4

He raced through trees, escaping light. Daylight was his enemy. He was now a creature of the night – pained, tortured by the caress of the rays of the sun. Days passed alone in silence. Sometimes she would come to him after the piercing of a needle. The Black Angel waited for night to dance in the moonlight and sweep down upon those whose names found their way onto a list.

Chapter 5

Loneliness was nothing new.

It was comforting really. Like being home. Much of the preceding two years had been a holiday, an extended vacation. Now, months after New York, reality had firmly set in. He was gone. He was dead.

She waited for the sadness. She waited every minute of every day for it. But it wouldn't come. She couldn't get past the hate to feel sadness. She was angry, damned angry. Lance shouldn't have been there when the bomb went off. She should have stopped the bastards from ever going to the World Trade Center. Should have killed them all. She had the chance to stop them, but failed. And Marta hated to fail.

She despised failure nearly as much as she detested herself. This hatred fueled the thoughts that kept her from submitting to the numbness the drugs were supposed to bring. She was a prisoner. They had locked her in this room, this cell, to protect her and to protect others as her wounds healed. She was dangerous, of course. But she wasn't thinking of killing those who cared for her every day.

Her reaction to the news of Lance's death had been violent. Even with the barrage of drugs in her system and the bullet holes and broken bones, she had reached out to grab Seibel's throat and choke the life from him. But there again, she had failed.

Marta was a wreck, a mess. She had injuries that would kill most humans. She drifted off as doctors reviewed the litany of her ailments in those days after New York. She couldn't help but think of her beautiful Lance lying beside her in the night naming every piece of her anatomy as he moved his finger across her skin.

Her wounds were just physical. They would heal with time. She instinctively rubbed the scar on her left hand; the one from the bullet fired by his gun back in Baghdad. She found herself rubbing and caressing and sometimes just staring at the scar on the palm and on the back of her hand where the bullet passed through. Her head would shake slowly from side to side as she realized these scars, plus the one on her thigh that he also caused with a bullet, were all she had left of him.

There were no photos of the two of them together. No love letters written. No flower petals pressed between pages. Their relationship was personal. They did not share each other with anyone. Their time together was all they had. And it had been passionate. It was a scalpel slicing away everything else, when they were in each other's arms. Marta looked from the scar to the window. She could see forever from that window and forever looked amazingly, hauntingly empty. So to keep that forever of emptiness at bay, she focused on the bitterness around the fraying edges of her anger, her hatred. If she stared directly into the anger she was blinded. She had to look to the periphery so she wouldn't completely lose her mind.

Marta was no fool. She knew full well that she had descended to a place somewhere south of sane. Her thoughts were no longer her own. The hate had transformed her into something she could not name. It wasn't human, that's for sure. If she had to put a label on it, she would say that she had become death. She wanted nothing more than to end the lives of those who had wronged her, wronged him. Killed him.

Footsteps in the hall told her it was 11 a.m. Stuart Braden was here for their weekly session. He wanted to come more often. She didn't need to talk more than once a week. The door opened and the good doctor walked in with guards in front and behind him. That was laughable. Guards, how ludicrous. If she wanted Braden or Seibel or Fuchs or Smelinski or anyone on planet Earth dead, guards would be her least concern.

She forced a smile and adjusted herself in the hospital bed. Moving any part of her bandaged, broken and battered body hurt tremendously. The chains in the handcuffs on her left wrist and ankle rattled as she scooted herself up. Handcuffs; laughable.

Chapter 6

There are people out there who believe that one person can change the world. And then there are a select few who know this to be true.

They would sit in silence for extended periods. Stuart Braden was patient and could wait for hours for Lance to open his eyes. But the thing was, the guy that opened his eyes this time was not Lance. The eyes were no longer hazel. They were black. Coal black.

Braden knew they had been changed at Lance's request, but seeing them a first time was unreal, unsettling. This human chameleon was now a living demon. The eyes were black holes where no emotion escaped.

"What do you have there?" Lance nodded to the envelope in Braden's hand. "Is that my mission?"

Braden brought the list up and touched his forehead with it, like he was honoring the piece of paper. "Yes. But this list is more than your mission, as you know. This is your life."

"I know. I know what I agreed to without having any idea. I'm ready."

Braden started to hand him the paper and stopped.

"What?"

"You don't have to do this. You owe him nothing." Braden squinted. Lance saw the facial muscles working underneath the psychologist's skin. The orbicularis oculi and corrugator supercilii muscles contracted to create the pained look on Braden's face.

"Seibel wouldn't give me this mission if he had anyone else who could do it. And Stu, you and I both know the only other person who could do it is dead."

Braden nodded and handed him the envelope. The trusted psychologist was a delivery boy for this top-secret assignment.

He was gone again, drifting. He agreed to this extended assignment mainly because he didn't care. He could go on autopilot, focus on nothing but the mission. His abilities were a gift of nature. His mind allowed him to ignore the guilt, the fear and restraint other humans were cursed to consider.

Although free to roam, to glide, unseen chains weighed him down. He was shackled to a ghost.

This new Lance Priest, this violent, smoldering, empty vessel cloaked human skin, was truly perfect. At 26, he was seasoned. And now, he was broken. He was the Black Angel.

The night was his domain and dangerous for anyone in his presence. Some would learn this last lesson within minutes.

Footsteps in the hall were out of place; shouldn't be there. In three seconds, he moved from the filthy bed to the wall. With his ear plastered to the surface and eyes closed, he "watched" the man walk down the hall on creaky wooden floors, sounding out every step. Try as he might, each fall of the person's feet gave away his amateur approach. But if these steps were being made in the hallway, other feet must surely be lurking below. Excellent.

Had they followed him? He smiled at that and shook his head. Following him was a joke, laughable. He chuckled. Then he looked over his shoulder at the bed and her fading image. Her transparent smile faded with her. And then he was pissed.

They'd interrupted his time with her and their lively discussion of which Caesar was the most effective Roman leader. Marcus Aurelius, although gone for most of his reign campaigning in the north, was his favorite. She considered Julius Caesar's reign to be the most successful as emperor.

No, these men weren't here for him. They were in and around this building because they believed it was occupied by Bosniaks – Bosnian Muslims. They were here for some good ol' ethnic cleansing.

As he watched her go, he followed Fuchs' guidance. His CIA special ops mentor always loosened his joints, especially his neck, rolling his head in all directions. The footsteps in the hall stopped about eight feet from his door. The man was on the other side of the wall. Black Angel stepped from the wall and fired twice with the silenced Sig. He put two bullets through the wall at four and two feet from the floor. The man in the hall was hit by both bullets and groaned while falling to the floor.

Black Angel flew to the door and pulled it open while rolling into the hall. The wounded guy on the hallway floor was in the process of raising his gun. Too late. One more silenced shot through the soldier's head ended his suffering. In the next moment, Black Angel was up and opening the window at the end of the hallway. He had chosen this dilapidated apartment building in Mostar, Bosnia because of its fire escape at the end of the hall, which was really just a set of rusted stairs down to a tight alley below.

Out on the fire escape, he was down to the brick paved alleyway in seconds and rounding the backside of the 12-unit building a few seconds later. He put his gloved hand to the wall as he peeked around and saw what he expected. Two men stood waiting, watching and holding guns. The moon was the only light on them. He didn't wait to ask what they wanted. He let his satchel fall to the ground and lay prone on the ancient Balkan stones to take aim.

The Black Angel didn't think about the fact that his ability to hit targets more than 30 feet away had vastly improved in recent months. It couldn't be as simple as wearing leather gloves. That was crazy.

He squeezed the trigger two times for each man, putting bullets in chests and heads. The natural elevation of a recoiling handgun made this shot pattern most prudent.

He sprung to his feet and was kneeling between the two dead soldiers five seconds later. They were wearing uniforms designating them as Serbs. His trap had worked. He took the coat and hat from one of the dead men and put the items on and raced to the building's main entrance. He waited a moment and listened.

This would be a five-man team as they always were. That meant two more were inside, most likely in the foyer and on the stairs. They were probably growing concerned about their comrade who had ventured upstairs and down the hall where he met death at the hands of the Black Angel 49 seconds ago.

He stepped inside and whispered in Serbo-Croatian, "What is happening?"

"Quiet." Came a whisper from the bottom of the stairs. Black Angel approached the man and saw the other up at the top. He raised his pistol and shot the one on the stairs twice in the back of the head and hurled the other soldier into the wall. The man shoved back and put an elbow in Black Angel's throat. It hurt. It felt good.

The soldier threw a punch with his left hand that Black Angel mostly avoided by shifting to his left. A knee from the man was a good move and it caught the angel in his side. It hurt. Which was also good. Pain is invigorating.

The soldier pushed further off the wall and began to throw a punch with his right hand. Black Angel was done with this little get-together and ducked forward delivering a head butt that shattered teeth and nose. With that, the capable Serb opponent collapsed. Black Angel thought for the briefest of seconds about why humans, men especially, continually ball up their fists to hurl punches when so many other parts of the body can do significantly more damage without breaking weak little bones. Just nature, he figured. He automatically ran through the 27 carpel and metacarpal phalanges comprising the bone structure in the human hand.

He bent and lifted the bloody-faced man onto the bottom stair and sat him up.

"Brother, you fought well. You nearly had me there." He slapped the man's face to wake him up. "Can you hear me?"

"Yes." The Serbian soldier muttered through haze and pain and blood. "I can hear you." The guy then tried to throw another punch. Black Angel was just inches away from the man's face so he brought an elbow up to pummel the fella's left temple. The blow sent the Serb soldier back onto the stairs behind him.

"No more of that my friend." He pulled the man back to a sitting position and took a knee. "Listen to me. I need to leave here shortly." He slapped the man's face again to liven him up. "Quickly now, are you here at the orders of Kryzgolov, the Russian?"

The soldier nodded. Blood spilled from his mouth and nose. "Yes. The Colonel ordered the killing of every Muslim bastard coming here from Afghanistan."

"Very good." Black Angel leaned in close. "And if you found any women here?"

"Our choice, our pleasure." The soldier smiled as he replied.

"Of course. Nothing better than being raped by a gang of savages. Even more pleasant when a knife is at your throat. Right?"

"Yes. That does make it better."

"Very good my friend. Your name?"

"Mesa."

"And it sounds like you hail from up north, Tuzla, correct?" The bloody soldier nodded again. "Good. Then I will go through your identification papers and pay a visit to your home and your wife and children." The words shook away the soldier's haze and he tried to rise and fight. Too late.

Black Angel shoved the blade deep into the man's stomach, wrenched it up and sideways while covering the man's blood-filled mouth. "No, no. Don't fight brother. Just die knowing you have brought dishonor to your family. They will pay for your actions, your sins. You get off easy dying here. Their suffering will be much more severe." Black Angel stayed there with the blade inside the dying man. He let him endure every painful moment, until the last. It was a bad death.

Four minutes later, the Black Angel walked a deserted alley into the early morning darkness of Mostar with war and death

all around. He left the dead soldier and his sins behind. He had
no intention of visiting Tuzla and the man's family. There was
enough suffering already in this stupid little uncivil war with its
brutal ethnic cleansing. Serbs killed Bosniaks. Bosniaks killed
Serbs. Croats killed and were killed by the others. When Tito
died and the lid was taken off the Yugoslavian cauldron,
decades of hatred and mistrust and vengeance boiled over.
Religion lay at the heart of this conflict, as it often does.

He was no one; Seibel's mission orders, delivered by
Braden. He lived by one rule – be a ghost. He was to stay so far
off the grid that he did not register as a blip on the radar of
official government records.

But there was so much else. There was the list. The names,
faces, titles, addresses, families, proclivities and other nuances
related to the humans on the list. Those first days after New
York were now just a blurred collage. Now, walking beside the
Neretva River southeast of Mostar, Bosnia at 4 a.m. on a
Tuesday morning was a blur as well. Almost everything was
experienced through a steady diet of opiates.

Others refer to it as heroin or opium or horse. For him, it was
her, Marta. He could escape the loss and emptiness and
loneliness and be with her.

The side effects of the drug were interesting. Memory loss
was the hallmark effect on him. With the lapses of memory
came the eventual loss of time and place and grip. He moved on
autopilot while under the needle's spell. He would insert the
needle in his vein in Vienna and return to earth sometime later
in Minsk or Zelenograd or Moscow. He'd find new artifacts

when he awoke. Sometimes a gash, sometimes bruises, sometimes gunshot wounds. Often a new tattoo.

Flashes would come to him. Faces of those on the list he'd tracked and those he'd killed. Five of the nine names had been crossed off in seven months. It was not a hit list, but some of them required dispatching. The only constant through all his mystery travels and ghostly visits and deep dives into the depths of grey and black was Neil Sedaka. Ol' Neil kept on singing and playing that piano day after day, night after night.

The songs tethered him to this world. They kept him from collapsing into himself. The songs were the structure, the foundation the rest of his being was built upon. He laughed at that thought walking now along a riverbank, but that was as close as he could come to figuring it out. She was gone and he was lost. Lance was up their floating but wasn't sharing his eyesight these days. All that was left was the list and the Black Angel and Neil Sedaka.

An approaching vehicle meant the usual. He ducked into the woods. Daylight breaking on the horizon meant he needed to find cover. He had indeed become a vampire of sorts. His only comfort was found in the dark, whether night or blacked out windows or tunnel or train car or ship's hold. Humans could not see his face. The ever-increasing cameras mounted on buildings or in shops or attached to ATMs must be avoided. He was a ghost, per his agreement with Seibel.

It was an impossible assignment of course, but he was the one person who could pull off the impossible. And he had no reason to be with others. Not anymore.

Chapter 7

Colonel Kryzgolov was given the freedom to do as he saw fit. The KGB, now called FSB, kept their distance and handled him with kid gloves. Kryzgolov had 13 men surrounding him. They were good soldiers who'd been with him in Afghanistan, and since. They were members of his personal army. But they would not be enough when the sun went down tonight.

The Black Angel had been watching, waiting, planning over the previous four nights. That was a long time to prepare to kill.

The first of the Russians to die did so silently at the edge of the woods, a blade slammed into and through his temple. The next took a vicious blow to the back of his head, the parietal lobe, to be anatomically specific. Problem was, another Kryzgolov guard sitting 14 feet away heard the thud of the blow. He turned to see the other man fall and then the Black Angel burst toward him. He screamed. That scream set in motion a ballet of chaos.

Men turned and ran to the scream, their AK-47s drawn. Several fired into the darkness that enveloped the edges of the small clearing the house stood upon. Three armed men inside the house came to the front door. Colonel Kryzgolov was one of them. Silenced shots fired from the darkness felled the two men standing on either side of Kryzgolov. The Colonel started to step back inside, but an explosion at the rear of the house blew out windows and propelled the Russian special ops soldiers out the door and down the steps.

A nice variety of explosives with the necessary detonators were easy to steal from Serb and Croat units. Planting the charges was only a little tricky.

Kryzgolov's men converged on their leader and took up positions firing in the direction the shots came from moments earlier. The team started a slow procession toward their vehicles parked 30 meters to the east. Two simultaneous explosions sent the eight remaining members of the private army to the ground. One was killed, nearly decapitated by a side view mirror. It was a good quick death.

Back on their feet, Kryzgolov's men, with the illustrious leader in their center, began yelling out status, directions, reports. They were professional soldiers who had faced enemy fire and countless explosions.

"To the tree line, 70 meters, go!" Kryzgolov ordered and all obeyed. Sergeant Osokin, a squat man, built like a spark plug, took point and moved rapidly into the woods. He then took a knee and scanned all horizons. Darkness was all around in the trees. Visibility was only feet. Not good. But to remain in the clearing meant death. The team that had attacked would not be prepared for a rapid deployment into the forest and then a flanking sweep back from the south. Kryzgolov's men knew the procedure well. They had learned it from their Mujahedeen counterparts in the mountains of Afghanistan.

The other members of the team moved past Osokin, who turned his aim to the rear and anyone tracking the squad. No one followed. Kryzgolov took his turn with the others kneeling and aiming into the darkness as the team progressed hundreds of meters into the dense forest. The journey took them up a hillside to the southeast. They pressed on in a methodical sequence with men intermittently taking point and then the rear. Soldiers moved up the sides, sometimes fanning out 50 to 60 meters. Other times, staying compact, within a couple of meters of each other. The group began their turn back northeast after three quarters of a mile.

It was at the turn that the troupe met resistance. Just 40 meters ahead in the darkness, a shooter lay in wait and put the soldier on point in his sites. The burst of shots fired sent the man onto his back with his chest turned into bloody Swiss cheese. The other members of Kryzgolov's elite team dropped and returned fire in expert fashion. The location the shots had been fired from was obliterated under a barrage of bullets. After 40 seconds when no shots were returned, two members of the squad moved in at 45-degree angles on the location. As they stepped into a small clearing, the explosion less than 10 feet from where each stood ended their lives.

Kryzgolov's select team of soldiers was down to five. This was a massacre in slow-motion. But order did not break down. Each man knew his duty, his job. They turned and moved to the south abandoning their flanking plan for now. This coordinated attack by a skilled group of what could only be elite assassins, had proven too much for Kryzgolov's bunch. So on, into the night and down into a darker valley they trudged. If they could get some distance on those attacking them, they could assume some high ground and counterattack. They just needed time and distance.

Pushing, thumping, gnashing, they moved on. At the bottom of a steep hill, they crossed a stream, turned west and began an ascent of another hillside. They had all seen the cluster of lights up near the top of this hill from the hillside across the narrow valley. It had to be the tiny village of Gora. No one could be sure with the disarray in which they had traveled since the attack started close to an hour ago. They pushed on, urged each other up the tree-covered hill toward the village.

This time, shots came at them from above. It was small arms fire, maybe a pistol. Four bullets found their home in the neck and chest of a sergeant from Vladivostok in far eastern Russia. He had been with Kryzgolov since the early days of the Afghan debacle. Dying here on a peaceful, bucolic hillside was better than Afghanistan. Kryzgolov's remaining four team members dropped to prone positions and obliterated the location the pistol had fired from. A minute or so later, a member of the team from southern Russia, near the Caspian Sea stepped out to the right, to the south 40 meters or so. His quiet path was excellent, nearly undetected, except that it took him past a tree where a killer held a blade. As the bloody metal slashed through the black of night, a hand cupped the man's mouth. The razor edge of the blade severed nearly all the anatomical aspects of the man's neck. Esophagus, pharynx, carotid artery, larynx, and the favorite neck muscle, the sternocleidomastoid, were sliced. Loss of blood was immediately followed by loss of life. A silent kill.

When the man from Caspian region did not return a minute later, order broke down. It was every man for himself as they spread out, raced in three directions. Kryzgolov was now alone and moving laterally on the hillside. He stopped after 40 seconds and dropped to his knee to pivot in all directions. Nothing. He raced on into the night. He did not plan to die on this hillside in this nothing of a conflict.

His lungs heaved, heart pounded. For a man of 53, he was in ultra-excellent shape. He had run three marathons the previous year; could still bench-press 140 kilograms and swim kilometers through the frozen waters of the Baltic. Kryzgolov did not need his men surrounding him. He was better off on his own. He told himself this as he ran for his life. He raced past a thicket of trees into a wide pasture. He crossed the clearing and leaned against a tree to catch his breath. He looked back into the tree line. A moment later, two heavy thuds smashed into the tree above his head. In the near distance he heard the spits of the silenced handgun. He was being tracked.

"Show yourself," he whispered between swallows of air. His body demanding oxygen, his heart pumping blood into depleted muscles. He turned away and ran again, not wanting to exchange fire here. He needed the high ground. Kryzgolov worked his way upward, toward lights on the hill, a village. He would lead those following him near the village and then break off his route and lay in wait for them. He would kill them.

He ran, pushing weakening legs, his AK-47 strapped over his shoulder, jumbling about as he huffed and puffed up the hillside. Adequate air was difficult to find. He had been running now for over an hour. He had the feeling he was being herded, driven to a destination. "You will show yourself shortly," he whispered and turned to the left, the north.

Grigory Andreovich Kryzgolov knew the thrill of killing, the feel of life ebbing between his fingers. He had killed dozens of humans, maybe hundreds. As a leader of men, he had ordered, maneuvered and positioned others to kill thousands more. He preferred smaller, more mobile and nimble units. Did not care for battalions and the headaches they brought.

His preference was guerilla warfare. Before Afghanistan, he traveled extensively throughout Southeast Asia and Africa with small teams of elite Russian killers. His personal brand of special ops left waves of death and destroyed lives in its wake.

He was trusted by the KGB to get the job done, wherever, whenever needed. The fact that Kryzgolov and his team were in Bosnia could only mean that Russia had an interest in the Balkan War ravaging the former Yugoslavia.

The Colonel expected to complete this piss ant mission and return to his home and family outside Moscow to await orders for his next special op. Kryzgolov certainly never anticipated being hunted by a team of killers. It was always the other way around.

Kryzgolov was slowing, limping. He'd twisted an ankle a couple of hills back. He needed to turn and take offensive action soon. So he did. The Colonel dropped, rolled behind a tree and aimed his AK-47 into the night behind and below him. He worked to control his breathing. He needed his lungs to slow down their rapid intake and his pulse to moderate so he could listen. After nearly a minute, he had control. He wiped his brow and scanned the forest.

The Colonel's complete attention to the rear was somewhat surprising to the Black Angel. He expected more. Actually, he didn't know what to expect. He just thought it would be more difficult to corner this illustrious soldier. But alas, humans can be so disappointing. Black Angel sat on his haunches 25 feet from the Colonel. He was actually in front of the man, but since Kryzgolov was facing to the rear, the angel was now behind him. He lowered himself to his butt and crossed his legs, watching Kryzgolov lay on his stomach and scan the woods. The angel had gotten control of his own breathing a few moments back and felt the easing of his pulse. His deep understanding of human anatomy, begun at the age of nine reading through a Grey's Anatomy reference book, gave him insight into the workings of humans.

Seventeen years later, he remained fascinated. He understood as well the effects and processes that occur during and after acts of violence. Like a surgeon, he knew a knife doesn't kill. It is loss of blood – lack of oxygen. People don't die the moment a knife severs a major artery or pierces a vital organ. It takes time, and usually, suffering.

Black Angel thought of all the people Kryzgolov had killed, including those he had exterminated just yesterday in a tiny enclave on the south side of Sarajevo. It was a brutal operation with women and children joining Muslim men in death. It was wrong; just plain horrible. But the angel wasn't here to right wrongs. He was here because of the list. And Kryzgolov's name was on it. He was number six of nine. And his reign of terror was over, as was his life.

The CIA agent playing the role of Colonel Kryzgolov may have taken on a secret, top-secret, covert assignment more than 22 years ago, but he had turned. He'd gone bad. He was no longer a reliable resource for the United States. In fact, he did more harm than good. Much more harm. But not any more.

After some time, Black Angel silently slid closer to the Colonel lying prone on the ground. "Don't turn around George," he whispered in English. "I only have one question for you."

The Colonel froze. "Who is George?" He answered in halting, heavily accented English.

"You are. Your name is George Thomas Russell. You are from Topeka, Kansas. You are an operative for the CIA. Or, you were."

"Who are you?" His English still accented, but less so.

"I am your executioner. You knew this day was coming, but still you went deeper, turned darker. I can only assume you have become an addict. You are addicted to killing. You forgot your mission George; you went off track years ago. It happens. You made your choice. For whatever reason, you have chosen to be a brutal, ruthless murderer. You forgot why Uncle Sam asked you to take on this role. I tracked you from Russia here, to this war zone where you came to kill indiscriminately."

"You punk. I've been hunting terrorists, killers who want nothing more than to exterminate people like you. You can go to hell."

"Hunting terrorists? Yes, I saw some of your handiwork last night in town. Those women and children were definitely terrorists. And don't worry about it George, I'll see you in hell soon."

Kryzgolov lifted his head to turn around. He wanted to plead for his life; convince his executioner he still had value. He had vital information to share with his CIA superiors. He could change his ways. His raised head only made his neck an easier target for the blade.

Codename Black Angel turned from the deceased deep, deep-cover agent and faded into the dark emptiness of night. There were no answers here, just a man who'd lost his way, a name checked off a list. The angel knew about addiction and it's needs. His mind turned to the next name on his memorized list.

He would make his way through the forest and 23 kilometers to the east to a small airfield. Small planes, Cessnas were his favorite, were his secret form of cross-border transportation. Pilots of these small planes were always hesitant at first and then very appreciative of payments in excess of $1,000 for a few hours of illegal work.

Catch your breath.

Chapter 8

Berlin, Germany January 12...

Night was bitter cold. His breath vaporized behind him as he hurtled through a dark and empty alley. His target just meters in front of him, leaving a vapor trail of frozen carbon dioxide behind.

The problem was the three men bringing up the rear of this little convoy. These men, members of German secret police, known as Stasi, were armed and shooting to kill. Black Angel needed to stay with his target. The man fleeing was another name on the list of nine. His name was Wilhelm Mueller. His profession, at least the occupation he displayed for most of the world, was a lawyer, a prosecutor. But for those who knew his secret, Mueller was a spy.

Black Angel respected Mueller's ability. That is why he had been following the man for five days and nights; watching. The angel kept his distance. He intended to follow the state prosecutor again this evening, but was surprised when he came around a corner 11 minutes ago to the sound of gunshots and explosions on the wall above his head. Luckily, he had been crouched when he rounded the corner. Otherwise, his head would have a couple more holes and his brains would have been introduced to the bricks of the wall. Mueller missed, but not by much.

Black Angel sprung to his right, shoulder-rolled and came up firing into the darkness. The echo of footsteps trailed away in the other direction. Chase on. He stayed close to the wall as he followed the man down a short alley and out onto an avenue. He crossed a street, careful to avoid the spill of streetlights. He could barely make out Mueller's outline up ahead approximately 75 meters or so. The angel pushed his pace up to full sprint and closed the gap on the man 16 years his senior.

The sudden appearance of the three-man Stasi unit four blocks later as the chase moved from a business district to block upon block of warehouses was simply no coincidence. It meant others were watching, waiting and had decided to take action. But who? Who brought these guys to the party? And who would know to have them positioned here, in this fairly isolated location, on this bitter frozen night? How did Black Angel know they were German secret police? The patterns. Their strategic tracking and approach gave them away as Stasi. He'd seen their work before.

The angel slid into a doorway as the Stasi agents fanned out across the broken bricks of the street. They were on a hunting expedition. Black Angel brought the collar of his coat up and breathed inside it to contain the freezing vapor of his breath. Forty seconds later, after they had moved on, he slipped out and doubled back to another alley that allowed him to move to the north, the direction Mueller had been headed. He rounded a corner and accelerated, running somewhat blindly into a tight alleyway. At the end of the block, he squatted on his haunches, brought his gun up and peered around the corner onto a wider street. Streetlights lining this boulevard made it a bad place to cross. He waited.

Seventy meters to the east, a barrage of bullets between two buildings shattered the quiet. Out of the mouth of the alley came a man, running for all he was worth. He veered left and angled across the street. Moments later, three hunters emerged from the alleyway firing their automatic weapons at the running figure. Mueller was fast for a man in his forties. He sprinted across the street into the yawning black mouth of another alley. The Stasi squad split up. One hugged the wall heading east. Another thug sprinted across directly after Mueller. The third drifted to the right, into the darkness between streetlights. Their attack and coverage pattern indicated professionalism, experience in hunting prey. But it unfortunately also brought one of them right into the welcoming arms of the Black Angel.

As the Stasi agent stepped into the alley's opening, the angel grabbed the collar of the guy's coat and swung down to pull and fling away the automatic weapon. Black Angel put pressure on the ball of his left foot and hurled the man to the left, into the darkness and pounced on him. He needed information more than he needed a quick kill. The Stasi agent was surprised by the attack, but was quick and alert.

The man used the momentum the angel generated, reached up to grab the sleeve of the Black Angel's coat and pull him to the ground. Both men rolled, struggling for advantage. They continued their roll into the black of the alley on filthy bricks. To stop momentum meant one of them would be on the bottom and lose all advantage. Each grasped the other's coat, not willing to let go or give the other any space to maneuver. The angel needed enough room to pull his blade from the sheath attached to his belt.

The Stasi operative needed help and was about to scream out to the others when the Black Angel brought up a wicked knee into the man's groin and then jammed a forearm into the German's neck, stifling the shriek. But the knee and forearm weren't all. The angel followed the first groin blow with three more.

In a blur, he rolled off the poor guy and shifted behind to put him in a vice-like headlock. From here, he could continue the intense pressure and induce unconsciousness or wrench the neck and skull in opposite directions severing the spinal column from the brain.

Instead, Black Angel leaned in close, his lips touching the struggling man's left ear. "We all die my friend. Tonight is your time. I wish you well on your journey into that long night." He liked how certain words sounded in German. "Night" was one of them. The German version "nacht," with its distinctive retching noise, just sounded better than the English version.

"Nein, bitte." The Stasi man sputtered.

"Warum?" the angel asked the fella why. "Death comes to us all."

"I can help you."

That was quick. As usual, the supposed tough guys, the bullies, are easiest to break. "Sorry, I don't want your help." He squeezed the vice around the man's neck and wrenched his arm upward. Cartilage and vertebrae neared the breaking point.

"Bitte. I will tell you everything." The man's whispered words spoke of his pain, his mortality. The Black Angel recognized the tone, the underlying message in the words. This man was done resisting. He was his for the taking, the breaking.

Three minutes later, Black Angel, carrying new information about the Stasi mission, crossed the partially lit street and ran into another alley. At the end of that street he crossed into another and then turned north toward the gunshots he'd heard a minute earlier. Ahead, warehouses and factories stood rusting, deteriorating. There was no third shift at work, no one at work. Production had been halted. Jobs gone, suffering had spread. This was not the winning side of the Cold War.

He dove under a chain link fence, sprinted across the open yard and then between two buildings. He leaned against a wall, closed his eyes and listened. After a few seconds, he heard a voice call to another. It was coordination. One voice told another where to go; the other accepted the order with a one-word reply. Footsteps across a metal grate were next. They came from the far end of the building on the right. Black Angel ran along the wall until he found a door propped open with a coffee can full of cigarette butts.

Black Angel stepped in and hugged the wall. He was in a short hallway. He slid to the end and peeked into the factory floor with idled equipment, stacks of boxes. Moonlight filtered through broken windows up near the tops of the walls. The building was frigid. No one was stoking the fires down in the boiler rooms. Looked like the facility had sat idle for some time, years maybe. The quiet was shattered by a barrage of gunshots at the far end of the huge open room. The shots from a silenced gun made a hell of a racket when they struck metal walls and stairs. Black Angel sprinted diagonally across the space.

He reached the other side and moved to his left, in the direction the shots had been fired. More running footsteps. This time, it was up above on an overhead run of grates. "Jetzt stoppen!" A voice shouted for someone to stop. "Jetzt." The voice reiterated the order to stop now. More shots were fired. This time, they were followed by a stifled scream and a moan. Someone had been struck. But who? He hoped it wasn't Mueller. He needed him alive, for a few minutes.

To shake things up a bit, the angel shouted and fired a few shots, "KGB. Do not shoot." The order issued in Russian certainly enlivened the situation. The mention of Soviet intelligence would create a few moments of uncertainty, if not chaos.

He stepped lightly along the wall until he came to a set of rickety stairs leading up the second level.

"Who is there?" a voice maybe 50 meters away and above asked. "NKVD? Who are you?" The voice asked again. Good. Doubt and confusion sown.

He climbed the stairs to second the story walkway running the length of the factory. He stayed low and then laid down with his weapon pointing into darkness. He waited for movement, waited for what was next. It wasn't long. A figure came running at him. The dim light made it next to impossible to make out who it was. As the runner approached, Black Angel rose to a knee. But instead of stopping or tripping the man, he let him run past and waited. Just four seconds later, another figure approached. This one moved with more fluidity, he was a hunter. Perfect.

As the man moved closer, the angel stuck his leg out into the walkway and brought his right hand down to the knife sheath. The hunter tripped over the outstretched leg. Black Angel reached out with his left hand to grasp at the gun in the man's hands to be sure it did not come around at him while the man cart wheeled forward. With his left arm straight out, the angel pushed off of his right foot and brought the knife up from his hip toward the flailing man. But, a flailing man is not a defenseless one. The guy falling forward had momentum on his side and used it to shoulder-roll on the metal grate. Because Black Angel had a solid grip on the man's silenced machine gun, the two of them stayed close in the darkness. Before the angel could bring his knife into play, the Stasi agent came up from his shoulder-roll and exploded into him, driving him into the wall and then down onto the grate. His hand slammed into the frozen metal and released the knife. He still held the barrel of the man's weapon.

The two men were now face to face. "Greetings comrade," the angel whispered in German.

"And you, mein freund." The Stasi man whispered his reply. There was just enough light to see each other's face. They smiled for a fraction of a moment. Each knew what was next. Each had killed many men.

Black Angel hurled the man to the right and rolled with him. His opponent knew what was happening and used the momentary release generated by momentum to bring his hand to the angel's throat where he gripped and squeezed. A good move, but not immediately effective. It would take a full minute of intense pressure on the trachea to induce unconsciousness. So obviously, this was not the real move. This was facade, subterfuge to hide the next move or series of moves. The angel liked it. Liked the challenge of someone thinking several moves ahead.

So without delay, Black Angel broke the pattern and head-butted his opponent. Not once or twice, but six times. He used his forehead as a battering ram smashing bone, breaking skin. And because he held the higher ground in this two-man telephone booth battle, the Stasi man could not pull his head away. It was jammed into the metal grate underneath them. The angel did not stop his brutal offensive with the head butts. He flipped the guy over and bashed the back of his head and neck down into the grate with his forearm and elbow.

The Stasi man had been playing a little possum and let his body go limp for a couple of seconds. The angel released his grip on the guy's jacket. He shouldn't have; because in the next second, the German secret policeman brought up his right elbow as he spun off the grating. The elbow cracked the angel right in the temple. It was a beautiful, concussive strike. Black Angel was nearly knocked out. All he could do was reach out and grasp clothing to pull the man close and keep the battle intimate, like a boxer wrapping up an opponent who had clocked him. Any distance at all would give the Stasi man room to increase the momentum of his punches, elbows and kicks.

Black Angel held onto fabric and onto consciousness. He needed time, a few precious moments to recover. The Stasi man knew this and pressed his attack with a left knee driven into the angel's midsection. Black Angel kept his grip and tucked his forehead into the man's chest. Each second pulled back the black that had encroached across his vision when the elbow struck his head. Black Angel was almost back, but he couldn't help but think for a few seconds about leaving the structure he had called home. It was a seedy apartment on the edge of downtown Berlin, nothing special. He wondered if this man he held close thought about killing other men when he left the place he called home earlier today. Did he leave behind a wife, a family? And then the thought faded as full alertness returned.

Black Angel was brought into this world to kill. Nothing more. He could think and plan and strategize and respond in a creative manner to any and every situation. But the end result of every action was to control, to eliminate, to destroy, to end. For this kill, he used his head again. Black Angel untucked his head from this excellent Stasi fighter's chest and exploded upward. The top of his skull struck the man's chin and continued upward driving the man's head up and back until it smashed into the metal wall behind him. This was a blow he could not play possum after. It was simply too severe. Black Angel would have liked to extract information from this resource, but Mueller was 30 seconds ahead of him. The angel grabbed his knife from the grate and ended this brief battle with a deep slash of the blade. He did not have the luxury of time to honor his opponent or reflect on how the lives of those who knew and loved him would be impacted by his loss. Killers kill and then they die.

He stood and made sure his feet were beneath him. Unsteadily, he started in the direction Mueller had gone almost a minute ago. He came to the set of stairs he'd climbed earlier, descended and continued along the wall to where he knew he needed to cross the open space. No telling if Mueller laid in wait, so he burst from the wall into the open, ready to zig or zag or roll. No shots came.

He reached the other side and hurried through the short hallway to the propped open door and the frozen night outside. He knew right away that Mueller had not come out this way. Didn't feel right. Too still. He slid along the wall a dozen feet and waited. His ear placed against the frozen metal exterior wall of the vast building, listening for any movement inside.

He thought back to the words the first Stasi man spoke before he died. He didn't have much information, only that Mueller had been compromised and was to be followed and engaged. The euphemism brought a smile to Black Angel's lips. "Engaged," he whispered. Why not just say what they meant – killed. This three-man East German government Stasi crew was assigned to kill Mueller tonight. Why? What did they know about the CIA/KGB double agent that he didn't?

Black Angel would need to figure that one out later. For now, he had the same mission. Engage Mueller. Movement at the end of the street interrupted his intense concentration. Someone hurriedly crossed the opening. Black Angel kicked from the side of the building, shot across the dark alleyway and raced up to the north end. He stopped at the corner and peered around into a wider street. He watched for several seconds. Approximately 80 meters ahead, a figure moved across another alley. A light from behind illuminated Mueller. The Black Angel burst into the street.

Mueller heard him and turned to fire three shots. All missed. The double, actually triple, agent took off down the next alley. It was pitch black down there; with just the faintest trickle of light at the far end more than a hundred meters away. Black Angel rounded the corner nine seconds after Mueller. The guy had to be tuckered. He had already run from the Stasi squad into the factory. The angel thought briefly about the shots and sounds of suffering and death he heard a few minutes back. Obviously, Mueller knew how to use a gun and had done so back on the second floor of the factory.

He ran through the Mueller file in his mind he'd built over the last five days. He'd followed, researched, delved into and sat for hours gazing into nothingness exploring Mueller in his mind. This exercise often unveiled pieces missed when reviewing physical evidence.

What drew Mueller out tonight? Black Angel wasn't planning aggressive provocation or confrontation for at least two more days. He was on no set timeline where the names on list were concerned.

Black Angel chose not to slow down as he reached the end of the alley and flew around the corner into the next street. The first shot exploded over his head, smashing brick. He jutted right and ducked but kept moving forward as the second shot whizzed past his head, missing by inches. He felt the rush of air, the lightning-like explosion of smashing air particles beside his ear. Still he ran forward. Mueller took off again, but because of momentum and physics and superior strength, the Black Angel was upon him. Mueller's decision to stand and fire these last two shots backfired.

Black Angel had his Luger in his hand. He raised the pistol to take aim at Mueller's legs and fired twice. One of the two bullets struck the rabbit in his left calf. Mueller screamed and cart wheeled in a rolling heap. But he also brought up his .32 caliber handgun and fired. Problem was, the angel had stepped to the side and squatted down to a knee against the wall on the sidewalk. He was virtually invisible in the darkness. He breathed into his open coat to capture his steaming breath.

Mueller pointed his gun in all directions. After several seconds, he tried to get up. It was slow and painful. When he made it upright and took his first limping step, Black Angel spoke, "You won't get very far comrade." The words were spoken quietly in Russian. "Don't turn around." He ordered.

"Who are you?" Mueller stopped and stood motionless. He did not turn to the angel.

"Not important," Black Angel answered in German. "My name means nothing. It is you who matters."

"Why? What do you want?" Mueller remained still, but his head adjusted minutely. The angel watched the movement. He knew it was a form of sonar at work. Mueller was calculating time and distance and precise location. So Black Angel took offensive action and shot the man in the other calf. It was a mean thing to do.

Mueller sagged and collapsed. Two bullets in his legs was not something he could stand for. Angel cracked up at the joke in his head, but stayed where he was, tucked against the wall. "Throw your gun away. Now." He said these words in heavily accented English. Mueller huffed and then obeyed.

"You are a bastard," the triple agent spewed the words with venom.

"Of course I am. I am a killer, like you. Remorse is not something I am troubled with. But unlike you, I am not a traitor."

"What do you want from me comrade?" Mueller rolled on his side so he could look in the direction of the angel's voice.

"I have been following you for days. I have most of what I need on you. I just wonder what you have done to inspire the wrath of our Stasi friends back there." The nameless angel stayed motionless, speaking into his coat to disguise vocal tone. He had not yet decided if he was going to let this name on the list live or die. It depended on the next few seconds, the answers to the next few questions. "What were they after tonight?"

"I don't know. I never got to ask them."

"Specifically now, be very deliberate in your answer. What did you do to bring this response from the Stasi?" Black Angel asked the question in a cultured Russian accent.

"I, I do not know."

"Last chance, comrade. Careful now, the next bullet will not find your leg."

Mueller was silent, but not motionless. Under his coat, he moved a hand. He brought out a gun, but did not aim it at the Black Angel. He put it to his chin, not his chin per se, the submaxillary triangle of soft skin between the chin and Adam's apple. He'd made his decision.

"So be it." Black Angel whispered. Mueller pulled the trigger of this second, hidden gun and ended the pain this world delivers unto us all. The angel rose and walked past the dead CIA sleeper agent gone bad and disappeared into the frigid Berlin night.

Catch your breath.

Chapter 9

South of Phnom Penh, Cambodia May 22...

Free-falling from 11,000 feet through low-lying clouds is fun. Doing it at 1:30 a.m. on a Tuesday morning makes it even more fun, delightful even. The rush, the scream of air collapsing, the force, the unyielding tug of gravity pulling ever downward. Fun is a word some humans use to describe this amalgamation of sensations. Black Angel is one of these people.

Clearing the blanket of clouds gave him approximately 2,100 feet to successfully pull off a night parachute landing in the dense jungle three kilometers west of the Mekong River and 12 kilometers south of the southern outskirts of Phnom Penh, Cambodia. He pulled the ripcord and stayed loose as the canopy of the chute opened overhead, yanking his body side to side. He rolled his head in all directions to relax.

Now, this is where hope becomes a strategy. He peered down into the quickly approaching jungle floor and hoped that his feet would find grass or mud or water and not a tree. He bent his legs and pulled them up moments before he struck the ground. Ground was good.

It was mud, thick and deep and heavy. The rains over the last week had made everything even more wet and marshy than normal in this swampy river delta. He rolled to his left, onto his back, letting the chute and lines fall on and around him. He gathered up the black fabric. So far, so good. No injuries. No soldiers shooting at him.

He was up and getting his bearings within seconds. He stuffed as much of the fabric canopy and lines as he could into the backpack container. He found a good clump of underbrush and shoved the parachute pack underneath. Black Angel pulled the ancillary pack off his chest and checked the contents to make sure the mini assault rifle and handgun were intact. He fingered the ammunition he brought along. Lastly, he gripped the knife sheath that he had wrapped and taped up so it wouldn't stab him during landing. He unwrapped it and clipped the deadly weapon to his belt.

Seconds later, he was jogging northeast toward the one-lane dirt, now mud, road that ran perpendicular to the Mekong two and a half kilometers to the east. The angel reached the road and headed north. No one was around.

The rain stopped for the moment, but would commence again shortly. The night air was sticky, heavy. Bugs hissed and hummed. Animals screeched and darted off the road as he moved along. After four minutes, headlights bounced toward him. He stepped off the road into the dense jungle growth and disappeared instantaneously. The vehicle, a beat up jeep with two passengers, passed by and rumbled off into the night. He bounded back onto the road and picked up the pace of his jog. He had something of a schedule to keep.

Just over 13 minutes later, he reached his destination, the outskirts of a tiny village. They would be here, his targets. Two men, the last two on the list he had memorized over a year earlier, would be here. He had tracked them across continents for months while attending to other names on the list. Their proximity to him at the moment was perfect, simply perfect. They undoubtedly considered this remote location surrounded by kilometers of untamed jungle to be safe, secure. The real action was miles away to the south and east in the jungles of Vietnam.

These last two names were tattooed inside his brain -- Nikolay Startsev and Aleksandr Berezhko.

They were with him night and day and across endless miles. It would take time. He was told that before he was handed the list and then ordered to destroy it at once. Nine names to start; now only two remained. He'd done his job, which didn't always require killing. Some he merely spoke with for a few minutes. It was all it took to cause them to change their ways. This was a strange assignment.

Movement. Up ahead in the brush beside the road, something moved. It wasn't right. The Black Angel stopped, froze. He peered into the night, waiting. He was ready, poised, coiled. Humans can't outrun bullets. The tiny projectiles are simply too fast. But some humans can move with a speed, a quickness that sets them apart. It makes them different and deadly.

Black Angel saw the very beginning, the first microsecond of the muzzle flash. He didn't know why, but he chose to slide his body to the left, adjusting his hips and applying pressure to the ball of his right foot. The bullet was fired from maybe 75 feet away. Traveling at approximately 3,000 feet per second, the bullet reached him in less than a 25th of a second. He heard it whizz by, right by his ear. Did his fade to the left allow him to avoid the bullet? He'd never know. Carrying the momentum of his sideways movement, he dove into the brush on the side of the road as six more bullets pierced the night. The element of surprise was definitely gone.

He rolled back to his feet and raced several hundred feet into the dense jungle in ankle-deep mud. He stopped to listen. He heard shouting, an engine revving. Headlights angled his way. He burst forward again, pounding his boots into the slosh. Not just one vehicle, but two tore off the road and barreled into the tall grasses, bushes and bamboo. Black Angel needed to stay on this course to make it into the trees, but didn't know if he had the time to reach them.

"Damn." He muttered and stopped. He already had his assault rifle out, but decided to reach into his pack and pull out the Luger as well. He had about 10 seconds until they reached him, so he rolled his head in all directions. He decided to shorten the distance and took off toward the approaching vehicles and their bouncing headlights.

His heart pounding out of his chest, legs burning from the struggle through dense growth and sticky mud and his lungs burning, he couldn't recall ever feeling better in his life. The first vehicle came upon him. Because he was running, the handgun was the better choice. He had the element of surprise on his side for that flash of a moment as he ran directly at the lead jeep. No time for deviation.

He brought his aim up to the spot where the vehicle's driver sat behind mud-splattered glass. When the jeep was only 30 feet away, he fired four shots into and through the windshield and dove to the right. The jeep bulldozed past him into the thick growth, but it began to slide to the right, out of control. Black Angel rose to his feet, but this time, he had the semi-automatic rifle in his hands and took aim at the second vehicle now 50 feet away and closing. He casually walked forward, firing a dozen rounds into the vehicle's windshield. None of the occupants in either vehicle expected their attack to be turned back on them by an individual. They weren't prepared.

The driver of the second vehicle was hit and fell on the steering wheel. The jeep did a radical spin to the left. Black Angel was splattered by thick mud from the jeep's tires. He exploded after the vehicle and raced up beside it just as a passenger began to take aim in his direction with what looked like an AK-47. The angel fired five shots into the guy and kept advancing to fire three more bullets into the other passenger. As the vehicle came to a stop, he reached into his pack to pull out a flashlight and shined it into each of the men's faces. There were three of them and they were all dead. But none of them were Startsev or Berezhko.

The engine of the first jeep roared as someone slammed on the gas pedal and the vehicle blasted forward, its spinning tires slinging mud skyward. It veered to the right, back toward the road. Black Angel hastily pulled the three dead men from the second jeep, climbed into the driver's seat, threw the backpack into the passenger seat and floored it. Engine roared, tires spun, mud slung. Chase on.

The other jeep bounced up ahead as it made it to the road where it turned left, toward the village. The cloud-filled sky blocked all moonlight so the angel couldn't see who or how many people were in vehicle. He kept both hands glued to the steering wheel as he fought to close the distance. His jeep went airborne as it shot up onto the road and slammed to the left. His visibility was hampered by mud flinging everywhere and the busted windshield. So he stood up to look over the shattered glass at the vehicle about 150 meters ahead. He sat back down when he saw the muzzle flashes. The shooter was taking advantage of the straightaway to fire a dozen or so rounds at him. A couple of them struck the already ruined windshield. The rest missed wildly.

He kept the gas pedal to the floorboard and kept his head down. He could feel the distance between the two vehicles collapsing. The lead jeep passed a couple of small buildings next to the road and fishtailed to the right. Black Angel reached into the backpack to retrieve the Luger. He brought it back to the steering wheel and gripped it with his available pinky finger as he spun around the same turn nine seconds later. As he brought the vehicle back under control from the turn, he raised the handgun on top of the windshield frame just in case the other jeep had stopped and waited in ambush.

The jeep was nearly 100 meters down the dirt road, but that wasn't the problem. The speed of light showed the angel the muzzle flashes before the bullets left the barrels of two guns about 40 feet to the right. He was already hunched over and diving into the passenger seat as the barrage of rounds exploded the remaining windshield of the battered jeep. He kept his foot on the gas and turned the wheel in the general direction the bullets came from. A second and a half later, the jeep struck something, then something else, and then rammed into the side of a hut.

Black Angel burst out the driver's side of his stolen jeep prepared to fire. Turned out he didn't need to. One of the two men who'd shot at him was lying about 15 feet to his left, moaning. The other was trapped and seriously crushed against the front of the jeep and the wall of the hut.

He stepped over to the man rolling and groaning on the ground and flipped him onto his back. Once again, not one of the two he'd come for. This man, like the others dead in the marshy field, was Asian; Cambodian most likely. The angel knew many languages and dialects from the area and used the standard Khmer while placing the barrel of the Lugar to the man's forehead.

"Where are they, the two Russians?" he asked hurriedly. He got no immediate reply, so he fired the gun into the ground next to the injured man's head. He screamed. "Now. Where are they?"

"To the north, past the village."

"How did they know I was coming?" He didn't expect an answer, but tried it nonetheless.

"I don't know. We learned just hours ago."

Black Angel got up from straddling the man and fired a shot into the poor guy's left kneecap to make sure he stayed where he was. He hopped back into the jeep and threw it into reverse, dislodging the bloody dead man attached to the grill. But instead of chasing after the other jeep down the side trail, he turned back to the main road and went right, to the north. He didn't care about the other vehicle, he wanted to see if the gentleman he had just left wounded and alive was lying about the two Russians being on the north side of the tiny village. He knew the general location of the structures on that end of the village from aerial photography.

The main road would take him past several offshoot roads until it came to a lane that led northeast to a loose gathering of buildings. That had to be where his two targets were holed up; if they hadn't fled. He reached the road and veered to the right. No time to play it safe. He barreled ahead at 70 kilometers an hour. Instead of slowing as he reached the compound, he jammed on the gas pedal and accelerated. He shot off the road and went airborne over a small levee beside the road designed to guide flood waters past the village.

Moving as fast as he was, he and his borrowed jeep were difficult to hit. The barrage of bullets that struck the vehicle as he exploded through a fence into the compound did significant damage. One bullet struck him in the left arm. Another implanted in his shoulder. He drove the vehicle between two buildings and jumped out with his assault rifle ready to do a bit of killing. He stepped around the corner into the open and sprayed bullets into a house across the courtyard. He ran to the right and drew fire from another building. Perfect. He turned and fired into the window the shots came from. Not more shots came from there.

All the while, Black Angel listened for the sound he expected. After crossing to the other side and taking out three more men, he heard it. Two engines roared to life just outside the complex. Tires tore into wet earth. It was them, the last two on his memorized list. He needed to move now.

He ran beside a house, around to a tall fence he scaled and jumped over, rolling to his feet and aiming his weapon. No one fired at him. He ran around a two-story building into the alley where he left the jeep. The angel jumped in, turned the ignition and pounded the accelerator to the floor. The jeep shot forward, blowing through the fence surrounding the complex.

Out in the open, he ducked down to avoid a few dozen shots fired from the compound. It appeared some of the men who had been cowering inside buildings while he stalked them, felt brave enough to shoot at him as he roared away.

He knew from the aerials that the road he was on led to the river and then went north or south. There was no bridge spanning the wide Mekong River here. It was upstream a dozen kilometers, in Phnom Penh. He didn't like that there were two vehicles fleeing. It could mean that each of the men he chased could be in separate vehicles and could split up.

He could see them up ahead. Looked like they were in Land Rovers. Not good. Very powerful engines. Still he floored it and powered forward. It was coming, the intersection. A perfect opportunity for them to split. And they did.

Damn.

He needed to make a decision quick-like. Left or right, which one to follow? He chose to turn right and fishtailed around the turn in a wide messy arc, spraying mud to the heavens as he negotiated the turn with his wounded arm and shoulder screaming in pain. He concentrated on catching the Land Rover in front of him and hoping like hell that at least one of the two names on his list was a passenger.

Damp night air rushed by him. He could feel the river just a few hundred meters or so to the left, the east. He reached inside his jacket to feel the holes in his arm and shoulder. The wounds were wet with blood. They stung like hell. He pulled his hand back out and squeezed the area. He hoped he could slow the blood loss until he had some time to clean the wounds and bandage them appropriately with the tiny first aid kit in his pack.

He pushed the stolen jeep to its maximum speed. He was gaining on them. Just a matter of time. Suddenly, the vehicle up ahead slowed and shot to the left. Black Angel kept his speed up a little too fast for executing the turn, but momentum and need for immediate conclusion necessitated his dangerous action. The jeep balanced on two tires for a few precarious seconds rounding the muddy corner to a road barely one-lane in width. He used his aching left arm to grip the wheel and his right to pull out the Luger and take aim at the vehicle now only 40 meters or so ahead.

He fired off a half-dozen shots. The Land Rover dodged to the left and then right. It accelerated, going off road onto a trail that ran just beside the black flow of the Mekong. Without any warning or indication, the Land Rover spun to a sloppy stop. He had no time to brake, so he jammed his foot to the floor and accelerated into the vehicle.

The violent collision pinwheeled the Rover to the left, throwing its passengers about. Black Angel switched the handgun to his left hand and grabbed the semi-automatic assault rifle and fired mercilessly into the Land Rover, obliterating its occupants. He jumped out of the jeep and circled around behind the other vehicle to see what he expected. Movement down by the river. The momentary roadblock was meant to hold him up for a few precious seconds to allow what he assumed was at least one of his targets to reach a boat resting on the riverbank.

He made sure the passengers in the Rover were no longer among the living and raced toward the river. As he crested the berm, a dozen rounds were fired up at him, requiring him to dive for cover. After a few seconds, he rolled back onto his stomach and aimed at where the boat had been. It had been pushed out into the water. The guy who had fired at him did so again while standing in the front of the boat.

The shooter then pull-started the outboard engine and it roared to life, driving the small boat away from shore and to the right with the river's strong current. Black Angel fired on the boat as it sped off downstream. The black night prevented him from knowing whether he hit anyone aboard.

Decision time.

Looked like there were three or four other small boats sitting beside the river. He could skip down there and see if he could get one of them started. Or, he could get up and run back to his stolen jeep, tear back down the path to the main road and go north to see if he could pick up the scent of the other Land Rover. Third, he could call it quits for the night, go break in to a store or doctor's office and clean his wounds before anything bad set in.

Not really that much of a decision.

He hustled down to the river. Reaching into his pack, he pulled out the flashlight and found what he was looking for in the third boat. The owners had left the key in the ignition. He kicked the gas can. It had plenty in it. The angel shoved the small boat, using mainly his right arm, out into the Mekong. He hopped in and kneeled in the back of the boat to pull the starter line. It took a fourth try before the engine kicked to life. He sat on the rear bench and grabbed the tiller handle, which both steered the boat and allowed him to turn the handle to full speed, like cranking the grip on a motorcycle.

Into the night, gliding on a river of black, the Black Angel closed off the world around him and concentrated all his attention, all his abilities on two senses. He peered into the dark downstream, seeking anything that disrupted the pattern of smooth, silky blackness. He listened for the sound of the other outboard motor. He scanned the narrow horizon. It came at him quickly with the boat's small engine maxed out. The rapid current added to the speed.

There. Less than 200 meters ahead, near the right bank, a boat. Even on this moonless night, a slight glimmer and reflection across the water was enough to show the craft. Angel pulled his pack close and had to use his wounded left arm to again to grab the flashlight, Luger and mini-assault rifle. He switched his left hand to the engine tiller and used his right to reload the weapons. He had no problem doing it in the pitch black, having done it blindfolded a number of times. Doing it one-handed in a rickety little boat on a fast-moving river made it a little more interesting.

He was steadily closing the gap. It wouldn't be too much longer until they crossed into Vietnam from Cambodia. These waters and surrounding land were not safe for most humans, with other humans on the prowl. Suddenly, the gap between the two boats shrunk. The lead vessel pulled to the bank. Black Angel cut his engine, angled the tiller to take him into the bank and picked up the flashlight and rifle.

Just 50 feet apart, he turned the flashlight on and lit up the two men pulling the vessel onto the muddy riverbank. One of the men had his hands full tugging on the boat. He was a sitting duck. Black Angel blasted the poor guy from this world to the next. Problem was the other guy. It was Startsev.

He only had one hand on the boat. The other held an automatic rifle. The other problem was the very precise pinpoint in the night the flashlight bulb created. It made an excellent target. Startsev let loose a couple dozen rounds toward the light before the Black Angel could extinguish it.

Several bullets struck and penetrated the flimsy metal comprising the small boat's hull. One hit his pack; another put a hole in the gas can. Black Angel took this as his signal to exit stage right into the water. He kept the assault rifle and backpack raised out of the water as he swam the remaining 25 feet to shore. He was up on one soggy knee ready to fire just moments after reaching the bank.

He pulled the flashlight and pressed it against the barrel of the gun as he aimed at the other boat and turned the bulb on. Nothing, no one. Startsev had fled. He turned the flashlight off and raced away from the river, over the berm, across the trail and into the jungle. He kept his path directly west, heading deeper into the thick jungle, toward the main road, which ran perpendicular to the river.

Adrenaline coursed through him like an electric charge. He was on a high as the hormone poured through his arteries and veins. The pain radiating out from his left arm and shoulder were kept in check by the spread of adrenaline. Black Angel lived for this rush.

He reached the road after racing through the jungle for nearly 300 meters. He continued his inhuman pace heading south. His instincts were in full control of his every action. On he ran. He needed to reach the tiny village ahead in the next minute or so.

While running at this wild, unreal tempo, he switched the assault rifle into his left hand and reached over his shoulder into the backpack to retrieve the handgun yet again. On he ran, a gun in each hand. Knees rising and dropping, pistons at work. Feet gliding through mud. Eyes scanning the road ahead, the jungle to the left. The small village appeared. Two bare light bulbs hung from a telephone pole. Several small buildings, huts really, spread out before him.

Black Angel tore to the left, between two structures into a tight lane with a small fence running beside it. Up ahead he saw the miniscule intersection he sought. He angled to the right side of the rutted out trail and then slid like a base runner stealing second.

He waited and breathed and melted into the muddy darkness, impossible to see on this cloud-obscured early morning. His wait was brief.

Forty seconds later, a man came jogging up the path, keeping a steady pace. When he was just a couple of meters from the shadow that was the Black Angel, the poor guy was blasted by three shots. He toppled forward, the bullets expertly placed in his thighs and knee.

As Startsev finished his forward sprawl, he tried to roll from his back onto his stomach to take aim with his AK-47. But he was too slow. A boot struck him in the shoulder, knocking the gun into the mud. A light rain began to fall.

Startsev was stuck on his back with a boot on his throat. He looked up at the demon standing over him and breathed deep with his mouth open. They stayed like this for a few seconds.

"You were difficult to find comrade," Black Angel smiled down at his prey.

"We had a job to do, a mission to complete." Startsev replied, wincing as he did.

"Don't we all." The angel stepped off his prey's neck and over to the man's AK-47. "You two just couldn't decide which mission to stay with. Whose side to take."

"We never take sides. We just follow orders." Startsev had something of a smile on his mud-covered lips.

"Ah yes. But again, whose orders do you follow? Is it Moscow or Washington?"

"What is the difference?" Startsev looked from the man standing over him to his ruined legs. "Go ahead and complete your mission. Do what you were sent here to do."

"I already have my friend. I found you. That is my mission. What I do after that is at my discretion."

"Then make your call. Finish me or leave me here to die, to bleed out into this muddy, wasted country." Startsev was done.

Decision made.

Codename Black Angel turned away from one of the men he had tracked for nearly a year, but not before putting a bullet through the traitor's forehead, which traveled through his skull and into the mud below. The Black Angel only follows one rule – let no one live who knows your identity.

CIA double agent Patrick Olgunsky from Rochester, New York just learned that rule. He had been KGB operative Nikolay Startsev for 19 years. But somewhere along the line, he and his partner had been turned. He was no longer a trusted resource for the CIA or United States. And he and his partner had made it onto a list of nine names. It wasn't necessarily a death sentence. But it usually meant life in prison or death six feet under. Or, in the case of Patrick Olgunsky, an inglorious end in a Cambodian jungle. Codename Black Angel needed to clean and stitch some wounds and track down number nine on the list.

Catch your breath.

Heroin can be injected, snorted/sniffed, or smoked — routes of administration that rapidly deliver the drug to the brain. Injecting is the use of a needle to administer the drug directly into the bloodstream. Snorting is the process of inhaling heroin powder through the nose, where it is absorbed into the bloodstream through the nasal tissues. Smoking involves inhaling heroin smoke into the lungs. All three methods of administering heroin can lead to addiction and other severe health problems.

Chapter 10

The slap was first. It was followed by more slaps and then punches, and finally, kicks. Between all the blows was the shouting, the cursing, the spittle splattering his face.

"Again, what is your name?" It was the same question he had been asked two days ago and all day yesterday.

"You will tell us who you are and whose bidding you do. Time really doesn't matter." The words were spoken in Russian, as they had been for the previous two days. This man's accent was much more cultured than the others who'd been doing the asking, the torturing. "I see here you haven't uttered a word. Not in this room, not at the station, not on the table or when you were picked up in the hotel room. Nothing." In Russian, the word was "nichego." And the word fit so well. Because there was nothing.

Nothing to say; nothing to feel; nothing to want, to desire. There was nothing these guys could do to hurt him. Cut and bleeding skin, broken cheekbones and injected chemicals were nothing. Nichego. He had turned himself off.

"I knew all four of them, you know." The well-dressed inquisitor leaned forward in his chair. This put him about four feet away. A safe distance with the prisoner's feet chained to the floor and hands chained to those chains. "They were good people, good resources that we could count on. I worked with each of them. I trained two of them myself."

This guy was taking a different approach than the brutes who had done the interrogating yesterday. He operated at a level above the others in the room, and those who'd been in this room the day before or in the interrogation room at the police station. This man was a leader, a giver of orders. Maybe he would be the one to finally get this thing over. He could raise a gun and pull a trigger and put an end to this show. But alas, no. The mission would continue.

The man stood and took a step back. He looked at the other two guys in the room standing in corners and switched to English. "I can see for myself what I've heard. You are young, 25, maybe 26." He switched to German and pointed to the prisoner's shackled arms. "You are an addict. Heroin has you in its grasp." He switched to French. "But you are skilled, trained, well-traveled. You are not Russian, not completely Russian at least." The last line spoken in English.

He stepped to the door and turned around. He returned to Russian. "I can also see what you are not telling me. You are in pain, but not from anything any of my men have inflicted upon you. No, your pain is not physical. I dare say it is the kind of pain that has no name. It is the brand of pain that insulates you from anything else. And I guess it is my job to find the source. When I learn that, we can get past all the rest of this nonsense."

He turned to knock on the door. A head appeared in a small window and the door was opened to let him out. The slaps and kicks and spittle started back up. Luckily, sleep came after a little while. Neil Sedaka sang him a lullaby, like usual. By now, he'd replayed the songwriter's *Sedaka's Back* album in his head no less than 800 times. It was both torture and salvation. Time slipped again.

Water filled his mouth and nose. He was awake again. They were forcing his head over the chair back and pouring the bucket's contents on his face. Water-boarding, they called it in the torture business. This went on for a couple of minutes. He gagged and coughed and took water into his lungs, which meant more coughing. He hoped this would be it, the end. But he knew it wouldn't. This was just more fun for his interrogators since they weren't getting anything from him.

When the water stopped, they released his head and he shot forward to cough and spit and vomit. It took him a minute or two to get his breath back. When he shook his head and opened his eyes, a stranger sat in front of him. This man was older, maybe 63. He was dressed in a suit, but not an expensive outfit.

"Hello." The man spoke in Russian. He sat only three feet away. "Do you know who I am?"

The question was simple and direct and asked by a man who needed no introduction in many, many places in Russia and throughout Europe. This man was a legend. He had fought the Cold War and nearly won. He kept order and discipline and fear in those who worked for him in the KGB, now FSB.

Gregor Smelinski leaned in closer. He had no fear in him, even with this prisoner no longer chained like an animal. The look in Smelinski's eyes was that of a scientist. There was no emotion. Nichego.

"I guess you do not. My face is known to some. Yours is not known to me. I thought coming here would possibly trigger something. I have looked at your photo the last two days and nothing. Your mug shot has been through our system, through the computers and nothing. Your fingerprints, again, nothing. Your dental work, a compilation of East German, British and Greek. Strange, don't you think?" Smelinski smiled.

"Your actions are just as strange. The deaths of four agents in a dirty little hotel room was excellent work. Two shot, one killed with a knife, the other by your hands. Yet, all done while you were evidently under the spell of your demon heroin. You just sat there afterword, waiting. Amazing really."

Smelinski sat back in his chair and rubbed his chin. "My first thought was a drug deal, of course. But there were no drugs on the premises. None, except those in your veins. So that theory was quickly negated." Smelinski turned to the table behind him and grabbed the folder waiting there. He opened it and looked again through the photos and printed pages. "You know, I went there myself, after the bodies had been removed. I wanted to see if I could ascertain what happened. But alas, no. The reason, the cause and motives escape me, as they do everyone else.

"Your silence has been impressive. Interrogations have produced nothing, nothing at all. The chemicals were useless. My associate who visited you yesterday has his theories and is hard at work tracking down information. I doubt the effectiveness of his approach, but he has been right more often than not over the years."

The KGB legend stood and paced. He was thinking, working through details. "Do you know what my favorite theory is now that drugs have been ruled out? I'll tell you. I think maybe it's Seibel. This just feels like him." Smelinski returned to the chair. "Do you know who he is? Oh, I forgot, you're not talking. So I did additional research into Seibel-related matters and even looked into an area no one besides myself knows about. And I thought I had found something, maybe."

Smelinski reached for another folder. He brought it over just a foot in front of the prisoner. He turned it around and leafed through several sheets and enlarged photos. "These are photos taken just before and just after multiple explosions in Moscow in 1992. These two individuals were captured by several cameras around the city." He held up three photos. In them, two bearded men were visible. One photo showed the two walking. The others caught them riding in a car. The photos were taken at night and weren't very clear.

"I don't know why exactly, but I see something in these pictures. In this man." He pointed to one of the two apparently Arab passengers in the car. "Something about this looks familiar. I know it is difficult to see, but," Smelinski turned the photos around and looked at them. "Of course, if this were you, then you would know something that very few people in this world know. You would know a person very few on this earth have met and lived to tell. It would make you very special. And I don't think you are that special. I don't know though, I see something in your black eyes."

He closed the folder, put it with the other and stood with both of the folders cupped in his hand at his side. The KGB spymaster was done with his visit. "You are being moved to another location. I apologize in advance for the facility. You will see what I mean. But it has its purposes."

And with that Smelinski turned to the door. It was just then that the prisoner noticed there was no one else in the room. His torturers had left the two of them alone. He also noticed his handcuffs were no longer chained to his leg chains. Smelinski had been sitting there two feet away, within reach.

"Prizrak." He whispered.

Smelinski turned back from the door. "Excuse me?"

"My name is Prizrak." The prisoner whispered the words.

"Prizrak?" Smelinski raised his eyebrows. "Your name is ghost?"

"Yes. And you need to be very careful. Do not allow anyone else to see me or see my photo." He bowed his head and rotated it in a circular motion. It was a motion learned from a deadly mentor and often followed by death.

Smelinski took a step back toward him, but only one. "And why is that?"

"Anyone who sees my face dies. You should know that Gregor Ivanovich."

The use of the name had its effect. Smelinski stiffened and squinted. But he said nothing.

Black Angel looked down at his unchained feet and hands, "Be sure to tell them to put a bag over my head before anyone else sees me. We don't want anyone to die who doesn't deserve to."

With Smelinski gone, the guards returned. There were three of them. It was the same three who'd been enjoying their time with the angel over the last couple days. Two men stepped over to him to violently lift him from his chair and shove him against the wall. One jammed a nightstick into his side; the other held a gun to his head. It was the first time he'd been on his feet in days. Even with heavy chains on his wrists and ankles, it was a death sentence for three of the men in the room.

Up on his feet with the chain that bound his handcuffs to his leg chains now gone, he stretched his back, even though he was pressed hard against the wall. He moved his head right and left and up and down. His feet were bare. The concrete floor was cold and soaked from all the water dumped on him. He did a head-to-feet analysis of his body, an anatomical review. There was significant soreness, pain. Several joints were strained, but not torn. Felt like two ribs were broken, numbers eight and nine on the right side. His right pinky toe was broken. But overall, not too bad.

It started with his toes, as every good move does. It was a series of movements that folded into one fluid action. Black Angel exploded off the wall, pivoting and raising his arms. He grasped the gun from the first guard's hand and twisted it while lunging forward with his forehead, crushing the bridge of the man's nose. Bone and skull fractured. The man's brain experienced fatal hemorrhaging as he began to collapse to the floor.

Simultaneously, he put the gun to the other guard's head with Guard One's finger still on the trigger. He put a bullet into and through Guard Two's skull. But before either of the first two guards reached the floor, he applied pressure to the ball of his right foot and dove onto the table standing between him and Guard Three. This third guard in the room was the key to the whole thing. The prisoner had watched with his head smashed against the wall as this guard lowered the gun in his hand to his side. That was the movement he needed to initiate the killing.

Guard Three was in the process of raising the gun in his right hand from it's lowered position when his hand was struck by a bare foot, which guided the bullet off target and into the concrete wall. The guard threw a left-handed punch that caught the prisoner in the chest as he came up off the table. The blow succeeded in delaying the guard's death by a whole second and a half.

When the prisoner spun around from the punch with his hands raised and fists clenched, the blow he delivered to the man's neck was sickening in its ferocity. Vertebrae inside the neck's structure were shattered from the viciousness of the blow. Sounded like C3 and C4, right in the middle of the cervical vertebral column. The guard crumpled in a heap and died 35 seconds later, his vertebral arteries crushed and severed.

All three guards lay dead. The entirety of the kill lasted an elapsed nine seconds from the moment the prisoner burst from the wall. He was the angel of death for these brutal killers.

He returned to his chair and sat with the gun in his hand. And there would have been one, maybe two more shots fired up through his own head if it had been anyone else besides Smelinski sitting there in front of him a few minutes earlier. He was ready to be done with all this.

He shook his head slowly and looked at the gun in his hand and smiled. He examined, for the umpteenth time, the tattoos on his arms and chest. He reached out and set the gun on the table and brought his hands back behind his head in resignation. He waited for them to come. They would be pissed, but what the hell. He closed his eyes and time slipped as Sedaka played piano and sang in his head.

The Black Angel was more real in this moment than he'd been in the previous months of subterfuge and killing and chaos in Russia and the Balkans. He'd brought hell on Earth to those on his list. To the world, it seemed he'd been brought to this place by forces outside his control. But alas, the Black Angel makes very few mistakes. And being sent to a prison known to most as the last stop before hell was no mistake.

The shaking started less than a minute later. It had been at least two days since he'd been with her.

Chapter 11

Yuri Sergeyevich Ludkovich didn't much care that four people were murdered in a dilapidated hotel in East Moscow. He did mind that he had not ordered the killings.

The four dead were KGB, or now FSB. Hell, who could keep it straight nowadays? But they were his FSB agents. He owned them, like he did hotels, dozens of gentlemen's clubs, nine banks, a number of corporations and hundreds of current Russian government employees. Yuri had risen in less than a decade to run the largest, most ruthless, and by far, the most profitable organized crime operation in the former Soviet Union. Most people called him a mobster. He felt the name a little insulting and preferred to be called a businessman.

Word of the killings spread in the hours after the bodies were found. Those killed held dual citizenship as FSB agents and mob contractors. They, like so many others after the collapse of the Soviet economy, relied on freelance work to keep their income at a respectable level. It was everywhere. People were out of work or working for a pittance or facing eviction from a landlord who had not existed two years earlier when the government owned everything.

All this destabilization made for good business for men like Ludkovich. KGB agents were trained in the ways of unscrupulous behavior and excelled at exploiting government agencies they once worked for. Ludkovich recognized the value of these professionals and began recruiting them in every state of the former Union. Now, he had resources everywhere. In almost every "business deal," his team included KGB spooks working side-by-side with mob thugs.

He personally knew only one of the four who had been killed at the hotel. The others were hired on by his mob captains. The one he knew, Popov, was good. He had earned his KGB stripes in the Ukraine before returning to Moscow. He was reliable as a negotiator and enforcer; a guy who could hold his own in any fight. He'd killed many.

In fact, Ludkovich had identified Popov as a potential leader in the organization. But now, he and the other three agents were worm food. Murdered brutally and efficiently. The facts surrounding the killings were still being assembled. It appeared one man, an addict actually, had killed all four.

Ludkovich couldn't help but be intrigued. One man, a junkie, killing four experienced spies and walking away from the incident. It was almost unheard of. These espionage types prided themselves on knowing everything when walking into any situation. How could they end up in the same room with a man who could kill them all? It didn't fit, didn't sit well.

Ludkovich would be meeting with Suvorov, Smelinski's right hand man, this evening and hear what he had learned about the suspect. Maybe he could arrange to bring this young killer to him so Ludkovich could see for himself what this man was made of. Killers like that could always be useful.

Chapter 12

"I should have seen that. Huge error on my part." Frank Wyrick, contract special surveillance expert for the Central Intelligence Agency, was ticked at himself. Seibel wasn't very happy either.

Wyrick had been working for much of the past year on a very special project and thought he had completed it with superb results. But he missed something; something big.

"I missed it. Don't know how it could have happened." Wyrick shook his head sitting across the table from Seibel in a café outside of Philadelphia where they had met maybe three dozen times over the past 25 years.

"But you got it all now, right?" Seibel took a sip of his coffee after asking.

"All of it. But months after the fact."

"You're sure you have it all?" Seibel was insistent.

"All of it. Been over it seven times. Confirmed through computer backend with two blind sources. It has all been removed now." Wyrick finished the coffee in his cup. He had learned just this past week that data featuring information on Lance Porter Priest was in a backup U.S. Military repository. It could have been tragic if it was discovered before being erased. But the information should not have been there. It didn't make sense really. It was like someone left it there for others to find. It felt to Wyrick like it had been done on purpose.

"Then everything should be fine. No harm, no foul." Seibel sat back against the ancient cushions in their booth tucked into the back corner of the diner. "Don't beat yourself up. This one was far outside the norm. There was a whole lot more to control than the last time we did this. Back then, it was contained to three counties in Western New York. This time, you had to penetrate what, nine different systems?"

"Eleven, when you include Texas Records and the National Parks."

Seibel shook his head and chuckled. "That's right, I forgot about Preacher's little incident at Yosemite with that poacher. Always dealing out his own brand of justice isn't he?"

Wyrick turned away. It was evident to Seibel by the set of Wyrick's face that he was still a little ticked about this assignment. Seibel had given him the orders over a year and a half ago. His dissatisfaction with the whole thing was obvious. Seibel knew the face well.

"I don't have to tell you how good a job this was Frank," Seibel tapped a finger on the table as he said each word. "I know how you feel about this, but that doesn't change the fact that what you did was magic. What you've done here is nothing short of genius. I didn't know if it was possible when you started."

Seibel's words did not soften Wyrick's face. He simply wasn't going to be convinced of the righteousness of this assignment. It wasn't the job really; it was the effect of the entire strategy that offended Wyrick. Doing this to someone was terrible. Doing it to someone they knew and were supposed to protect was deplorable, unforgivable. "Just a job." Wyrick muttered. He'd done so many unsavory ones for Seibel over the years. He knew he'd given up his right to protest dishonorable acts such as this. He'd sold his soul decades ago.

"Like I said, I know how you feel. You're not alone. Mikel is not speaking to me right now, or at least not returning my calls."

Wyrick shook his head. "I don't want to know, you know that."

"Okay, okay." Seibel sat forward to be sure he had Wyrick's attention. "This will work. It is already working."

"I don't need your mad scientist stuff." Wyrick cut him off. "I know what you're doing, what we are doing, can work. If anyone can get himself out of this alive it is Preacher. It's just..." he looked down at the remains of his breakfast on his plate.

"It's just that I shouldn't have done this. I shouldn't have cut him off at the knees and thrown him to the wolves. I know." Seibel pursed his lips.

"It's not that. No one should have done this. No, its how you did it. Like I said, I don't want to know. Hell I don't want to know anything about this, but Fuchs can't talk to anyone else in the world but me, so I got more details than I want." Wyrick sat forward now, agitated. "You didn't have to do it this way. And if I had known what you and Braden were planning a year ago, I would have stopped you. You have destroyed at least two lives here, many more when you include family. This God act you and your evil genius shrink are pulling off here will undoubtedly come back to haunt you, haunt all of us."

Seibel often reacted quite differently than others expected him to. Wyrick had been around Papa long enough to know this as much as anyone. So he wasn't surprised to see the smile come across Seibel's face now. "Undoubtedly."

Wyrick just shook his head. "And then there's her."

"Indeed." Seibel nodded his head. "This will be the proverbial unleashing of hell on Earth."

"But why? Why did we do this?" Wyrick raised his hands slightly. Seibel watched the movement. Wyrick saw the way Seibel's eyes moved. "So you think maybe I'm here to act?"

"You said yourself you'd stop me."

"I should have."

"Frank, just relax. You've been through enough with me to know I've got my reasons. And you know that some things I need to keep to myself. This is one of them."

"It may work, but at a cost no one should have to pay. You could have done it differently. They didn't have to be treated this way."

Seibel shook his head at that. "This was the only way. He needed a clean break, a severing of himself from the world. You know him."

"Not just a clean break. You and Braden felt you had to break him, like some wild horse or some animal in an experiment. You, we, had other options."

"Wrong. This is literally the one and only way, for both of them." Seibel's smile was gone.

"Christ, literally? You went into your little lab and mixed up some concoction here that is going to literally get people killed. And you and I will be among them."

And the smile came back to Seibel's face. "I have no doubt. Me for sure. You may be spared. But I don't stand a chance. This is terminal this time, no doubt."

"Listen to you. I've watched all your Machiavellian schemes for years and no one has been better, no one has come close.

But this little scheme is sick. I can only imagine what is going through Preacher's mind, wherever he is. He's probably thinking of only one thing."

Seibel reached across the table and grabbed Wyrick's forearm. "Exactly. He is thinking one thing and one thing only. And you and I both know what that is. He is going to kill everyone. He has no distractions any more. She is dead. He can focus solely on what he was meant to do. This mission will change things."

"Man, look at you. I was wondering and now I know. You are losing it. I think you've been in this so long you can't see out. You are not seeing this clearly."

"Wrong again." Seibel pulled Wyrick's hand across the table until they were basically in a position like two men about to arm-wrestle. "I've never seen anything more clearly. This scheme, as you call it, is where we have been headed for decades. It took time and tide and the ideal ingredients, but this is exactly where we were headed 25 years ago when we started this. We are there."

Wyrick tried to pull his hand back but Seibel held it in a vise. "Where are we? Wholesale death and destruction at the hands of two killers you brought into the world?"

"No, no Frank. We are at the dawn, the birth of two perfect spies, two perfect weapons. And thanks to you and your exceptional work, neither of them exist."

"Except for the memories in his family's head. And don't think for a moment that I didn't believe you capable of wiping those out as well. Maybe you have a little humanity left in you." Wyrick relaxed his arm.

"Very little. They lost their son, their brother. That's all they need to know. They wouldn't want to know him now anyway. He's not Lance any more. Just as she ceased being Jenny 15 years ago. You'll see. This is perfect. It's uncomfortable and wrong, I know. But perfect nonetheless."

"Let me just remind you that your perfect scenario here involves two people, two ruthless, and I mean absolutely friggin' ruthless, coldblooded, merciless killers. And let me remind you that neither are dead like they've each been convinced. When they eventually learn the other is alive, we are likely to see a killing spree that will make Bonnie and Clyde look like scouts." Wyrick was not amused. In fact, he was scared.

Chapter 13

Sarajevo continued to rage, to boil with death and destruction and overflowing despair. He could see the muzzle flashes in high-rise windows from his hillside perch. Down below, people scattered and screamed. Some fell. Others died. He looked for a pattern in the shooting. *Could that be him?*

Fuchs was here tracking a ghost, a violent angel. The trail had gone cold several weeks ago until whispers started coming out of Bosnia, out of the war raging in the former Yugoslavia. Russians had come here and so had a team of deadly killers who wiped out the elite Russian squad and vanished into the night. Sounded like the work of the Black Angel.

Fuchs' skills were perfect for deteriorating situations like this. This city, like others in Bosnia, was being torn apart by ethnic violence. It was primarily Serbs against Bosniaks and Croats. But the code underneath was Christian versus Muslim. Fuchs had listened as Seibel worked through the very scenario being played out before him below in the streets of Sarajevo. The words "ethnic cleansing" were spoken by news anchors, reporters and pundits in relation to this horrific conflict.

If those words were used in their actual meaning, they could be applied to most, if not all conflagrations currently roiling across the globe. From Africa to the Middle East to Tibet, ethnic and religious differences fueled killing and torture and forced relocation. But that wasn't what occupied his mind at present. He needed to see if a certain angel had lost it.

Fuchs, Foxy to his closest CIA compatriots, rose from his perch and made his way down the hill. He was clothed in black and pulled a ski mask down over his face as he reached a ravine at the east end of a park. He skirted along the tree line. The evening light was completely obscured by surrounding hills as he stepped out from the trees onto a blackened city street. He took his pace up to a steady jog and hugged buildings as he made his way into the center of the city over the course of several miles.

Nineteen minutes later, he entered the southeast door of an 18-story structure. In the minutes prior to entering the building, he had killed two sentries posted 70 yards apart on the street. Their deaths were silent. An experienced vicious killer expertly wielded the blade that ended their lives. Now, rounding floor after floor in the stairwell, Fuchs kept his climbing pace steady. His daily physical regimen was only surpassed by Preacher's; the Preacher of old at least. Fuchs pushed himself to outer and upper limits on a daily basis in preparation for moments like this.

Suddenly he stopped. The leather sole of a boot or shoe scraping across metal created a noise above in the stairwell. Fuchs stepped sideways to peer up into the darkness. He was between the 11th and 12th floors. The noise sounded like it came from two levels up. He stood silently listening for movement. A few seconds later, he heard a belch followed by a sigh and then a muttered word. He waited a another minute.

No other sounds came down. Fuchs began taking the steps slowly, his silenced assault rifle aimed upward. The person above adjusted his weight and leaned against the railing. It was the sound of a guard lacking attentiveness; the sound of boredom. So Fuchs continued his ascent until he was on the floor just below the man. He leaned to his left and looked up to see the man's elbow leaning on the railing. He took aim but didn't fire. The stairwell was darkened; lit only by small bulbs on every other landing. The sentry was positioned just below one of the unlit landings. Fuchs took in a small breath and continued his climb.

As he approached the flight just below the guard, he turned to climb backwards with his weapon aimed up at the man. Although it was dark, Fuchs saw all he needed to see. The sentry had on a dark suit with a rifle slung over his shoulder. It was not a sniper rifle, just a normal Kalashnikov. Fuchs silently stepped onto the stairs below the guard. The man took the cigarette from his mouth and looked down at the black figure just 10 feet below him. The move was his, but he was frozen. He stood no chance and he knew it. Fuchs nodded and put a silenced bullet through the man's head. In the enclosed space, it sounded like a cough. He rushed up to catch the body and rifle as the now lifeless body collapsed.

He left the sentry there and continued up to the next floor. From the landing, he listened through the door and heard no movement, no activity. He opened the door and stepped into a darkened hallway. The siege mentality of the place hit him smack in the face. There was no one walking about on the floor. All doors were closed and locked. The next part should be fairly easy if he made it here fast enough. He walked down a hall, turned right and down another hallway. His hunch was proven true less than 30 seconds later when a single shot rang out through the building. He knew where it came from. There was no hurry now. He had reached his destination.

Six units from the end of the hallway, Fuchs stood outside a door and listened. He didn't want to wait for another shot to be fired, but needed to. So he stepped back and prepared for his next move. He prepared to explode.

Twenty-one seconds later, another shot was fired. The loud explosion shook the building. In the same microsecond as the gunshot, Fuchs sprang forward and kicked the door with such force the casing split and burst as the door slammed open. He was through the doorway and into the small apartment in the same second. To his left, a man, woman and small child cringed together on a sofa in a tiny living room. Fuchs turned to his right to move down the short hall, a stealth panther stalking the night. A second later he was on his belly sliding into the doorway of a bedroom on the left. In the room, a man with a pair of binoculars in one hand held a handgun in the other. Fuchs put a silenced bullet through the man's neck that traveled through the raised windowpane where the sniper turned to look in Fuchs' direction.

It was not Lance. Not the Black Angel.

The sniper was seated on a chair with a can of soda sitting on a shelf beside him; a burning cigarette in his mouth. He started the useless process of moving the sniper rifle from the window to aim at Fuchs. The CIA operative with well more than 50 kills in his illustrious and completely top secret career, put another silenced bullet through the shooter's right shoulder. The shot caused the man to drop the rifle to the floor where it crashed and rattled. Fuchs got back to his feet and stepped over to the whimpering man.

He knew it wouldn't be Preacher doing the shooting, but still he followed the hunch. Fuchs liked to rid the world of the occasional vermin, like the scum sitting in a window picking off innocent civilians on the streets below.

Fuchs gathered the information he needed and ended the sniper's life the same way he had ended many others – a clean bullet through his head and a mess for someone else to clean up on the wall and floor.

Fuchs stepped back out to the family cowering on the couch. The husband and father positioned himself in front of his wife and young daughter. Fuchs was not happy with these people, but he realized they probably didn't have a whole lot of say in the matter. The sniper and his spotter had probably made it exceedingly clear that regardless of their ethnicity or political affiliations, the family would be slaughtered if they tried anything funny. They were prisoners in this city just as much as those scampering about below.

He turned and walked out of the apartment and made his way from of the apartment building through the black of the Sarajevo night into the woods. He had learned from the sniper a good bit of helpful information that would provide the basis for future incursion operations in the area. He had the name of a few ethnic Serb commanders who would prove useful. And he learned a little more about a troupe of elite Russian soldiers slaughtered the week before.

"I'm glad it wasn't you." Fuchs thought to himself as he reached the jeep he stashed two miles away from the hillside. He drove off and disappeared into the night. He'd been tracking the latest Black Angel through Russia, Ukraine and into the Balkans. He'd learned to start with local heroin dealers as the best resource, but was always a few days behind Preacher.

Chapter 14

Stuart Braden kept a secret that only four people in this world knew. It was one of those secrets that people die for, literally, die for. To tell the truth, he wished he didn't know. He only had this knowledge because he was handed a copy of a hospital medical record.

With time, all wounds heal. The human body is truly an amazingly resilient super organism. Broken bones will set and fuse together even stronger than before the break occurred. A fractured pelvis may require surgery and an external fixator device with screws inserted through the skin. Skull fractures my require surgery and leave scars beneath hair, but they too heal with time, leaving only a scar and maybe some screws and a metal plate or two.

The patient will eventually regain health, partial mobility, and hopefully, normalcy. There may be reminders. Scars and limps and dull aches can be a part of life after these injuries.

The part of the body that may have the most difficult time finding the benefits of healing is that which can't be seen on an x-ray or MRI. The human mind, although as resilient as the rest of the body, can sometimes be unable to enjoy the miracles of healing touch. Sometimes the wounds sustained here never get better. Never.

And when a mind has been exposed to a reality not expected, not ever expected in wildest dreams, it may be unable to accept another reality. This new existence may be rejected, just as a body rejects a transplanted organ.

If Marta had to say, that is how she would describe it. She was rejecting life without him, without Lance. She was rejecting his death. Marta knew it was real, knew he was gone. She'd been shown the evidence, as minuscule and fractured as it was. He was too close to the rented van as it exploded in the underground parking garage of the World Trade Center. Most likely, he was right there trying to deactivate the bomb.

Marta knew the facts. Seibel and his team had meticulously traced Lance's final hours and his detective work that alerted authorities to the bomb threat in the Empire State Building before he headed south to the World Trade Center.

He'd gotten close, obviously. But he'd been unable to stop the explosion. Lance was only human after all. She'd witnessed the limits of his abilities before. Marta nursed him after the disastrous adventure in the Philippines when Fuchs had to carry his bullet-riddled body out of a terrorist training camp. She'd heard the frustration of his failure in Baghdad, when he had Saddam in his sites but was unable to rid the planet of that menace.

She just had so much faith in Lance. She simply never expected him to be gone before her. He was such a marvel, such a gift...

She turned away from Braden to look out the window in the small community room she and he had walked to during the last 30 minutes. They had walked slowly in silence into the facility's main building from her bungalow. Her extensive injuries required her to move at a snail's pace and use a cane. The slow pace gave her time to think, too much time. When she turned back to him, she was a vulnerable woman mourning the loss of love. She let only Braden see this face. He was the only one she trusted with any display of emotion. Only Braden knew the extent of her pain.

He could never betray this moment. Seibel had surely asked him, ordered him, on numerous occasions to tell him what Marta divulged to him. But she was sure Braden protected certain elements of her psyche from Seibel.

Braden reached out and took her hand. He had spent many hours with others going through similar situations. Death and loss go with the territory in the espionage and black ops game. He counseled hundreds of patients, ranging from field agents to agency directors. He had held many hands to reassure his patients of his trustworthiness. But sitting here in this room with Marta, he knew once again that he was dealing with the loneliest person he had ever encountered. There was now no one else like her in the entire world. The only one had been lost.

Marta's impenetrable wall of loneliness was palpable. It was tangible. He could feel her solitude, her abandonment, the complete and total isolation in her touch. He could not help but feel sad for this lethal killing machine.

In his decades of duty as a CIA psychologist, he sat beside patients who had attempted suicide for various and sundry reasons and had always felt that their plight was self-imposed. While this was true to an extent for Marta, her history, with its descent through every single level of Hell, was carved in stone. She was a killer, an agent of death and destruction and pain and misery. Her eventual return to the living world was coupled to Lance. She was bound to him, like a pair of swans mated for life. Braden understood that Marta's role of Juliet to his Romeo required her to follow him into that sweet hereafter. Sooner or later.

What was he supposed to say to her? 'Come on honey, you'll get over it. You'll meet another cold-blooded, ruthless, merciless, pitiless killer. Just give it a little time.' He really had no right to offer her any advice. He was a part of a system that brought her here to this lonely place. He was complicit in falling in love with the idea of Lance Priest going out and altering the world as a glorious agent of change.

"You're thinking that I'm planning to end my life soon." Her words pulled him out of his haze.

"Actually, I was thinking that very thing. It makes me sad." His response was honest.

"How's that?" She smiled slightly.

"It making me sad?"

"Yes. I think I should be the sad one."

"Yes, of course. But it makes me sad thinking of this world without you in it. I've come to think of you as much more than a patient, you know." He smiled back at her.

"I understand. I do. But you shouldn't do that."

"Do what?"

"Think of me as anything more than a patient, a project. I appreciate your time and your efforts and I understand why you're doing this. But we both know it is more about him than me." She looked down before the tears came. She squeezed his hand. He let her be; held her hand and let her go where she needed to.

Marta Sidorova knew the rules. She was anything but naive. She had done terrible, horrible, no good things all through her life. She murdered her brother at 11; killed another boy in a facility a few years later and permanently injured two male guards at another institution who thought they could have their way with her.

She was rescued from that world by Seibel, who saw value in her personal brand of malevolence. She was trained and released into the wild in Russia where she completed every mission assigned to her by Seibel. She caught the eye of the KGB. She was recruited trained and released into another wilderness where she never failed to exceed expectations.

Gregor Smelinski, Seibel's Cold War counterpart, hatched a secret plan where Marta went AWOL from the KGB and built a rogue network of mischief and mayhem. She was the perfect double agent. Her entire life was a lie, a facade. And then there was Baghdad, and that young man who walked through the door and stole her breath and her heart, before he shot her. Twice.

After five minutes and a million miles, she was back. "Did you know about his satellite vision?" She asked Braden.

His brows furrowed. "His what?"

"His extra-sensory visual acuity."

"No, I mean he pulled his little seeing behind my back trick several times, but..."

"That's it. He could see down from above." She looked up into the corners of the room. "I know it sounds crazy. Hell it was crazy. But after several hundred times doing it, it was more than a trick. He could see things in a different way, see more than the rest of us."

"Like what he saw in you?" He got another smile out of her with that one. She even laughed and wiped away a tear.

Marta instinctively rubbed the scar on her left hand. He watched her do this for the hundredth or so time since they had lost him. He watched her look up again into the corner of the room and understood now why she had done this hundreds of times in these sessions. She was looking for him. It was a little bit of relief. He had mistaken these glances to be a form of psychosis.

It was just Marta seeking to hold on to something. That was understandable. And that brought him back to the secret he kept. It was a secret that Marta could never know. If she ever learned of it, she would surely lose whatever hold she had on reality. She would likely turn to murder and mayhem on a scale not seen before. Seibel would be a goner. Braden would be slaughtered for keeping it from her. He had tossed the pages into his fireplace at his home in Pennsylvania just a minute after reading the words on a sheet of paper.

He did his best not to think of it while with Marta, but sometimes it just crept in when he looked at her. She was beautiful in a way that couldn't be defined. Her personality and aura influenced those who gazed upon her. Her beauty came in layers. That was the best way he could describe it.

And Lance, well he was such a chameleon all the time that looking at him was like looking at the sky or the ocean. It changed constantly. But he was just such a good-looking kid that he invited you in. He, like Marta, attracted one's eye because of unique aspects, no matter how much they each worked to be anonymous.

Braden knew he was biased when it came to each of them. He had gotten too close. His relationship with them crossed a professional boundary. He couldn't help but think of their blended uniqueness. He couldn't help but think of the baby, the unborn child they produced. The child they had created before it died inside Marta when she was caught in that horrific explosion. The blood test ordered by the doctor in the hospital ICU confirmed what he saw in a pelvic x-ray. The doctor ordered an ultrasound to confirm his initial diagnosis. The fetus captured in one of the images was indeed dead. It was simply the kind of news that no one could ever share with her.

He squeezed her hand and smiled again and helped her get up to make her way slowly back to her cottage.

Of course, Stuart Braden possessed another secret that very few humans knew. He knew that Lance Priest was not dead. This little tidbit was possibly more dangerous than the other piece of withheld information. Braden knew that he and Seibel were dead men. She would one day find out. And she would make that murdering child and teenager she had once been look like a saint. Her vengeance would not be contained.

Back in her bungalow, Marta replayed the session with Braden. She could only assume he knew. He is a doctor after all. She could see him holding back.

It had to be difficult for Stuart to come here and see her like this week after week, month after month. Had to be shocking for him to see her reduced to what she had become. But how could she be any different? What else could she be but empty? She had lost her love and her baby, their baby. Instead of rubbing the scar on her hand, when she was alone, she rubbed her belly and the unseen painful scar there. She had been ready to tell him, tell Lance her news. She would have told him later that day in New York. On her trip to the drug store for the cold medicine she spiked and forced on Lance so he could get a few hours sleep, she also purchased a pregnancy test kit.

She shook her head for the millionth time. How could everything come crashing down in a matter of hours? Damn.

But still, she was Marta. She was the same person deep inside. She had a job to do, eventually. Her bungalow was nice, but it was undoubtedly bugged. She had inspected it a number of times and found several devices. But some were just too easy to find. That meant there were others, most likely planted by Wyrick.

So she focused on one room. The bathroom.

She pried loose light switches, loosened light sockets and electrical outlets. The fan in the ceiling had no device. Evidently, they left her alone in this one room. Mistake.

In the bathroom, she would turn on the shower and proceed to push herself through tight little workouts that maximized the tight space. Thousands of pushups, sit-ups, squats and curls using two one gallon jugs were her release from bondage. Outside this tiny room, she was a pained, miserable, hobbled remnant of what used to be. Her back was always stooped. Her limp always pronounced.

But inside her bathroom, Marta became something else. She knew that one day she would emerge from this small room and burst forth into a world not prepared for a new Marta.

Heroin enters the brain, where it is converted to morphine and binds to receptors known as opioid receptors. These receptors are located in many areas of the brain (and in the body), especially those involved in the perception of pain and in reward. Opioid receptors are also located in the brain stem—important for automatic processes critical for life, such as breathing (respiration), blood pressure, and arousal. Heroin overdoses frequently involve a suppression of respiration.

Chapter 15

The shaking, constant bone-jarring, teeth-chattering, never-ending, death spiral shaking stopped. The itching and sweats that followed the shaking also stopped. Problem was, it all ended because the bastards stuck a needle in his vein and injected pure friggin' Grade A heroin.

To get the needle in his arm, six heavily armed and armored guards rushed him while two standing back from the others shot him with tranquilizer darts. The darts hit him in the chest and shoulder while he sat in the chair with his hands behind his head. And then the bodies were on him. They were brutal in their assault, which was understandable since three of their own were dead on the floor in the small room. Lance just took it all without any resistance. He went limp and was face down on the smooth concrete floor when the additional needle was inserted into his arm. He knew right away it was heroin. It was her.

He had no idea what the drug felt like just a few months ago. He worked back through the months as best he could, but they were all murky, distant. They were like a rounded and smooth rock wall that didn't give him any hand or footholds to work his way up. He lost days and weeks sometimes. The only thing he was sure about was that Marta was dead.

He worked through the last four days. He was found at the hotel where he had killed four FSB agents. He was arrested and taken to a local police station where he was beaten. He was transported from the police station to the Lubyanka, the headquarters of the KGB, where he was beaten and tortured some more. And today, he had been transported from the Lubyanka to Lefortovo Prison. The facility was famous, almost mythical, for its place in Russian, Soviet and Cold War legends as the house of death and torture. Great.

"She's gone Lance. I'm so sorry."

Braden was as hurt by it as anyone. He had come to love and trust and care for Marta in the months since she and Preacher returned from Europe to track Anwar, the terrorist bomber. Lance had to comfort Braden when the psychologist brought him the terrible news about Marta.

Lance also knew that Braden was sent to convey the news because if Seibel had, he would have killed him on the spot. Lance would have broken free of the straps holding him to the bed and killed Seibel with his own hands.

He could only return to the hospital in his mind for a few seconds before the image overtook him and brought the rage. Holding her hand as she lay barely alive in the ICU was his goodbye to her; his goodbye to unexpected and undeserved love. He had exploded a few minutes later when he accused Seibel of not acting to stop the WTC bombing. But the rage was really his reaction to losing her.

Lance shook his head for the thousandth time since he'd lost her. It was a helpless movement, resignation.

They'd always known their time together was tenuous, limited. They would never be allowed to grow old together, to live a life of peace and family and contemplation. There was no chance of that.

But still, there was hope.

He'd been changed by her; and she by him. It was one of those irreversible things that once experienced, could never be negated, never refuted. She may have been working for Seibel the whole time they were together, but that didn't matter. Hell, she could have been the Devil's ugly stepdaughter and he would have felt the same.

The connection he and Marta shared was the kindred spirit type. Few could relate to it. That made it special, maybe unique. That was what he missed most. Not her smile, nor her welcoming eyes. Not her warm touch and smooth skin. It was her understanding of who he is. It took one to know one; to be one.

Nothing more.

A question answered yesterday no longer troubled him. He'd been wondering about the 'why' behind all of this. That answer came when he opened his eyes to see Smelinski seated before him. Several things came into focus in that moment. Chiefly among them was the realization that Seibel had worked his magic yet again.

Coupled with Smelinski coming into the picture was the realization that Lance's identity had truly been wiped out, erased. He recalled somewhere in the haze of the lost months hearing from a disembodied Seibel that he was now a free man. No strings held him in place anymore.

His prints had not registered on any databases. And undoubtedly, the FSB had inroads into U.S. law enforcement and military databases. Removing all information connecting Lance Porter Priest to the unknown tattooed soul in this concrete prison box required a little magic as well. Lance assumed it was Wyrick's handiwork.

Someone really had to know how to dig to find and remove biographical and biometric information. No one could completely wipe out a person's history, especially when there is family involved.

Erasing fingerprint records, driver's license numbers, photos and military personnel records would take time and know-how. Something like this wasn't done in weeks. It had taken months, maybe longer. Friggin' ingenious yet again, Mr. Seibel. He smiled into the concrete floor his bloody face lay upon.

On the "why" front, the best Lance had come up with was to remove him from any semblance of normalcy in order to sever him from the past. He was basically primed and perfect for this Black Angel mission. Seibel did it again.

But then there was Neil Sedaka playing piano and singing in his head. Those songs from an album his mom played endlessly on a huge record player, refused to let him go. Sedaka's songs playing on a repeating loop in his brain insulated him from death and pain and heroin and withdrawal and memories.

Gregor the Terrible was on full display. He had put six people in their place in the last hour. He prided himself on being unemotional, but some things just got him going. Yuri Ludkovich was one of those things.

The upstart mobster had taken over where the corrupt government left off. The fact this street trash had risen to elite status and now held a position that the FSB had to kowtow to was unconscionable. It was a direct result of the complete and utter collapse of the Russian economy. The damn mafia was often the only place spies could find good paying jobs nowadays. Smelinski could not compete with them on a cash basis.

Because of the mass defections from covert operational status to mafia employee, the FSB had been forced to deal with the likes of Ludkovich. Smelinski could order the bastard's assassination, but another ruthless creep would ascend to the throne within days, after a few hundred mostly innocent people were killed, of course.

Ludkovich demanded an audience to discuss the killings in the hotel. He wanted details. Smelinski had no fewer than 25 agency resources researching this one. Nothing was coming up on the mystery prisoner. His prints produced no hits. His photo was circulated through virtually every database and came back with nothing more than 10 to 15 percent connections. The dental exams and x-rays showed a mixed bag of results. And then there were the tattoos. Damn.

The markings this character bore were those of a mafia special soldier. The 37 teardrops leaking from that eye on his chest translated to 37 kills. Christ, 37 kills by a man no older than 25. A boy really. But that number needed to be updated after the hotel three nights ago. Then the mystery man decided to give a few of his guards a little payback just minutes after Smelinski had left him.

"Black Angel." He whispered the words. If this mystery man was indeed the mythical Black Angel, Smelinski should go down to Lefortovo right now and put a bullet through the murdering bastard's head. But this young man couldn't be the Angel. He was just a boy. The Angel, if such a creature really existed outside of KGB legend, was an experienced killer who terrorized the agency in the late 1950s and then again in the early 70s in Southeast Asia. More than 20 years had passed since Gregor the Terrible heard the words "Black Angel."

Gregor knew he bore the blame for the killings of the three guards in the Lubyanka by having the connecting chain on the mystery man's hands and legs removed. To tell the truth, he wanted to see what the killer would do. How he would respond. He just didn't expect him to be so clinically effective. The killings evidently took a total of 10 seconds. And the guards killed were very experienced interrogation specialists.

Who was this man? The Lubyanka warden had authorized the use of heroin to subdue the prisoner somewhat permanently since Smelinski had placed a strict no-kill order. The mystery man was probably so high right now he wouldn't come down for days.

Smelinski needed more information. And he wanted to see just what this character was capable of. His skills could be useful, undoubtedly. The question was, could this ambiguous, unknown and vicious animal be tamed?

And just how did the murdering bastard know Smelinski's name?

Chapter 16

Ludkovich sat at his reserved table in the café he visited almost every day of the week. If someone wanted to kill him, they need only put a bomb under the table. No one had the balls, yet.

Smelinski entered the dining room through the kitchen door. He preferred to use the rear entrance the few times he'd been to the café.

"Tea." The KGB veteran said to the waiter after he removed his coat and sat.

The two of them just looked at each other while they waited for Smelinski's tea. After it arrived Ludkovich smiled. "Those men were well executed. It was clockwork, very professional." Ludkovich smiled broadly.

"Are you referring to the hotel or Lubyanka?" Smelinski asked as he sipped the steaming tea.

"Both." Ludkovich continued to smile.

Smelinski didn't return the smile. "So what did you need to talk to me about? I'm sure you have more pressing matters."

The mafia kingpin laughed. His men sitting at tables around the café looked in his direction. He avoided their eyes. "Of course Gregor Ivanovich. I have very pressing matters to talk to you about, as always." He leaned even closer and dropped his voice to a whisper. "The particular matter we have discussed on several occasions involving a certain member of the leadership team is still unresolved. I will have to take action within days if this is not corrected to satisfaction."

Smelinski knew this was the reason he'd been summoned by this mobster trash. The member of the leadership team Ludkovich referred to just happened to be the current president. The issue Ludkovich alluded to involved a large mob debt the man had incurred prior to being elected. His office did not excuse him from his personal debt. And Ludkovich was growing impatient, very impatient.

Smelinski nodded, "I am aware of the situation, perhaps more aware than yourself. But you must remain patient Yuri Andreovich. This will be remedied. I have given you my word that a workable solution will be reached. The debt will be repaid."

Covering a gambler's debts was just about the last thing Smelinski wanted to do with his limited time. But the need existed for his involvement because of the source of the funds in question. The obscenely stupid current president had not merely placed state funds in jeopardy, he had utilized KGB sourced monies in his off-book ventures. So now, the nation's premier intelligence agency owed a debt to one of the nation's preeminent ruthless mobsters. It was surreal. And Smelinski intended to have someone pay dearly for the action.

He was glad when Ludkovich returned to the topic of the mystery man being held in Lefortovo.

"I think I'd like to meet him." Ludkovich raised his eyebrows as he kept the smile on his lips. "He sounds like a very interesting man."

Chapter 17

Unhinged.

He was unhinged. Lefortovo Prison caused people to become deranged. The arrival of Prisoner 77H3 caused a stir the place hadn't seen in years, decades even.

The guards wanted him dead. The FSB agents back at the Lubyanka wanted him to suffer terribly before he was killed. But Smelinski's orders could not be disobeyed without repercussions.

However, the orders did not preclude prisoners in the general population from doing the deed.

So it was with a bit of theater that the prisoner was ushered through dingy hallways into a small common yard five days after arriving at Lefortovo. The chain connecting his leg chains and handcuffs was removed as he was pushed into the yard with six other inmates.

Six dead men.

It took the Black Angel exactly 32 seconds to kill the first prisoner who attacked him in the yard. The next man died 14 seconds later. Well, actually, he died a couple of minutes later, but the blow delivered by Black Angel's right elbow to the man's left temple caused immediate and extensive subdural bleeding and swelling. Death ensued.

A third man barreled toward him. He was as big as the first two combined. He was mammoth, with arms significantly thicker than the angel's legs and a torso that alone weighed 250 pounds. The problem was the giant's momentum and the Black Angel's understanding of physics. The giant's key problem was his inability to stop his momentum as he roared toward Black Angel kneeling on the ground next to the first two dead men.

The giant probably didn't know Einstein's universal law. $E=MC^2$ and all.

Black Angel saw the kill well before he dealt the death. A glance to his right showed four guards standing behind two closed gates. The look on their faces was not the satisfaction they were hoping to witness when they pushed the lone inmate into a small yard with six ruthless killers.

Instead, the guards looked at each other and fumbled for the keys to open the gates. The angel had about 20 seconds to become further unhinged and complete a mission component.

He rose to his feet and turned to his left as the giant began to throw his mammoth right fist at his head. The next move was simple. It was even easier to see it unfolding in ultra slow motion. The guards had waited too long to play this game. Five days was enough for the heroin to leave his bloodstream and brain; long enough for the ravages of withdrawals to flood through him and ebb. Five days meant the Black Angel had a clear mind.

And finally, the one thing this brilliant killing machine had that no one else in the world possessed was the gift of a second set of eyes looking down from above. He noticed it the moment the guards shoved him through the gate and to the ground. Again, five days meant no mind-altering drugs lingering in his system. Lance may not have come back, but his vision from above returned as Black Angel entered the yard and the sky above beckoned. He saw everything. Everything.

The rust flaking on the ancient bars. The worms swimming through the tiny patch of grass beyond the bars. The four swallows perched atop a 30-foot wall. The initial muscle twitch in the left forearm of the first inmate to attack him. The distinct limp in the right leg of the second man. The barbed wire tattoo on the neck of the gargantuan prisoner swinging an immense fist at him.

It was all quite beautiful. It was a stop-action ballet unfolding before his eyes. He even smiled.

Black Angel waited for the punch to be fully extended and reached to grab the monster's wrist as he simultaneously dropped to his knee while turning away from the behemoth. This wrenching, dropping and spinning motion used the giant's momentum against him. Black Angel pulled down on the man's arm, which caused the giant to tumble forward and down. The sound the man's head made when it impacted on the concrete slab was sickening. Literally sickening. Bone crushed, skin split and matter seeped out.

The angel then leapt from the dead giant to burst toward the next closest inmate. He grasped the man's left arm and broke it at the elbow and then spun and shot his fingers up and into the soft tissue of the man's submaxillary triangle between the Adam's apple and chin and spun to fling the man up and over his shoulder crushing skull and brain on the concrete underfoot just like the monster's head.

The other two men in the 40 by 30-foot space were either frozen by the display or cowering back against bars and brick. Black Angel was a frenetic tornado delivering elbows, knees, shoulders and kicks. The next prisoner was dealt blows to the back of his neck that shattered vertebrae and spinal cord.

The last fella was hurled into the bars and received a blow to his sternum that crushed rib, dislodged cartilage and punctured lungs. Black Angel sustained several blows during the chaos, but nothing too serious. As usual, he was simply too fast. It was like his mother's huge stereo that he had to pull a chair over to and climb up to put another record on the player. The prisoners, now mostly dead, spun at 33 rpm while Black Angel moved at 78 rpm.

By the time the four guards came through the double security gates at the far end of the small yard, six inmates were either dead or dying. The guards, instead of rushing the angel, only took a couple of steps into the space. They stood 30 feet away from him with their sticks in hand. Black Angel took a few deep cleansing breaths and looked their way.

"Today is as good as any to die comrades. Why wait?" And he waved them on. None of them stepped forward. In fact, they moved back behind the gates and closed and locked them. They spoke into radios calling for assistance. Preacher could only shake his head. He turned to pick up the man lying closest to him, the one with the shattered sternum, and set him on a bench.

The prisoner, a bald man with coal black eyes and a dragon tattoo on his neck was the reason the Black Angel was in this prison hell hole. The man's name was on a list memorized in his killer's head. He had tracked the prisoner down and found out just nine days ago that he was an inmate in Lefortovo. To get to him, Black Angel needed to do something heinous and shocking; something the FSB would be compelled to respond to by sending the perpetrator to hell on earth.

Something like killing four corrupt FSB agents who were basically evil henchmen. After following and witnessing some truly disturbing acts committed by the FSB agents doing the Russian mob's dirty work, Black Angel put his plan in action. He paid the four men a visit in the filthy hotel room and dispatched them in a most efficient manner. Then he sat and waited for others to come.

Now, coming to Lefortovo did not guarantee him exposure to his target. But time and tide seem to always flow in his direction. Being placed in an open yard with six deadly and murderous prisoners brought the two of them together. Life just seems to work this way for Preacher.

He sat down beside the man on the bench. He would die within the hour from internal bleeding. He was laboring to breath. At least one of his lungs was filling with blood already. Preacher sat beside the man and pulled up his own shirt.

"Brother, what is the meaning of these markings?"

The man was in pain and perplexed. "What do you mean?"

"These tattoos. I want to know what they mean, quickly now." Lance took off his shirt to show his chest and shoulders. His muscled body with countless bruises, several wicked scars and an array of menacing tattoos, shocked the grizzled inmate.

The doomed man whispered. "Well, the eye is the sign of both God and the devil. I think the devil suits you. These teardrops signify your kills. I see why there are so many." The man waved at the human carnage in the yard and coughed up some blood.

"And this web?" Lance pointed to his left shoulder.

"Ah, that is the sign of the horse, of addiction. Opium." The man shook his head while his brow furrowed. He breathed heavily, became weaker. "How can you have these tattoos and not know their meanings? How did you get them?"

It was Preacher's turn to shake his head. He did so while looking at the guards now assembling behind the gates at the other end. It looked like 14 or 15 of them had gathered. "That's easy. I got them when I died."

He turned and smiled at his fellow prisoner as he stood. "I'm sorry to kill you. You probably don't have much time left brother. Your internal injuries are severe. I think a lung is punctured and your spleen is ruptured. I don't believe you will get the care you need here in this place. What is your name?"

"Lev." The man winced and hugged his own abdomen.

"That's not your name. Not your true name. Good luck in the next world. Your secret, your treachery, will die with you Martin." Lance smiled at Martin Rice, number seven on his memorized list of CIA traitors and nodded. He was once a promising CIA operative who was sent deep under cover in the KGB. But he, like the other names on the Black Angel list, had turned, been lost. And this name on the list was too far gone to merely be paid a visit by the Black Angel. Death was required for Martin Rice from Pittsburg, Pennsylvania.

Codename Black Angel stepped to the middle of the open yard and lay down with his arms and legs stretched out as far as the chains would allow. Moments later, a dozen men were on him, beating with nightsticks and jamming knees into his back and neck. Others stood around waiting for their turn. He did not resist. His eyes were closed. He was listening to Gerry Rafferty sing about that street in London. It felt wonderful to hear a song by someone other than Neil Sedaka.

Chapter 18

He awoke in a warm, comfortable bed with clean sheets and a fluffy pillow under his head. Not bad for heaven, just as long as she was here. She had been with him just a little while ago. He had seen her and fallen into her warm touch. The sensations lingered.

He opened his eyes to see that alas, it wasn't heaven. It was a bedroom with a dresser, wardrobe and a door to a bathroom. Lifting his head told him that days had passed. The stiffness and soreness of a severe beating was not too bad. He still hurt, but not nearly as bad as he should. He swung his legs over the bed and rubbed his head and face before standing. The growth on his face felt like four days, maybe five. He was wearing only a pair of grey shorts. He didn't have them on a few days ago.

His feet felt steady underneath him as he stood. He instinctively stretched and then dropped and counted off 50 push-ups before rolling over and knocking out 100 sit-ups. He stood and did 50 squat-thrusts. Everything seemed to be working properly. Before walking to the bathroom, he took in the room again. He had missed a small table by the door with what looked like medical equipment and supplies. Someone had been taking care of him. Interesting. He waved to the video camera mounted above the door.

He stepped to the bathroom. When he turned the light on, he got the shock of his life from the creature in the mirror. Holy shit. He hadn't looked into a mirror in months.

If he had been wavering, it was 100 percent confirmed now. Lance Priest was gone. The guy in the mirror was a stranger, a total stranger. It started with his eyes. They were black. Not brown; not dark brown. They were coal black with no differentiation from pupil to iris.

He remembered asking Braden to help him. It was the third time the psychologist had visited in the hospital that was more of a prison. The second time he came to visit Lance after telling him that Marta had died.

It was the time after Braden had brought Lance a sealed envelope. It was sealed with a round stamp that bore the CIA's telltale "top secret" symbol. Another stamp to the right of the seal read "Destroy after opening."

Braden handed the envelope to Lance and told him the obvious. "If you choose to open this, you will be required to memorize its contents, commit to the mission and then I will burn it." And Braden pulled out the lighter in his other hand.

With Marta dead, Lance Priest was an empty galaxy. He was black and cold and lifeless. Perhaps that is the reason he snatched the envelope from Braden's hand and ripped it open.

He put his back to Braden and unfolded the single sheet of paper. On it was a list of nine CIA deep-cover operatives and their cover names.

At the bottom of the page were two sentences. "Codename Black Angel will hunt these traitors and determine their worthiness to live. Black Angel will be a ghost and never show his face in the light of day."

Lance looked over the list again and let his photographic memory kick in. Without turning, he handed the sheet of paper to Braden.

"The envelope also." Braden said. Lance turned and held out the envelope. Braden had already flicked the lighter and touched the flame to the corner of the sheet of paper.

During the next visit, Lance turned away from Braden and looked into the mirror over the sink in his tiny cell-hospital room. "Tell Seibel I'll take the mission. But I need to make a couple of changes."

"I'll tell him. He will be pleased. What kind of changes do you need to make?"

He looked at himself in the mirror. He found it utterly impossible to gaze into his own eyes without seeing Marta looking back at him. He had so completely fallen into her that he and she were now one and the same. "I need to change my eyes. I think black will do."

After the eyes were transformed from hazel to black via a surgical procedure not unlike Lasik eye surgery, Lance was able to again look in the mirror. Healing from the eye surgery took a couple of weeks. The following week, Lance Priest was gone. He disappeared into the night and into an empty galaxy, but not before sticking a needle in his vein just two blocks from the cleared lot where a house had exploded and killed the love of his life.

The eyes alone changed his appearance. But there was more now, nearly a year later.

The face had changed. It was subtle. The nose had been broken multiple times. Cheekbones were enhanced, swollen. The jaw line more pronounced. It was a different face. He didn't recognize himself in it.

Then there were the tattoos. Jesus, the tattoos.

At least a dozen of them covered his skin, with the huge crying eye on his chest the largest of them. In the mirror, he could see the entirety of the artwork. They were all the same dull green, almost grey color. There were birds, clouds and the intricate web on his left shoulder. The tattoos served to alter the appearance of his body. Combine them with the scars from the bullet wounds and the guy standing before him in the small bathroom mirror was one truly frightening son of a bitch. This guy looked like a killer, a cold-blooded murderer with lifeless black hole eyes.

"Man," he let the English word slip from his lips. He shook his head and smiled. He spoke in Russian this time, "You are one scary dude comrade."

He somehow pulled himself away from the macabre image in the mirror to step into the shower where he took it to full hot before ending with half a minute of straight cold, like usual. The only time he had ever broken this routine was when she had joined him... Stop.

He forced those images out. He couldn't help but wipe the fogged glass and look at the freak in the mirror again after getting out of the shower. This guy looked like the Black Angel, a creature of the night – not fit for daylight.

In the wardrobe he found several articles of clothing that looked like they'd fit. He settled for a pair of black jeans and a grey long sleeve pullover. The black shoes fit as well. When dressed, he sat in the chair beside the bed and picked up the book on the table beside it. It was *The Brothers Karamazov*, Dostoyevsky's last novel. He had first read it in Monterey, California at the Defense Language Institute.

His Russian language instructor was adamant that students read the classics by Dostoyevsky, Tolstoy, Turgenev. The artist formerly known as Lance found each and every one of the Russian classics to be the bleakest, most depressing things he'd ever read. But they did help him understand the austerity of the people and culture. Russians are a bleak people. Of course, who could blame them after living under Tsars and Great Leaders who killed off tens of millions. And then there is the cold, the miserable friggin' cold winters.

A few pages in, there was a knock at the door.

"Prihodyat." He called in Russian while staying seated.

Yuri Ludkovich entered. Two bodyguards stood uncomfortably in the hall. They wanted to be in there between their well-paying boss and the nameless stranger. "Greetings. Good to see you up finally." Ludkovich took a couple of steps in, but stayed about 12 feet away.

"Good to be up." Preacher replied in a Russian accent from the south, near Ukraine maybe.

"You look better. And you smell better for sure."

"I'm sure I do." Preacher kept his head about him even though it was spinning, screaming. He controlled every fiber in his being by moving his head side to side and up and down.

Ludkovich set a small pouch down on the table between the door and bathroom doorway. "Come and join me for dinner when you are ready." He turned and closed the door behind him as he left. He did not locked it.

Preacher had a good idea what was in the pouch. The fact that he was not shaking and sweating and itching like hell meant his addiction was being fed. He set the book on the table and walked across the room The leather pouch did indeed contain a full syringe and needle. Seeing the slightly cloudy liquid in the syringe set his heart racing. He tried to monitor the changes in his body, but they were involuntary. The immediate thirst and craving took control. He was a slave to his next movements as he sat down, pushed up his sleeve, applied the tourniquet to his bicep and deftly injected the substance into the bulging vein.

The euphoria was an immediate lifting of reality's veil and he remembered without a moment's hesitation why the demon heroin brought him such pleasure. It was her. Here in this place, this timeless momentary space, he could be with her. He could say her name, Marta. His Marta, sweet Marta, love Marta.

He could reach out and caress her face, brush his fingertips across her lips and trace her cheek to her jaw and down her neck to her lovely shoulder and then down her back where he could put his lips to her warm skin and pull her hair aside to taste her neck.

When Neil Sedaka began to sing, time started back up again. Those sappy songs were his buffer, his alarm clock for a return to reality. It meant he would have to leave her. But he would be back. This was the only place he wanted to be.

Downstairs a half hour later, Preacher stepped into a dining room to find Ludkovich seated at a table set for two. The bodyguards stood in opposite corners. He sat down across from the mobster who was reading the Wall Street Journal. Ludkovich set the paper down and smiled at Preacher.

"Do you know who I am?"

Preacher smiled as he put the napkin on his lap. "Yes. You are the boss."

"Yes, I am. Someone has to be, right?" The mafia kingpin raised his eyebrows and smiled.

"Someone has to keep all the crooks in line I guess."

Ludkovich just looked at him. He was giving Preacher the opportunity to take him in. He didn't need to. Preacher had already looked him over, up in the bedroom and since he walked in this room. He had catalogued it all – 43, maybe 44; 240 solid pounds, 6 foot 3 inches; big, powerful, strong, right-handed, capped teeth, too perfect, not very gangster; blue-grey eyes, scars on forehead, right cheek and right hand; slight limp in his left leg. He had a commanding presence about him. He did not demand attention, but he got everyone's respect. And by the looks of the newsprint he'd been reading when Preacher walked in, he speaks English.

It looked like Ludkovich had already taken in everything he needed to see. He'd obviously seen the wasted, gaunt, hollow man brought to this place some days ago. The why of it still escaped Preacher, but he was sure they would get around to that soon enough. And he was right.

"Why waste time, right?" Ludkovich spoke the words in perfect English. He turned and waved at the men in the corners and spoke in Russian. "Go on. I'll be fine. Leave now." The two hulks didn't like it and looked with disdain at Preacher. They moved slowly toward a doorway into the kitchen. He returned to English, "We'll have our dinner and then we need to talk."

On cue, a woman entered. She carried two plates heaping with food. She did not look either of them in the eye and left immediately after placing the plates in front of each of them.

They ate in silence. It took about eight minutes for each to clean their plate.

The woman entered and cleared the plates away and left.

"Now we talk." Ludkovich wiped his mouth and took a swig of wine.

"Great, let's talk." Preacher spoke the words in English with a heavily Russian accent.

"You don't need to do that with me." Ludkovich's smile broadened.

"What?"

"The Russian accent, the Russian language."

"What do you mean?" Preacher returned to Russian for the question.

"Everyone works for someone. You know that." Ludkovich pointed at himself. "No one is free from reporting to someone. A king has to keep his people happy or they will revolt and hang him. A president has the pesky Senate, House and Supreme Court, not to mention business interests who invest in him. The Pope always needs to be looking over his shoulder at his cardinals while he is supposed to be looking up at God. Everyone has a boss."

Preacher sat and listened.

"I have a boss. You have a boss. And so does he."

"Who?" Preacher rubbed his chin. "God?"

"No. The man who appears to have no higher authority. The man who walks between raindrops and tells the heads of CIA, NSA and the President only what he wants them to hear. The man who created his own army, his own system, his own world."

"And who is this man?" This was beyond interesting all of the sudden.

"You know." Ludkovich was not smiling now. Just boring into Preacher with those blue-grey eyes.

"He sounds interesting. Impressive." Preacher's feet tightened in the black shoes. The opiates moving through his blood slowed his reaction just enough to give away his next move. Because he was stoned, when he closed his eyes for a microsecond longer than a blink, he did not get the escape from his head. He could not see down on the room and the two men seated at the small table. He was trapped in his head. Lance was gone, off somewhere up there.

"I know why you are here." Ludkovich nodded.

"And why is that?"

"You are here to clean up, to clean house. Time is up for some resources, correct?" Ludkovich waited for a reply. Preacher waited for more. "But I don't understand the timing. Why now?"

Well, this was an interesting development. It seems this mobster had figured quite a few things out. Very astute.

"So who was your target inside Lefortovo?" Ludkovich brought his fingers together and weaved them together with his forefingers pressed to his lips.

"My, you have spent some time on this. Figured it all out."

"Not all of it."

"Lev Petarik. Do you know him?"

"No. But I recognize the name from the six prisoners you executed in the yard. That was quite a scenario you put together to get into Hell on Earth. All to get one man?"

"Yes. Took months to track him down."

"Amazing. And which one of the four you killed in that hotel room was your target?"

"Maybe it was two of them. Maybe all four. Maybe none." Preacher was matter of fact.

"You must be his greatest weapon." Ludkovich smiled.

"No. Just a mission." Black Angel leaned in, his elbows on the table.

"Wait. Please," Ludkovich raised his hands. "I know you can easily kill me and my men. It is evidently what you do. But you need to ask yourself two things first. Why are you still alive?

And why am I still alive sitting here across from you? Neither one should be, yet here we sit."

Preacher coiled again. Maybe this was it. Maybe this was the man who could and would actually kill him. Only one way to find out. He was within a baby's hair of exploding when Ludkovich unloaded on him. It wasn't a punch or kick or bullet. It was much worse. And it meant he would not die today as he'd hoped. It was a word, just one name.

"Marta."

After an intravenous injection of heroin, users report feeling a surge of euphoria ("rush") accompanied by dry mouth, a warm flushing of the skin, heaviness of the extremities, and clouded mental functioning. Following this initial euphoria, the user goes "on the nod," an alternately wakeful and drowsy state. Users who do not inject the drug may not experience the initial rush, but other effects are the same.

Chapter 19

Black Angel balled his right hand into a fist. This kill would be painful for the target.

"Wait. Don't." Ludkovich sat back with his hands up. "You have to wonder how I know her."

"I can wonder about that later."

Preacher exploded up and forward. The table between them came up with him and then came crashing down on Ludkovich. He kept moving forward bowling the mafia leader over and moving past him to the doorway where he dove to his left. He slid past the stunned female cook standing over a stove toward the two bodyguards who were both pulling guns from shoulder holsters. Preacher was within a foot and quarter of a second of delivering a vicious blow to the first when the shout came from the dining room.

"No guns. No shooting." Ludkovich's order changed Preacher's motion. Instead of striking the large man in the neck, he delivered a chopping blow to his chest and pivoted to kick the other in the midsection instead of the bridge of his nose. The blows allowed the men to absorb the force and respond with their own attacks, which they shouldn't have.

When the guy on the left came forward, Preacher pivoted again to deliver a knee to the man's right leg which instantly obliterated cartilage and tendons. The bodyguard on the right took this moment to begin a kick with his right foot. Preacher was already near the floor so he adjusted his momentum to the left as the boot came toward his head. It glanced off his shoulder and kept going so Preacher immediately followed the rising boot and leg with is left hand carrying the man's leg into the air as he rose. The movement caused the fella to fall to the floor where Preacher proceeded to stomp on his chest, cracking ribs in the process. But he did not kill them. Something had stopped him.

Marta.

He rose back to his feet and looked at the cook in her kitchen. Something in her eyes was not right. A door to the right led somewhere. If he had to guess, it probably led to more guards he would have to incapacitate or kill before finding his way out. He was turning toward the exit when Ludkovich spoke from the dining room doorway.

"You can run, leave. But then you will not get any answers." Ludkovich's nose was bleeding. A cut was starting to bleed over his left eye. "And you want to hear this Lance."

How the hell did he know that name? Preacher was ready to blow and take the world with him.

"How do you think I got here, got to where I am?" Ludkovich asked.

"From your barrage of hints, I assumed Papa put you here. And now he is taking you out. You have outlived your usefulness. It happens."

"Nope. Not Seibel. I've never met him."

Preacher got a quizzical look on his face. His procerus tugged at his eyebrows. Then he figured it out. "Marta. She put you here." And it all became clear. She had built up a few networks during her years of running wild through Europe. Ludkovich was one of her operatives. "I can see it now. She tore down a few or your obstacles and paved the way for you to move up the mob's ladder."

"Yes. She removed many barriers."

"And why do you think she did this?" Preacher looked at the guards still on the floor. Ludkovich stepped forward into the kitchen.

"She keeps her reasons to herself."

"Kept."

"I'm sorry?"

"She kept her reasons to herself."

Ludkovich staggered. "Are you saying?"

"Yes. Last year in New York. An explosion. She lived for several hours after, but did not regain consciousness. She is gone."

"I am sorry."

"Why?"

"Why am I sorry?" Ludkovich asked.

"Yes. How did you know about me, about her and me?"

"She told me almost three years ago. She mentioned a young man and described you to me. She said only that he, that you, would be a chameleon, a killer, a human hurricane. She said if this man ever came to me, I was to help him."

This was touching, moving. A Russian mob heavy told to watch out for Marta's boyfriend to come around some day and offer him assistance, salvation. Preacher cracked up.

"What is it?" Ludkovich asked.

"So you are saying that Marta, the fiercest, most brutal thing most humans will ever encounter, asked you to help me."

"Yes. It is that simple."

"And is it that simple that she was fooled by you, that she did not know your past?"

"My past?" Ludkovich now had a quizzical look on his face.

"Do I have to do this?" Preacher shook his head.

"Do what?"

That was it. Black Angel picked up the gun from the counter and turned lightning fast to put a bullet through each of the guard's heads. He then turned his aim on the cook, who was more than a cook, and did the same to her. In the next moment, he was down the hall and out into a garage where three men waited with guns pulled. Their fingers were too slow on their triggers and each received multiple bullets from a rolling, diving ball of fury.

After checking the exterior doors and windows, Black Angel returned to the kitchen and Ludkovich who was now holding a gun.

"Come on Steve, put that down before you get hurt." Black Angel walked right up to the ultra deep-cover CIA operative and snatched the gun from his hand. "Let's go."

Yuri Andreovich Ludkovich was actually Stephen Rainier Torrence from Spokane, Washington. He was placed in service as a Russian CIA operative 19 years earlier. His goal was to infiltrate the mob and work his way up to a mid-management level. Marta, working under the blind directive of Geoffrey Seibel, elevated Torrence to the mob's upper echelon. And during the process, he became the mob collector for the extreme gambling debts of a politician who just happened to hold the office of President of the Russian Federation.

It was brilliant, a marvelous operation; unrivaled in recent history. A CIA operative had the Russian President in his pocket. And yet, this operative's name Steve Torrence – Yuri Ludkovich appeared on a list handed to Lance Priest nearly a year ago. It made no sense.

Wait. It did.

Preacher just saved this resource's life by wiping out all witnesses. Torrence's cover was still intact. He had blurted out information about Marta and Seibel in front of the guards and cook.

Ludkovich wanted Preacher to take action. He knew that Preacher would kill everyone in this safe house once Marta's name was uttered. Ludkovich was a prisoner of sorts.

Damn. A mystery wrapped up in an enigma. Black Angel to the rescue.

"Porcelain protocol and olive wine." Preacher spoke the code in German into a payphone.

"Green grass, red linens." Came the reply. Also in German.

Preacher hung up the phone on a street corner in Moscow. He knew the process for tracking down his field mentor was still in place years later. Just over 1,194 miles to the southwest, Mikel Fuchs hung up a payphone in a train station in Vienna. The senior operative agreed to come to Moscow and do a little high-level babysitting for a few days.

Chapter 20

She was running, nearly limp-free. The moon in the night sky lit her way. It was so vivid. So real.

She raced across on open field and then through trees. She came to a road and hit the dirt to avoid the spray of headlights from a vehicle approaching, her heart pounding.

She stayed flat on the ground until it passed and was up and across the road and into another treeline. She moved through the woods like a wolf hunting prey. She came to an obstacle, a tall fence. She assessed the situation and then scaled the fence, snagging her shirt on the barbed wire at the top.

She breached to top, dropped ten feet to the ground on the other side and raced into a thicket of trees.

She was nearly home. Her home for now.

No need to wake. This was no dream.

Chapter 21

Saint Petersburg, Russia April 4...

He was beside a river, a canal really. Running, racing for all he had. His feet floated across the grass of the park. He was gaining on his prey up ahead. Behind him, he could hear the trample of footsteps. He was both the chaser and chased.

Overhead, the moon lit the night sky. Streetlights provided fountains of manmade light spilling down on empty streets and expanses of grass and gravel underfoot. The woman trying to evade him just 30 meters ahead now, had burst from the safety of her hotel minutes earlier. It was a mistake. Not so much the running, but the drawing of attention. She had reacted badly when presented with orders passed through a bellman.

The woman should have stayed calm, walked to the elevator and gone up to her room to await further instructions from the Black Angel. Instead, she bolted from the boutique hotel's lobby and ran west on Ulitsa Pestalya to the canal where she crossed on one of the countless bridges in Saint Petersburg, Russia. She followed the canal north and then crossed the street into the Summer Gardens. Preacher was enjoying the short tour they were taking through the Venice of the North. Even at a few minutes after midnight, Saint Petersburg was beautiful, truly striking as cities go.

The runner, Tanya Rusak, was one of two women on the list. She was number nine. The last name.

Rusak was not all that important from what Preacher could tell. She was a double agent, a courier of sorts between official and unofficial entities in Moscow, Odessa and Saint Petersburg. Yesterday, Black Angel followed her to the Leningradsky train station in Moscow and drove the 380 miles northwest in a stolen Peugeot to wait and watch as Rusak got off the train at Moskovsky Station in Saint Petersburg.

The overnight train brought the courier into Saint Petersburg at 5:40 a.m., just before the sun found its way to the eastern horizon and the Black Angel descended into shadows for the day. Now, 17 hours later, with injected opium coursing through his veins and Marta with glistening hair flowing, gliding effortlessly beside him, he delighted in the moment. This particular moment was perfect as so few were these days. He reached out to take her hand but she only giggled and shook her head. He laughed at her and exploded ahead as if he had been standing still the moment before.

He caught up with Rusak and danced beside her like a clown in a circus ring. The smile still on his face. Rusak, a middle-aged woman closer to 50 than 40, could not respond to the speed. Black Angel looked back over his shoulder at the approaching group of three men. A screech of tires a block away sounded like it was coming this way.

In the dark with the brim of his hat keeping light from his features, Black Angel was a shadow. He stepped closer to Rusak. They had 30 seconds or so before the following group arrived.

"Tanya, you should not have run. You were in no danger."

"Who are you? What do you want from me?" The double agent gasped for breath as she heaved.

"I only have one question for you. You must answer honestly and immediately." He stepped closer but kept his head bowed. It was menacing. "Why have you betrayed your homeland?"

Rusak could only stare at him. The look on her face transformed from quizzical to fear. "What?" she asked.

It was her eyes. They were honest. There was no lie behind her words. She was not a traitor, not a double agent. Black Angel looked around. He knew immediately. This was a trap.

"I have no time to chat. I will see you again, soon." Black Angel turned toward the approaching trio of men and decided on the one on the right. He burst forward, closing the gap in seconds. Ten feet apart, he jumped into the air and dealt the man a vicious kick planted in his chest. The guy's head snapped forward from the collision.

Black Angel rolled to his right and sprinted into the darkest portion of the Summer Gardens. Seconds later, several silenced shots were fired after him. But they weren't bullets. He recognized the distinct noise made by the firing of tranquilizer darts. Damn.

Seconds after that, the two remaining men were joined by two others on foot and two cars taking opposite routes around the perimeter of the park. The men communicated via radio. One stayed with Rusak, the other three gave chase into the dark.

He made it to the dead center of the beautiful park. A flame burned in a small square concrete box. No tourists were around as the Black Angel raced through the scene, now traveling from south to north. He hugged the shadow of a set of tall manicured bushes as one of the cars giving chase crossed his path 100 yards ahead. He considered diving under the bushes to watch the followers and see which one he would pick off for a little interrogation.

But lying down right now just felt wrong. He needed to move, to divide and conquer and then find out who the hell these guys were. He raced across the lawn. At one point he got a little too close to an overhead light and he heard four spits from behind him. One of the darts whizzed by just feet away. He veered left, away from the light while keeping to his northerly course near the edge of the park.

Behind him, the four men spread out to cover more ground. The car that passed seconds earlier slammed on its brakes and turned around in the center of the street, returning to intercept him.

He picked up his pace and raced across the street to an embankment next to another of the endless, endless friggin' Saint Petersburg canals. This one bordered the Letniy Sad property, formerly the summer palace of Peter the Great. Running next to the canal, he thought of the lack of planning that brought him here in this moment. He had let Rusak lead him to this open public place surrounded on all sides by water. Not smart. So he stopped and sat down in the shadows next to the frigid water.

He waited like a snake in the grass, only deadlier. He pulled out his silenced weapon and knife and breathed slowly while looking up to the beautiful, wondrous stars. The drugs in his system were being flushed with his exertion and adrenaline. He could not see her face any longer. The billions of stars in the clear night sky were no comparison to her, well, at least the memory of her.

Twenty seconds later, a man approached on foot. He was on the street above the embankment. He slowed to peer down into the canal. Moments after he passed, a shadow burst from the dark and pulled the man down toward the water. His grip so tight around the man's neck no sound could escape. The radio in the guy's hand was snatched and kept. Next to the water, the Black Angel lay across the man's body, keeping him facedown while the knife's point caressed the skin of the man's neck.

"We all die brother. Are you ready?" The voice a whisper.

"No, please no. I only do a job. I only work for hire." The man's plea carried an accent from Eastern Europe, sounded Polish.

"But you do the work of a killer do you not?" There was no answer this time. "So you can take life, but not give your own, is that it?"

"No please. I do not know you. I will tell no one."

"Who do you work for tonight?" The whisper deeper now.

"I don't."

The knife pierced skin. "Quickly now, I have several other men who can tell me what I need to know. You mean nothing to me." A vehicle raced by on the street above. "Nevermind, what is your name?"

"Jacob." The man sputtered.

"Goodbye Jacob." With that, Black Angel rose and delivered a violent blow to the base of Jacob's skull. An incapacitating blow, not a kill. The lucky man had not seen the Black Angel's face.

He rolled off and ran along next to the water, staying in a crouch. He reached a bridge and pressed himself against the stone wall. Above him, a couple out for a romantic late night stroll talked casually. From here, his options were to move up onto the street, which would put him in view of those searching for him, or he could slip into the frigid water and either cross or travel with the flow to the west which led to the Neva River just a few hundred yards away.

He closed his eyes and listened. As he did, he attempted to summon Lance and his vision from above, but he wouldn't come. Damn heroin.

Screeching tires on the bridge above were followed by car doors opening and men shouting in Russian. He heard words like "Vody" and "Bol'she muzhchin" the Russian words for water and more men and forget capture, and knew he had to prepare to bolt. Then he heard "naiti i ubit" which literally translates to "find and kill." The capture portion of the mission was evidently now over.

With pistols in each hand, he pushed off the wall and climbed up the embankment to the sidewalk. Just as he feared, the couple was right there between him and the two cars stopped in the road.

Standing around the two sedans were five individuals. He turned and pushed the young couple over the railing into the water below. He then turned and faced the group who had all stopped talking when the young woman screamed. The problem for this assembled group of men and one woman was that a Black Angel with the brim of his hat hiding his face had two guns aimed at them. On cue, they all either went for guns or began to raise those in their hands. Too late. He stepped forward casually putting bullets in all five heads of those standing. He then adjusted his aim to the drivers of each car. It was over in seven seconds.

He saw the lights with his peripheral vision, lots of them. It seemed the Saint Petersburg police had been called in to set up a perimeter for the hunt. He looked in all directions. There were dozens of police cars out there. Damn.

He kneeled and pulled out the closest dead man's wallet. He had only seconds. In the wallet he found money and credit cards and identification. He reached into the other pocket and found what he'd feared. It was another small leather wallet. Inside this one he found an I.D. card and badge identifying the man as an FSB special agent. Oh damn. The Black Angel just wiped out an entire FSB unit. But looking the men over quickly, something seemed wrong. He couldn't pin it down. They simply looked wrong.

No time to figure out why they were tailing Rusak or why this whole night felt like a set up. This team basically appeared out of nowhere and assembled quickly to follow him. He'd definitely missed something.

Police cars began to move in from the perimeter. He pulled a crackling radio from the guy's pocket, opened the door of the closest car, yanked the dead driver out and got in. He was right in front of the Mikhailovsky Zamok – St. Michael's Castle. He knew the streets of the city like he knew those of Istanbul or Mexico City or Tokyo. In that, he had memorized them from above, via map and satellite imagery. He took four seconds to do a mental review of the streets and avenues and bridges of central Saint Petersburg as police cars bore down on him. He rolled his head from side to side and up and down. He let the image of Marta driving cross his mind. Her driving skills were far superior to his. Black Angel gripped the steering wheel with gloved hands.

His eyes opened and he was off. He went east to Ulitsa Pestelya, swerved around three police cars and accelerated into a shallow canyon of buildings. The procession of vehicles behind him stretched out several blocks. Many peeled away in an attempt to head him off. He screamed around a corner onto Liteynyy Prospekt where he accelerated even more. When the first police car appeared up ahead, he put the pedal to the floor and jumped into oncoming traffic lanes.

A patrol car slammed into him from the right, attempting to force him to the left, he hit the brakes and let the police car get in front of him, where he crashed into it, spinning it around and leaving it behind. An excellent move. Problem was, a dozen more waited up ahead. He veered right on Belinskogo Street and pushed the vehicle to its top-end limits even though three police cars blocked the way ahead.

He drifted for a moment, remembering sitting beside her as she drove like this through the streets of Moscow minutes after they had blown up half the city. Smelinski showed him photos captured during that wild chase just a few days ago. Marta was a marvel. His driving skills, like his shooting, were a pale imitation of hers. He would never be as good as her. Driving like this now was something of a joke. He didn't care at all about any of this really. But he knew he did not want to be caught, be captured here in Saint Petersburg. They could not have him, no way.

So he swung the wheel to guide the Mercedes up onto the sidewalk on the right side of the street and flew around the temporary roadblock. More police awaited him as he crossed yet another bridge in front of the Bolshoi Ballet Theatre. "Cool, the Bolshoi," he muttered to himself. Three bullets struck the windshield. Not cool.

He veered left and then back right and gunned it for all the car was worth. A moment later, another Mercedes was beside him. Same make, same color. Had to be more FSB arriving at the party. And unlike their police friends, these guys were quite comfortable shooting at a haphazardly moving target. He spun the wheel to the left to slam into the car and then jammed on the brakes to let them moved ahead and make a nice target for him to ram. He was gunning the engine to do just that when he was struck from behind. The collision caused him to lose control and fishtail to the right. He used the momentum of the rotation and gassed it to continue in the direction he'd been spun.

A few seconds later, he turned right onto Nevskyy Prospekt, the main drag for all of Saint Petersburg. A bunch of new friends joined the party. A dozen more police cars and a couple large SUVs were added to the mix. He busted out in laughter. This was really something. Getting out of this one alive would be nearly impossible. And for the moment, the thought of shuffling off this mortal coil delighted him.

Not death. Just peace.

This would be a hell of a way to go. He instinctively reached over to the gun lying in the seat beside him and brought it into his lap. He hadn't shoved a gun into his mouth or under his chin in months. Maybe this early morning would bring an end to all this nonsense.

But in the next moment, something interesting happened. There on Nevskyy Prospekt, with Russian police and FSB resources assembling about him, the Black Angel could suddenly see everything from above. Lance had swept in from the heavens to join the fun. Then another funny thing occurred. Lance's voice bellowed in Black Angel's ears.

"Don't do this Preacher. Not today."

"Do what?" He responded.

"Don't disappoint her, dishonor her like this."

"Screw you." He screamed. "You gave up months ago."

"Think about it Preacher. When did you ever tell her the truth or pull down your endless curtain of charades."

"Just leave her out of this." Preacher spun the wheel to the right and then back left and back right again. The move spun out one of the trailing SUVs. "This isn't about her. You know that."

"Really, then what is this about? Why are you here? Why are you alive?" Four more bullets struck the back right quarter panel and rear window. Preacher barely noticed the shots.

"Who said I'm alive?" He spun the wheel to the right to turn onto another street beside yet another canal. Up ahead, he could see the towering spires of the Khram Spasa – *the Church on the Spilled Blood,* with its colorful bulbous parapets. He wasn't looking at the road in front of him. He was driving blind, because he was watching the car and all the other activity from above at about 500 feet. It made it easy. He could see everything. Every police car and FSB Mercedes and the large black SUVs.

"You are alive. You are working your mission. That's what you do." Lance's voice was calmer.

"What mission?" He approached the colorful church and rounded a corner forced by the road's turn. Even at 1:00 a.m. in the morning, the building was spectacular. "Cool," he whispered before returning to the action below.

Up ahead, more police cars waited for him in a blockade. So he slammed on the brakes and came to a screeching stop directly in front of the church. The vehicles trailing him slowed and stopped 50 meters from his bumper. They spread across the street. Two men jumped out of one of the SUVs and prepared to fire. He closed his eyes for just a moment to let Lance show him the scene from above. And, of course, a song started up. It was a classic by Manfred Mann's Earth Band. One of his all-time favorites. He was thrilled it wasn't Sedaka.

He could see all the sites, all the vehicles amassing to stop and kill him, all the streets and canals and baroque-style buildings. Just a half mile to the north ran the Neva River. He needed to reach that ice-cold water. He opened his eyes as the bullets shattered the remainder of the back window and rear driver-side window. Glass shards struck the back of his head as he put the gas pedal to the floor and burst forward, crashing through a heavy gate between tall ornate pillars.

Once through the gate, he was in a pleasant park with trees and grass and ponds. He tore up the grass under his tires as he chewed his way across the lawn, dodging trees along the route. He realized as he looked to his right that he wasn't really in a park, he was tearing across the back lawn of the Russian Museum. "This is what I call sightseeing." He muttered to himself. Lance laughed 500 feet up.

Now, across the museum's picturesque lawn, he came to Sadovaya Ulitsa once again. He was right in front of St. Michael's Palace. He roared onto the empty street squealing as he swung to the left, gaining speed to push through the blockade of four police vehicles just ahead at the intersection. Two of the policemen shot at him as he approached. He ducked down as far as he could and blasted into the rear of one of the police sedans, shoving it out of the way as he crossed the street and glanced at the patrol cars parked in the middle of the bridge around the human carnage he had created six minutes earlier.

He had his destination in sight now. Up ahead, just a few hundred meters, he could see the Trotsky Bridge. It was across the park he had sprinted into and through just 15 minutes earlier. Between him and the bridge, he could count at least a dozen police cars. And Lance noticed something neither of them wanted to see. Two police snipers had climbed on top of two SUVs up ahead and were sighting in on him as he barreled toward them. This could get dicey.

He swerved off the road into the park and tore across grass and gravel to put a few visual obstacles between him and the sharpshooters. Then, looking past the snipers, Lance pointed out the next deal breaker. The drawbridge on the bridge's middle section began to rise. His route of departure was cut off. Damn.

"What are you going to do?" Lance asked. Preacher was just happy to hear the voice after almost a year of silence.

"I guess we're all going swimming." He replied as he began to swerve the vehicle side to side in a zigzag pattern to make it tougher for snipers to get a clean shot at him. He knew the bullets would come any second now.

"Turn around, evade them. Take another route. This is a no-win." Lance shouted. It wasn't like him. Preacher laughed. That's because it wasn't Lance. It was just his crowded skull. He settled down in the seat to take his head out of view. If it were him up there ready to shoot, he would have one go for the driver and the other take out the tires. Right on cue, gunshots exploded and the front right tire took a direct hit. Bullets ripped through the windshield and seat above his head. Great shots. He floored it and continued his zigzag as he was now less than a hundred meters from the snipers on top of the SUVs.

Other police officers standing beside their vehicles began to fire. The barrage was tremendous. He ducked fully down in the seat and let Lance guide him. He jammed the wheel to the right and then back left as his bullet-riddled Mercedes flew onto and across the street careening into several police cars, which slowed, but did not stop his progress. So he floored it and flew toward the bridge with its raised mid section.

He stayed down as the shots from behind took out both back tires. That left the front left as the only working rubber. He struggled to keep it straight. An SUV following close behind crashed into him and crushed a good bit of the back of the sturdy sedan. His time was just about up. So, he did the usual, which, of course, was the unusual.

Black Angel slammed on the brakes and brought the vehicle to a sparking, screeching halt. He jumped out of the car and raced 30 feet to the SUV behind him. He only had a few seconds to turn this thing around on its head. No problem.

He reached the vehicle before the driver could throw it in reverse. The passenger was in the process of raising a gun to aim at him. He nodded at them both before putting six bullets through glass and into each of them. He then pulled open the driver's door and yanked the dead man out just as the bullets from the snipers came. Too late. He had the pedal to the floor and was squealing around a corner onto Dvortsovaya Avenue beside the Neva River. In 10 seconds, the powerful vehicle was up to 70 miles per hour and flying toward another bridge.

"Not bad. You had me fooled." Lance sounded like he was laughing now.

"Not now. We're not clear yet." He turned to the deceased passenger beside him. "This is going to be close buddy."

Up ahead, the Dvortsovaya Bridge beckoned. The road ahead was clear for the moment. It seemed the Saint Petersburg police didn't think he could make it this far. And then time collapsed again. He saw from 200 meters away the drawbridge for the structure starting to rise. A quick calculation in Lance's head told them it would take about 9 seconds to reach the rising drawbridge. Holy shit, this was going to be like a stunt in an action movie.

He swerved to the left to give him the best angle to turn onto the bridge. He saw out of the corner of his eye the approaching police cars moving in. Nothing he could do about that. He adjusted his angle to prepare for the impact of one of the police sedans. The impact did indeed occur right in the intersection, but the collision helped him into his turn and did not slow the SUV down too much. He punched it and pushed back straight-arm from the steering wheel after grabbing the seat belt and pulling it around his lap.

"Not enough speed." Lance muttered.

"Shut up."

"You won't make it."

"Byt spokoinym!" He shouted for Lance to be quiet.

He glanced down at the speedometer as he hit the bottom of the rising drawbridge. He had it up to 65 m.p.h. It didn't feel like enough to get up and over.

And it wasn't.

At the top of the ramp, the 3-ton vehicle took flight, but the trip up the incline had slowed its speed. Instead of flying across the yawning gap between the two raised bridge portions, the heavy front end of the vehicle immediately began to dip. The dip continued and turned into a flip. When the SUV hit the icy water flowing below, it landed smack dab on the top of the roof like a bad belly flop.

Preacher was thrown about, but the seatbelt did its job. His deceased passenger slammed into the top, now bottom, of the vehicle. The man's knees cracked the windshield as he struck it. In seconds, frigid water rushed in through the cracks. Preacher undid his seatbelt and waited for the water to equalize pressure inside and out as the vehicle began to roll with the strong current. For the briefest moment he was alone. No one around, no one in his head, no extra set of eyes floating overhead. Manfred Mann was wrapping up his favorite song about being blinded.

So he just closed his eyes; let himself drift as frigid water began to envelope him. The light from the dashboard was the only illumination. The SUV rolled along with the river's powerful current. He did not panic. In fact, he couldn't recall ever being more calm. He just wished he could see her, remember her face without the aid of opiates. As water flowed over his head, he took one last deep breath and relaxed every muscle in his body. The roar of the rushing water drowned out everything else. He was alone. What now?

This was it. He could simply let the air out of his lungs and breath in suffocating H^2O. It would be that simple. Hell, he shouldn't be alive anyway. The bullets and falls and explosions and collisions and beatings and drugs should have done him in. Why did he care? What was left for him to do? He finished the list earlier this evening.

The calm and cold were soothing. He stayed this way for another half minute. Then it happened.

He started to see a fuzzy image. It became clearer every moment. It was her, her face. It was from above, looking down on her. Had to be Lance's view from his memory. He was glad to have Lance back up there. How long had it been? He'd lost track.

Her face came sharper into focus. She was beautiful from this angle, every angle. She was stunning, but not smiling. She was not happy. Marta was so lost, her cheeks tear-stained, her eyes swollen. Lance spoke to him. "Watch."

Preacher opened his eyes under the black water to look around. It had been too long since Lance spoke to him. It both soothed and irritated him.

"Watch." Lance's calming voice made him close his eyes and gaze at the memory. In the vision, Marta ran her hands through her hair and brought them down to her knees. She was seated in a chair at a table. A cup of coffee on the table next to a stack of manila file folders. She turned away from the table and rose slowly, putting her hand on the chair's back to steady herself. She then took slow, limping steps across the room.

It was wrong. This was no memory he recalled. She was not the same. She was… older.

Marta was weak; broken was a better word. "Where is this? When? I don't remember this." He called out to Lance in his mind. He couldn't see his personal phantom anywhere around in the freezing water and rolling vehicle. "Tell me." He demanded.

"Just watch." Lance's whisper was barely audible with the water filling his ears.

Marta made her way across the small room to a window looking out over an expanse of lawn with sidewalks and benches and paths and people walking, many wearing hospital gowns and robes. "What the hell is this? What are you showing me? This isn't real. I don't remember this."

"Watch. Here it comes." Excitement in the whisper now.

In the middle of the Neva River, between two sections of Saint Petersburg, Russia, Preacher heard a knock at Marta's door. She turned and limped slowly over and opened the door. Standing there was a smiling Stuart Braden. Lance's view of the scene moved to just above Marta and Braden standing in the doorway.

"How are you today?" Braden asked pleasantly.

Preacher was already holding his breath or else he would have inhaled deeper. He was in a state of euphoria, like the moments just after the needle has delivered its payload into his vein. He couldn't wait to hear her voice. And when he did, it was like she had never gone away, never died and left him to find his way through an empty world.

"A little better, thank you." Her spoken words were a symphony. It was as if he had boiling water running through him. The warmth her voice generated within him set his body aglow. This was torture.

In Lance's vision, Braden handed her an envelope and a folded newspaper. "Are you up for a short walk?"

Marta smiled and it nearly caused Preacher to exhale the fading oxygen in his lungs. He smiled with her. "Sure. I think I can walk a little. Let me set this down." She turned and put the envelope and newspaper on a table beside the door and turned back to Braden. "Ready."

"Great. Nice and slow." Braden reached out his hand to help her out the door. Preacher was ecstatic. This was wonderful, a wonderful fantasy before dying. Very comforting in these last moments of his brief but violent life.

"No. We're not going." It was Lance again.

"Why not? Let's go for a walk. I want to stay with her."

"Stop." Lance's voice was like an anchor holding him in place in the midst of death and drowning. "The paper."

"What? No. Let's go." Preacher pleaded to follow Marta and Braden as the door closed behind her. She was getting away. "Follow her. Please."

"The paper. Look."

Preacher was pissed. She was gone. He feared he'd seen her for the last time. Even though it was fantasy, he wanted more of it. The pain of the last few moments was the best feeling he'd felt in months.

He turned away from the door and slowly swooped down to look at the newspaper folded in half. The headline mentioned something about a politician. "What am I supposed to see? I don't care about the news." He wanted to get outside and watch her with the sun shining on her face and hair. He wanted to see the squint in her eyes. He loved the delicate muscles that pulled at the fascia under her skin creating those beautiful wrinkles.

"The date." Lance's calm was still intact. Excitement crept in at the edges of the calm. "Look."

Preacher moved his eyes from the headline to the top left corner of the page. It took seconds, which felt like weeks and months down there in the freezing cold with the last of the usable oxygen fading in his lungs. He read the date and read it again. The date was April 4, 1994. "Why show me this?"

"It's today." Lance's words didn't register. They were just words, lies really. Figments of a lying, cheating mind in its last moments. But why?

"Why show me this? Why show me now?" It didn't matter. "And why did you chose now to come back to me? Where have you been?"

Lance chuckled in his mind. "Where do you think I've been?"

"I don't know. I figured you were just pissed at me for some reason, probably all the drugs and the damn Neil Sedaka. You just took off up there and didn't come back."

"Jesus buddy. You don't know me very well." Lance suddenly appeared right in front of him. It was peaceful seeing him. He looked like he was supposed to. Not beaten and bruised and no black eyes. "I was up there. But I wasn't staying away from you, I was looking for her." Lance smiled at his alter ego.

"Looking for her spirit, like you?" Preacher was fading now. Only seconds remained.

"No, looking for her. I knew I'd find her and I did. She's alive brother. I found her just today. She's alive."

Chapter 22

There is magic in this world. Like it, or believe it, or trust it or not. Magic is a part of this universe.

Lance Priest was endowed with magic at birth. He'd been blessed by whatever element or higher power or black hole that imbued this world with unexplained wonder. He had a disease with no cure.

His ability to see the world from above, from a view that only birds and pilots and satellites share, is nothing short of supernatural. The logical type explains it away as mental dexterity; ultra sensitive visual acuity. A heightened perception, not unlike a blind person's ability to smell fabric and skin and blood or a deaf person sensing the slightest vibrations, even the earth's rotation below their feet.

But logic could not explain this.

Reason held no sway in this equation. There was no explanation for a person's ability to travel the earth and the sky and the stratosphere, to span the surface of the globe hunting for a dead girl. But then again, Lance had another magic quality. He could lie. He could lie every minute of every day to every person he met.

But there was a limit to this magic. Lance had never lied to Preacher; never lied to himself. And now was not the time to start. This only meant one thing.

That crazy son of a bitch Seibel had pulled off one doozy of a charade. He used Braden to convince Lance she was dead and done the same to Marta. Damn. A brilliant friggin' deception.

Preacher opened his eyes again in the spinning, swirling watery blackness and reoriented himself to the world around him. He couldn't die here. He had some killing to do.

He braced himself against the dashboard and steering wheel to grasp the door handle. The pressure had equalized some time ago and the door opened easily. He squeezed through and out into the flowing water of the river. The clock in his head told him he'd been under for just over four minutes. Not bad. He had once held his breath for six minutes, but that was in a calm and clear swimming pool back home in Tulsa, Oklahoma.

The current of the Neva was strong and propelled him forward, toward Neva Bay and the Baltic Sea beyond. At four and a half minutes, he was done and needed to breath or die. He struggled to the surface and finally breached to take fresh air into his depleted lungs. He took a huge swallow of air and dove again, swimming with the rapid current. This breath only lasted two minutes. When he came to the surface again, he was another half mile downstream. He floated along looking back at the police lights and helicopter spotlights shining down on the bridge and surrounding water now over a mile away. He dove again and held this breath for three minutes as he gently swam with the current a dozen feet below the surface. When he finally reached the northern bank of the river, he was actually in the beginnings of Neva Bay. He bobbed past a large vessel docked at the shore and pulled himself ashore on a hill beside a warehouse. He dashed into a parking lot and tried several parked cars before finding one unlocked. He slid in and closed his eyes to catch his breath and clear his head as best he could.

He wanted to fly, to cross the globe and find her. It had to be real. She had to be alive. Lance had never lied to him. That thought made him shake his head. Lance.

He was Lance. He is Lance.

"Crazy son of bitch," he muttered to himself in Russian.

And then the beginnings of the answer started. His body was obviously cold and chilled from the frigid waters, but the tremble that started was not caused by the cold. It was the first moment of withdrawal. The chase and exhilaration and adrenaline followed by a pleasant night swim in frigid water had pushed the remnants of his last dose of opium out of his bloodstream. And his bloodstream wanted more. It always wanted more.

His need to escape and be with her for blissful hours, apart from the world and the light of day, had controlled his life more than his mission. How had he missed this? How had Seibel fooled him? Why was he so quick to accept her death, to accept Braden's words?

He knew the answer.

It was guilt. He had let her go, let her get out of his sight that night, that early morning in New York when she tracked down Ramzi Yousef, only to be caught in a deadly blast. He should have been with her.

He'd relived that night a thousand times, ten thousand times. In his dreams he was able to stop her, to save her. Before he left America to begin his Black Angel mission, he went there, to the empty lot where a row of houses stood in Jersey City, New Jersey. He stood right where she was severely injured, where she was loaded into the ambulance and taken to St. Vincent's in New York. Marta supposedly died the next day, after he visited her in the ICU and held her almost lifeless hand. Thinking back on that moment, he recalled two things. Standing in front of that empty lot was the last time he saw Lance, until tonight. And it was the first night he inserted a needle into his arm.

"How about that for cause and effect?" He asked himself as the tremors in his extremities turned into full-body quaking. He'd been alone since that day. His only company for months were Neil Sedaka and the names on the list. And her ghost. She only came to him when he was high as a kite. He was forced to admit there were huge black spots in his memory. He had no idea where or who he'd been much of the time.

But he had somehow completed the mission. Earlier this evening, he spoke with Tanya Rusak, the last traitor on his list of nine. He did not kill her, just like he had left several of the names on the list alive. But he had changed them. He guided them, let them know their lives, their double lives, were over. Each CIA operative on the list had been compromised in some manner and acted against the United States. Their treacherous actions were discovered. Black Angel visited each and redirected or killed them. Mission accomplished.

But he didn't care.

He needed to find Marta and he knew where to start – Braden. But he saw the problem. If he showed up and asked Braden where she was, they would move her, or worse.

He noticed the shaking had stopped. At first, he thought it was warm feelings coursing through him as he thought of a new reality and the possibility of her in this reality.

But that was not the source of the warmth, the heat emanating from within. It was not love generating this inner glow. It was hate. And hate was a blue flame burning within him, wanting nothing more than to kill Geoffrey Seibel.

He pushed everything out of his mind and looked clearly at a mission for the first time in recent memory. He was Lance and Preacher and Black Angel all rolled into one. And he was going to kill Geoffrey Seibel, which basically meant declaring war on the CIA.

She finished reading the article and closed the newspaper, tossing it on the fake wood vinyl of the coffee table. Today's paper, like most, held nothing for her. There was plenty of news, but none of it interested her. To tell the truth, she had been distracted most of the day. Now, at the end of the evening, with nothing more to do, she picked up the envelope Braden handed her this morning along with the paper.

The oversize envelope contained more of the documents she'd been reading and analyzing lately. Seibel arranged for her to be sent dossiers on certain espionage players for "translation." This translation involved the decoding of language, since it was primarily written in Russian. The analysis basically called for her gut feelings on the person or persons detailed in the report. She had a gift for reading these particular tea leaves.

But today, she was just too anxious. She tried not to think about it, but that was impossible. She was shaken by the incident this morning in the moments after Braden knocked on her door. It was good to see him and get out of the house for a little while, but it was the image she saw, she felt, as she turned to put the newspaper and envelope on the table beside the door.

In the flash of a moment, from the corner of her eye, she saw something. She saw someone, or at least an impression, a fragment of someone. In that flash, as she turned from the door, she saw Lance. He was hovering. She looked over in the corner of the room again now. He was there this morning for just a blink, like a briefest flicker of a flame in a breeze. He was indistinct and transparent, like a ghost. But it was him up there in that flash.

She had never seen him in all the times she glanced or stared up into the corners of rooms. Preacher told her endlessly about Lance being up there, hovering, floating. The way he described it was so real, she couldn't help but look.

And for a year now, she had peeked up into corners and trees and clouds and windows and seen nothing.

Nothing. Until this morning.

She closed her eyes and brought the vision back into her mind's eye. She smiled.

Maybe it meant she was finally reaching the edge and letting go. Maybe her struggle with sanity and reality was nearing its end and he was coming to join her as she stepped off that edge. Maybe.

Chapter 23

"Well, that's certainly a way to wrap up a mission." Fuchs was standing at a window looking down on the city. He had arrived back in Berlin a few hours ago after seeing Ludkovich through a couple of interesting days.

He, like Seibel, who had just walked into the apartment, was still uncomfortable standing in the open on the eastern side of the city. They were both still caught in the previous decade and the ones that preceded. Yet, here they were 25 floors up in a building funded by western money flooding this former Soviet stronghold.

"I'll say." Seibel put his jacket over a chair and poured himself a cup of coffee. "Body count, significant destruction and an underwater disappearing act. Just so he could get close and say a couple of words with Rusak."

"Just as you ordered." Fuchs walked from the window to a sofa. "Monitored, but not harmed. All that chaos for Tanya Rusak?" It was more of a statement than a question.

Seibel stepped to the window. "She wasn't on the list." Seibel's words were measured, emotionless. They were also a bombshell.

"What? Then why would Preacher go after her?" Fuchs shook his head.

"That, my good man, is the question. Why did he track Ms. Rusak, a woman we did not even consider a player?" Seibel turned from the window. "He didn't happen to mention anything to you or Ludkovich before he left Moscow did he?"

"Nothing. Nothing about Rusak at least. He was gone before I arrived at that safe house to take over."

"How the hell does he keep ducking you?" A little accusation seeped into Seibel's question.

Over the last year, Fuchs had been unsuccessful in nailing down Lance's location or network of drug dealers. He identified more than a dozen sellers who told of dealing with a nameless, faceless customer who purchased in large quantities. But any surveillance on these illegitimate business owners had proven fruitless, as he and Seibel knew it would. "We are not dealing with the same person we were 11 months ago. He is not only deadly and unpredictable; he is strung out on a heavy diet of opium. Hundreds of thousands of dollars worth of the stuff."

"I'm aware of his consumption. I just can't believe we can't discern a pattern in his consumption. His network reaches from Paris to Baghdad to Moscow. And it is my money he's spending on all this stuff." Seibel was travel-weary as well.

"Your uncle's money." Fuchs corrected him. Their conversation provided evidence of their time away from each other. It had been nearly five months since they had seen each other face to face. Fuchs still had serious reservations about the entire mission, but could not refute the evidence of Seibel's success on similar projects. Hell, he was living proof. And there was no denying the results achieved by Seibel in the good ol' days of the late 50s. Papa was also living proof.

Fuchs kicked his feet up and lay on the sofa.

"You don't have to sleep there. Take the bed." Seibel gestured to the other room.

"Don't be ridiculous. You're the boss. Take the bed." Fuchs already had his eyes closed. An experienced operative, he knew the value of sleep and could pass out anywhere. A small sofa was luxurious compared to where he'd been sleeping during the previous weeks. He'd been on floors and in cars and sometimes skipped sleep altogether in his efforts to track Lance. Following the latest Black Angel was a full-time job that seemed utterly useless.

Preacher did not want to be found. Fuchs thought to himself, like he had many, many times, that the boy wonder probably didn't even know where he was most of the time. And Fuchs was right, up until a few days ago.

It was Fuchs' turn to ask a question. "And that raises the biggest question of all."

"And what is that?"

"How the hell did Ludkovich end up on the list? Where did he turn?"

Seibel turned from walking down the hall. "That is indeed another mystery we have to figure out."

"Where Ludkovich turned?"

"No. How he got on Preacher's list. Ludkovich wasn't on the list I gave him."

Chapter 24

Dreams overtake the day's reality, like the spill of paint across a virgin canvas. They change perception and invite fantasy. Dreams return us to isolated moments. Mikel Fuchs lay dreaming on a sofa in East Berlin, but his mind drifted to another continent, another decade. He was alone in an alternate reality created by distant war, political chaos and fear of dominos falling.

Black Angel. The name drifted in and out of his dreams.

The idea of resurrecting the lethal shadow avenger had evidently sprung from an unusual source in 1972. A newbie CIA psych-ops analyst presented the resurrection scenario to Geoffrey Seibel after reviewing several classified files from the late 50s and early 60s.

The name itself, Black Angel, apparently was first recorded in transcriptions from a debriefing with a resource abducted from Bratislava and secreted across the border into Vienna in March 1960.

The resource detailed the killings of three KGB agents in Moscow and Eastern Europe. The brutal slayings of the deep-cover resources sent shockwaves through the entire infrastructural underpinnings of the KGB. It was the way the agents were dispatched. The graphic details of the murders were the only signature of the work.

Police work and initial investigations by Soviet intelligence machinery pointed to one individual performing the killings. Each murder occurred at night. Each without witness. Canvas of the area by authorities uncovered two locals in Bratislava and one in Moscow who spoke of seeing an individual who never left the shadows, never showed his face. This sparse information started the myth that grew over the ensuing decades. The Black Angel was nothing less than the angel of death for those in the KGB who encountered him.

The myth did not spread through the general populace. Instead, the supporting mythology for the prizrak, the ghost of death, was shared only among members of the elite Soviet intelligence agency. The myth held a certain value for both sides of the Cold War.

And so, it was this lingering myth that inspired reincarnation of the Black Angel in Southeast Asia in 1973. And Mikel Fuchs would serve in the lead role of this second act. The 23-year old Green Beret killer, murderer, hunter possessed the innate skills needed to become the new Black Angel.

With Seibel's guidance, Fuchs disappeared from the world into the jungles of Vietnam, Laos and Cambodia. His undocumented assignment was to hunt and kill CIA traitors who were also Soviet operatives.

In the weeks and months that stretched into nearly two years, Mikel Fuchs racked up a portfolio of impressive kills. The legend of the Black Angel spread throughout a new contingent of KGB resources stationed across Southeast Asia. The killings forced the KGB to reallocate interests. They also eliminated potential problems for the CIA.

All the while, Fuchs gained experience, bloody, messy experience. He stayed off the map and off the radar, moving from city to city, village to village. He crossed borders into Cambodia, China, India, Malaysia and crossed bodies of water into Africa and up through the Middle East into Europe. For 21 months, the Black Angel again spread terror throughout the KGB. Then the angel of death was gone, never heard from again.

Until 1993, that is.

Seibel learned long ago that a little goes a long way. He also learned that very few people in this world can be as dark and deadly as the Black Angel requires. Few individuals can give up everything and indeed, it was Fuchs' need to reconnect with a certain female individual from his past that forced him to shutter Black Angel version 2.0. in early '75. Fuchs was only human after all. That was the problem. Seibel needed someone lacking certain basic elements of humanity if he was ever to have the role reprised. If he was ever presented with another list.

That person would need to lose everything, be stripped of the little hooks that fasten humanity to his, or her, skin.

Standing in that apartment in Berlin, looking down on a sleeping and now-graying Mikel Fuchs, Seibel's mind drifted to Marta and her particular set of skills. He once hoped she would one day be his next. But she held onto hate too tightly, she could not let go of this most powerful of all emotions. But who could blame her. She too was only human.

Lance, now that brought a smile to Seibel's face. Lance was virtually perfect in his creator's image and even more perfected after New York, where he lost his life's one true love. Unlike the others before him, including Seibel, Lance lacked that certain defining element, that soft spark the makes one human. He was simply something other.

Nothing, no one would ever be this perfect again, ever. Lance had been under for nearly a year now and the results were nothing short of miraculous. He performed like he was training for the role every moment of his life. It was a marvel.

Under the pretext of peaceful sleep, Mikel Fuchs kept his breathing normal. He fought the urge to open his eyes and look up at his mentor, his tormentor. Fuchs lived the life of a second son, even though he was welcomed into this world long before the preferred heir to the throne. It would be easy now to just roll over on the sofa and put a bullet through the back of Seibel's head. It would be over. Simple.

But for the thrill of the ride.

He was shamelessly addicted to the violent magic show that only Seibel could conjure. Fuchs knew he would never be the one. He was the chosen one a long time ago, but that time was gone. His time as the Black Angel was over nearly two decades ago. Papa had found his new angel, the perfect angel.

Chapter 25

"You owe me nothing. But if you do me this kindness, I will repay you with any favor asked."

The words were spoken in German, through static and ambient noise. They were spoken into a telephone from some distant land and received in the ear of a U.S. Naval Reserve pilot.

"Sir," the reply in German. "I am afraid I don't know what you are asking." Lt. Stan Meadows stood beside a Navy Gulfstream jet resting beside a hangar in San Diego. His cell phone had rung 30 seconds earlier with a number he did not recognize. He regretted answering.

"I cannot be specific. You will be contacted within two days. At that time, you will need to consider the request."

The line went dead. Meadows squinched up his eyebrows and shook his head.

Forty-four hours later, Meadows' pager beeped as he walked from the Gulfstream to the pilot's quarters at the Antwerp airport. The display did not list a phone number. Instead, it listed an address a mile and a half from the airport.

Meadows again squinched up his forehead and eyebrows. It took him about seven seconds to tie the two events separated by two days and thousands and thousands of miles together. His next flight was not scheduled to depart until the following morning at 06:20. He needed dinner and sleep. But he was intrigued.

Twenty-five minutes later, he walked into the tavern located at the address on his pager. He glanced around the dim establishment and saw no one looking at him. He looked over at the bartender. The portly man gestured for him to come over. As Meadows approached, the bartender reached down and picked up a telephone and placed it on the bar. He said nothing to the tall lieutenant as he pulled out a sheet of paper and proceeded to dial a number. A moment later, he handed the phone to Meadows.

The line rang twice and was picked up. "Thank you for coming Lieutenant. Please walk outside and then west." It was English this time. The line disconnected.

Meadows handed it to the bartender. "Who gave you the number?"

The bartender responded in broken English, "It was just a phone call with your description and the number to call. No more."

"Nothing else?"

"No sir."

Meadows had a choice. He had avoided all things cloak and dagger these past five years flying military leaders and dignitaries to destinations around the world. His job was to fly the plane and ask no questions. He was very good at both.

He didn't care for the situation he now found himself in. He had been brought into several CIA missions over the years, but again, that was behind him. He preferred the straight and narrow. Black and white. His choice now was which way to walk when he left the pub. If he walked west, to the right, he entered something he did not wish to be involved in – uncertainty. If he turned left and walked east, he could avoid that uncertainty and go about his business.

Meadows turned left to leave uncertainty behind. He walked toward a café he knew well. Afterward, he would catch a taxi over to his preferred Antwerp hotel. He was breathing easier as he rounded the corner just a hundred yards from the café. But a dark alley changed his plans.

"You chose to walk east. Just as you should have; just as expected Lieutenant." A heavily accented voice from the alley stopped him in his tracks. He could not see who spoke the words.

"What do you want?"

The shadow stepped forward, but still remained in darkness. "The favor mentioned two days ago will now be asked of you."

"Like I said, what do you want?" The Texas drawl in Meadows' voice was less than its usual friendly.

"You will have another passenger on your flight tomorrow morning. The passenger will not be known to you or your co-pilot. This passenger is to be allowed onboard without question and will depart upon arrival without processing through customs. Again no questions."

Meadows looked at the figure and shook his head. "I cannot allow any undocumented passengers on my plane. I will not. It is that simple. Your request is denied."

"I understand your hesitation, your refusal. As we mentioned two days ago, this favor brings with it repayment, reimbursement in the form of a returned act of kindness with no questions asked. You are under no threat. Your life is not in danger. But this offer carries with it significant knowledge. Your history, your past actions have played an important role in your country's safety and security. Know that this action on your part reaffirms your commitment."

"It is not my decision. I am only concerned with the safety and security of my flight and that of my passengers. Again, I refuse your request. Now, I need to get some dinner. Goodnight." Meadows turned from the alley to walk toward the café just a few steps away.

"Lieutenant," the voice now carried a definite refinement in its German accent. "This request will not be denied. You will allow the passenger on your flight tomorrow morning and you will ask no questions. This is nothing you haven't done before for your government and its clandestine services. That is who makes this request. This comes from Papa and higher up. Thank you for your cooperation sir."

The voice faded into darkness and was gone.

Lt. Meadows did not recognize the fourth passenger lining up to board his Gulfstream. The Army officer carrying a briefcase did not make eye contact. Meadows and his co-pilot had already gone through their initial pre-flight checklist and stood beside the stairs and the open door. He said nothing as the passenger moved slowly past him with a nod. He looked at his co-pilot and shook his head when the man's eyebrows and forehead furrowed. The co-pilot looked to him for an answer.

Meadows merely pursed his lips and began his last walk-around inspection of the aircraft with clipboard in hand.

Minutes later when he came back around to the jet's stairs, his co-pilot, Second Lt. Schwarzman from Bergen, New Jersey, was ready for a confrontation.

"Lieutenant Meadows, our passenger manifest lists three souls. I am fairly certain I counted four passengers boarding."

"Yes." Meadows, at six foot six inches, stood a full 8 inches taller than his co-pilot.

"Why is that, sir?"

"Three plus one equals four."

"I can add, use my fingers and toes if needed. Why do we have an extra passenger and why do you seem unsurprised by the fact?" Schwarzman leaned forward just a hair; it was a very "Yankee" move.

Meadows knew the move well. Being from Texas, he didn't have a Yankee bone in his body. He'd been around this type thousands of times during his life in the Navy. They just do things differently up there. He was not offended and not insulted. He was not threatened by the move either. "What is your job?"

"To fly my plane and make sure my passengers, my approved passengers, arrive safely at their destination."

"Correct. You are to fly the plane beside me and that is all. We are tasked with transporting individuals, important individuals. We are not tasked with discovering their identities." It was Meadows turn to lean in now. "I counted three passengers and one ghost boarding our aircraft. In my experience, my years of experience in this particular line of work, I have learned that I serve several masters. Generals, admirals, colonels, ambassadors, Senators, I've flown them all.

But the most important ones have been those with no title, no name."

"That is not acceptable." Schwarzman persisted, stood his ground. "We have our orders. I will not allow this."

Meadows leaned in closer this time. Close enough to whisper into his co-pilot's ear. "There are people in this world who do not live by the same rules as the rest of us. They do not respect orders or the law or even our lives. I do not want your wife to be a widow or your daughter to lose her father. Do not invite these people into your life. Just fly the god-damn plane."

And the Lieutenant stepped past his co-pilot onto the Gulfstream and into the cockpit. Three minutes later, his co-pilot joined him without saying a word. They completed their pre-flight checks and then piloted the Gulfstream III over the Atlantic Ocean. The aircraft landed seven hours later at Teterboro Airport in New Jersey.

Three passengers proceeded from the jet to the customs office in the executive hangar. The fourth passenger, an Army Captain wearing sunglasses at night and carrying only a briefcase, walked in the opposite direction.

Lt. Meadows looked away as the nameless passenger walked into the night. He wondered to himself what favor he would need repaid by Preacher. It had taken Meadows an hour over the Atlantic to finally recognize the fourth passenger. He was last called in to transport codename Preacher and three additional passengers from Cairo to Athens nearly three years ago. It was maybe the fourth time he had flown the young CIA spook. He had changed. He was a scary creature now. Black eyes.

Meadows shook his head. Anything associated with Seibel was dangerous and Preacher made it deadly.

With regular heroin use, tolerance develops, in which the user's physiological (and psychological) response to the drug decreases, and more heroin is needed to achieve the same intensity of effect. Heroin users are at high risk for addiction—it is estimated that about 23 percent of individuals who use heroin become dependent on it.

Chapter 26

Newark, New Jersey, April 15...

The world is flat. Don't believe it? Just ask someone who fell off the edge.

Scoring heroin shouldn't be easy. It should be difficult, next to impossible. But it isn't. When one knows what to look for, finding it is simple.

Heroin looks the same, whether Baghdad or Minsk or Moscow or Sarajevo or New York. You can see it in doorways and alleys and darkened, broken windows. Heroin is a distinctive neighbor in any community.

Preacher knew these neighborhoods all too well. His trip and fall off the edge was preceded by his need, his addiction to be with her. He couldn't recall when it started. Whatever the impetus, the addiction had moved in and taken up residence.

A short taxi ride brought him to a neighborhood on the Jersey side of the river where heroin set up shop years before. New drugs moved in over the years. Cocaine lived next to crack with meth on the corner. They would not suffice. Only she would do.

For him, heroin had become Marta. Even now, with Marta possibly only hours away from where he stood on a darkened street corner, the injection that was only minutes from his arm would settle his nerves, ease his shaking. Preacher needed it, needed her. Lance could just wait up there, all pissed off and uppity. He had the luxury of avoiding the previous year of death and destruction.

He'd ditched the uniform. The change of clothes from the briefcase was now on his back. The comfortable leather gloves were on his sweating hands. Just under $150,000 dollars was in the ultra light backpack slung over his shoulder. He had no gun at the moment. That would be remedied shortly.

He didn't need a watch to tell him it was just before 1:00 a.m. He knew the passing of the night. The shades of darkness passed from hour to hour until the first embers of dawn began to glow to the east. Newark, New Jersey could just as well have been Zagreb or Warsaw or Kabul. He could already see where he was going and who he needed to interact with. He stepped down the street and into a tight alley. The ghoul crumpled in a filthy space between a water meter and dumpster emitted the odor Preacher needed to smell. A delightful fusion of urine and sweat and tears of euphoria. Preacher bent down to the skeleton.

"Brother, brother." He spoke with an oatmeal thick Russian accent. The African-American junkie took a few moments to come down to earth.

"What-you-want-fool?" It was one word.

"I need my sister. She comes to me through a needle. I need her desperately. I have $200 here if you will direct me to your closest friend who knows my where my sister is."

Mention of the money caused the man to shake his head and rub his filthy face. "I might know a guy."

"Good. Take me to him within five minutes and I add another $200."

"Okay, okay. You ain't no cop, right?" He struggled and then sat up.

"No cop. I am just lonely for my sister." Preacher pulled the man up. The odor would have caused most to turn and hurl. It unfortunately smelled a little like heaven to him. He handed the junkie $200 and helped him stay up. They crossed the street and then climbed the steps of a three-story dilapidated townhome.

The insides of the building were as bad as the exterior. Preacher stood back as the fella rapped on the door.

"Arnell, why the hell you back here? You know I'm gonna have to blow you away. Get the hell outta here." The voice through the small slat was tired, barely awake.

"Bebop, no. I got a friend here. He needs to see his sister. You got her in there."

"You ain't got no friends fool. Get the hell..."

Preacher stepped in. "Arnell does have a friend and his name is Benjamin." He stuffed ten $100 bills through the hole. "And my sister needs to come with a new slipper. She needs to bring along friends too." He slipped another ten bills through the door.

"Shit man. I don't know you and don't know your sister. Get the fu-"

"Give me all my sisters in there. Preacher stopped the small window from closing and stuffed a roll of bills inside. It was $5,000 in hundreds. "Quickly. I need to take them to a party."

The voice on the other side of the door cussed a few more times and then stepped away. He returned a minute later with a brown paper bag he stuffed through the hole.

"Go to your party Igor. Come back when you need more party tricks and sisters."

"Thank you my friend. I will." He and Arnell walked down the steps and back across the street to the alley. As promised, he handed the junkie two more $100 bills and then another for fun. "And now I need a brother to protect his sister Arnell. Who do I need to see about him?"

Nine minutes later, Preacher added a Beretta 9 mm and two boxes of shells to the bag of heroin and needles in his backpack. The seller tried to upgrade him to a larger piece. He stuck with tried and true. Welcome back to America Black Angel.

Chapter 27

Frank Wyrick had a bad taste in his mouth. The emptiness within the loosely affiliated team of operatives banded together for decades by Siegel was apparent. Fuchs stayed over in Europe. The Jordanians were nowhere to be found. No one gathered at Harvey Point for training or strategy or shooting the breeze. It was just work now. And that is how Wyrick kept his mind clear of some of the bad stuff still hanging on.

He was fairly sure Lance Priest was now one of those pulled under never to be seen again. He was gone. He had helped the kid disappear from the face of the earth. The girl, Marta, was another casualty. She was frozen in time. They served their greater purpose, of course. But still, it seemed a waste.

During the past year, he worked a surveillance job in Montreal, followed by a detailed background fact check on a prospect in London, and an extended multiple unit bug installation in a Berlin office building slated to be occupied by a few FSB shell companies. Technology continued to improve, allowing Wyrick to place ever smaller, more powerful and difficult to detect transmitters. The work kept him busy.

He, like Braden, lived in a suburb of Philadelphia in a condo he came home to for maybe three or four months of the year. It was home in that it was where he came when he was not invading the private lives of others through audio, photo or video means. But it wasn't much of a home, just four small rooms in 1,100-square feet.

Returning home this evening after being away for three weeks was no different than usual. The place was dark and empty. The alarm beeped upon his entry. He entered the code to deactivated it. The Spartan furnishings were straight and clean. The temperature was cool. The air a little stale, but there was a scent, a smell and moisture. There was a quiet noise. It was the bathroom. Water was running, the shower. *What the hell*?

He pulled his gun, closed the door behind him and ducked to the floor. The darkness enveloped his shadow. He waited 15 seconds for his eyes to adjust. He rose and took three silent steps across the room. He saw that the bathroom light was on. Light slipped out from under the door.

If someone meant to kill him, they could have done it already. He was beat-tired, not sharp. He took three more steps and stood in the short hallway outside the bathroom. His mind raced to all the possibilities. The easiest one to settle on was the obvious – Seibel. This was something he would do. He'd never done it before, but this was his modus operandi – unpredictable.

No reason to delay, he reached to turn the doorknob and open the door. The light from the room spilled out, along with warm, thick steam. He was struck from behind, crashing him into the wall. The gun was wrenched from his hand. Then he was thrown to the floor. The continuing motion brought a body down on top of him.

"Too easy," the thick Russian accent whispered in his ear. It was Seibel.

"Man, get off me."

"Not yet my friend." The voice sounded thick with vodka.

Wyrick laughed, even with his face shoved into the wood plank floor. "Come on, man, cut the shit. Let me up Siebel." Then Siebel laughed. But it wasn't Siebel.

His attacker rose up off of him and continued to laugh as he walked into the front room. Wyrick got up after a few seconds and turned on the nearest light. Lance Priest, or someone who looked like him, sat on the couch smiling. It looked like Preacher.

The two of them just stared each other. Lance broke the silence.

"So, I guess you've never seen a ghost before, huh?" The eyes were black, all black. "The ghost of someone you killed."

Wyrick took a couple of steps into the room. He had been around Lance in person maybe a dozen times in seven years. He'd spent significantly more time delving into his life. And then, of course, erasing it.

Looking at this human being sitting before him, he was perplexed. People change. They age, turn grey, sag. It happens. This, this was a transformation. He would have walked right past him on the street. The only word that fit was black. Wyrick's forehead furrowed as he processed. The ghost was in no rush. He just looked back at him.

"Where?" Wyrick muttered and moved his head. "How?"

"That's easy. Have a seat." Preacher gestured to the chair. Wyrick did as ordered. He kept his eyes on the black orbs that used to be another color. He couldn't remember what color they were originally. Wyrick sat down and watched as Lance, the ghost in front of him, proceeded to pull out a paper sack from a backpack on the floor.

From the paper sack, he pulled out a bag with small crystal-like rocks, a syringe and a bottle of water. Wyrick watched as the junkie sitting before him went through a routine he had perfected. Preacher took off the black jacket and rolled up the sleeve on his left arm. Wyrick sucked in air when he saw the bruising, the track marks. He couldn't look away from the damage done and the extensive tattoos. They were, menacing. That was the only word that came to mind.

Preacher looked up from his practiced routine and basically snickered at its effect on the old surveillance expert. "You'll find things interesting in just a few minutes. Hold on." He spoke the words in Russian. He could tell Wyrick caught half of it, but enough.

He poured water into the bottle cap and then siphoned out a precise amount into the syringe. He then poured some of the powder into the spoon he had pulled out of the bag. He squirted the water into the spoon and stirred it with the needle. He put the needle down and lit the lighter under the spoon. A few moments later, the liquid mixture began to agitate. He then placed and tiny bit of cigarette filter into the spoon, which sopped up the liquid. He inserted the needle into the filter and extracted the liquid out into the syringe. It was an impressive exercise, especially wearing leather gloves. "Turn the light off."

Wyrick got up to flip the light switch off.

This is where Preacher usually picks a vein and injects Marta into him. But this time, he set the syringe on the coffee table. It took incredible strength of will. "Please, help yourself." Lance nodded to the needle.

Wyrick shook his head. "No thanks."

"You sure? It takes away all that ails you. I can see that your mind is troubled. It will help." Preacher was having a difficult time avoiding looking at the syringe. Its pull was gravity on steroids.

"No. I appreciate it, but I don't think it would help."

"I have one question." Preacher asked.

"What is it?"

"Why did you leave them?"

"Leave what?"

"My dreams. Why did you leave my dreams, my memories? Why didn't you erase them?" The two of them sat in the dark. Wyrick waited for the next question. He was stunned by the last five minutes. He was intrigued and fascinated and excited and pleased that Lance was still alive, but troubled by the macabre character the 12-year-old boy he had first investigated 15 years before had become. This was a Seibel experiment gone terribly, horribly wrong. This was scary.

Wyrick was ready for the next question from Lance. He wasn't ready for the Black Angel.

He saw and heard movement and tensed, but before he could even bring his arms up to protect his face, an object struck him. It was heavy, but soft. "Move radio man. You're up." Wyrick was lifted along with the object. He felt like a ragdoll being tossed as he was shoved toward the door. It opened and an arm locked around his torso propelling him onto the porch and then down the stairs. He recognized the object in his arms as his own well-traveled duffle bag. There was no time to stop. It was a continuous motion.

Frank Wyrick is a strong, lean individual. He has kept himself in impressive shape over 25 years in clandestine service through running, weight training, martial arts and basketball. He knew a good many ways to disarm, overpower and seriously hurt most people. He decided to take a stand at the bottom of the stairs.

His first move was to plant his left foot, throw his right shoulder forward and bring his left elbow whirling around to make contact with his captor's head. It was an excellent move, strong, solid and powerful. It was karate and judo combined.

Problem was, even though he was in excellent shape for a man closer to 50 than 45, he was simply not as fast as a cobra or the speed of sound or electricity moving from brain to nerve to muscle.

The first tensing of his left big toe sent a message to the rest of his body which was felt by the lethal killer holding his midsection in a vice. The Black Angel could just as well have been Wyrick's shadow. There was never any possibility of the older man taking the younger killer by surprise. Especially with his senses undiminished by heroin. Black Angel felt that initial tension emanating from Wyrick's foot and released the vise to deliver a smashing blow to the man's right shoulder. The effect was to propel the man forward and to the ground.

Wyrick adjusted his body in flight to begin a roll that would carry him onto his back and then to his feet. Problem was, a Bon Jovi song had started playing in Preacher's head back up in the apartment. That and the fact that Preacher, through Lance's eyes, could see everything going on around him.

Wyrick had no idea. If he did, he wouldn't have tried any funny stuff. He would have known that anyone but Neil Sedaka playing in Preacher's head meant he had his wits about him. It was as if he could see and feel everything at once, all of it, everything. He hadn't felt this in a year of darkness, emptiness. Heroin got in the way.

The moon's caress on skin; the leaves wrestling each other in the trees; the decay of the trash from the dumpster across the parking lot; the strong latissimus dorsi muscles of the man in his grip; and, of course, the most minute change in a person's body brought on by a brain sending signals through nerves.

When Wyrick came back up from his well-performed roll, he expected to find Lance in front of him. Lance was nowhere around. The person occupying the skin of the guy who'd kidnapped him was not Lance Priest. He was much worse. Downright evil at times.

Wyrick threw an uppercut but no one was there. Preacher had already seen this move in the tensing and subtle rotation of Wyrick's shoulders. He had jumped in front, which was now behind Wyrick as the older man turned to deliver the blow. When the surveillance expert realized what had happened, he turned his head just in time to see the knee rising to impact the dead center of his back.

The blow was horrific, painful and a show-closer. Wyrick basically flailed up and back to concave around the knee before falling forward in a gasping heap. The air burst out of his lungs and pain exploded throughout his body. He convulsed on the ground. It was ugly. Preacher was immediately on him, lips at his ear. "Let's not do that again Frank. We have places to go and people to kill."

Wyrick felt himself lifted and tossed over a shoulder. Moments later, they were in Wyrick's van. Lance, or Preacher, or the Black Angel, whoever, behind the wheel. They drove north on damp city streets.

"Frank, you with me?"

"Yah." Wyrick leaned to the right in his seat; still trying to catch his breath. His back obviously hurting something fierce.

"I know you're in pain. But you can stay with me, right?"

"Mostly." Wyrick muttered.

"When was the last time you saw… me?" Preacher tripped up on the question. Wyrick had never seen this person before.

"In D.C., two weeks before... New York, the explosion. So, March last year."

"Yes, I remember. That last briefing with Papa." Preacher noted for maybe the thousandth time there was no literal Russian translation for Papa. It was just *Papa*. "And then you completed your assignment of erasing me and Marta."

"Yes."

"Very good work. Very thorough. Had you done that before?" Preacher nodded while keeping his eyes on the road.

"Only on a much smaller scale. I removed files, the history on computers... Never a person and most of their life. Took a long time." Wyrick struggled to get a full breath. He turned toward Lance and looked at him in the glow of the dashboard. Lance could pass for a good many people out there in the world. His features were changed. He could be any of several ethnicities. The eyes were black, but there was more. The jet-black hair allowed him to look Middle Eastern or Italian or Spanish.

"Again, very thorough. I have found almost no traces. But, of course, I know more places to look than others." Preacher smiled and looked over at Wyrick. "I'm going to need your help."

"I was pretty sure you didn't come to me for a friendly visit." Wyrick smiled back.

"What do you know about my mission?"

"Very little. He moved me on to others soon after. Honestly, I was glad to see you earlier; see that you are alive. I didn't know..."

"I don't really care why you're lying to me. But you are lying."

"Not lying. No reason."

"You've got reasons. And if you don't now, you will soon enough, after you help me." Preacher turned back to the road and the headlights spilling on the wet asphalt. "You're going to have to use your impressive skills."

Wyrick turned ahead. He didn't need to consider the statement. He knew he had a debt to pay here. It was a balance due that could lead to his death. He began to think of others. Luckily, his children were grown, not that he saw them much anymore.

Preacher read his mind. "We all make sacrifices Frank. Especially in this line of work, you know that. You won't be able to see your sons. They can't know. No one can. You need to forget them, forget everyone. Anyone you hold in there," Preacher reached over and tapped Wyrick on the side of the head. "Their only chance now, is to leave them out of this."

"So you chose only me for this mission." A statement, not a question from Wyrick.

"I think it's more like you chose me, but that doesn't matter. And no, you're not the only one I've visited."

The two of them rode in silence for several miles, until Wyrick began to smile again.

"What?" Preacher asked in Russian. "Chto?" He asked again.

Wyrick laughed and turned back to the black-eyed figure beside him. "It took a few years and required you to go through your own little hell, but it happened just like everyone knew it would." He trailed off and shook his head.

"What's that?"

Wyrick turned back to Lance. "How many ways could you kill me right now?" The question sounded off topic.

"Sixty-one." The answer showed that it was indeed a part of the equation.

"Did you include pushing me out the door?"

"That's number 34, right before wrapping the seat belt around your neck and pushing you out to drag along for a little ways. And right after putting your side of the van into and under the trailer of that semi a half-mile ahead."

"Jesus. Sixty-one. I could only see about eleven."

"Need to be more creative. I didn't get started on your torture options. You'd talk alright."

Wyrick shook his head again. "See, like I said, it took some time, but you've become him. There was no avoiding it."

It was Preacher's turn to shake his head at that. "Siebel. He was something." The past tense was not lost on Wyrick.

Chapter 28

The video was grainy, not the best. The audio sucked, basically worthless. But it wasn't the quality or the sound that mattered. It was the subject. And the subject in this video was doing something rather interesting. Pieces fell into place after viewing the footage.

Stuart Braden went through a routine on most mornings that bordered on the sublime. He rose before 4:30 a.m., stepped down the hall and down the stairs to the basement. He then went into a small room in the basement and closed the door behind. Once inside the room, which had no windows but did have nearly a dozen large posters of nature scenes, he turned on quiet music and worked through a qigong routine.

Qigong, the Asian practice of aligning movement with breathing and meditation, is performed by millions each morning in the Asian world. Americans call it tai chi.

Performing a morning ritual of aligning one's life force with their "Chi" or being, is nothing special. But doing it each and every morning while lost in a trance provided connection. As Preacher watched the series of video snippets of Braden pieced together by Wyrick, he had something of an epiphany. A light bulb came on in the deep recesses of his messed up brain.

"You've got hundreds of hours of this?"

"Yep" Wyrick answered without looking up from the screen.

"Over what period?"

"Two years."

"Two years? The same thing every morning?"

"Every morning that he was home."

"Why?" Lance asked.

"Why what?" Wyrick asked back.

"Why take the video. Why plant a video camera in Stuart Braden's secret basement room?"

"Why do you think?" Wyrick leaned back in his chair at his video editing studio in a rundown office complex in a rundown part of Philadelphia. The equipment Wyrick sat in front of was anything but rundown. It was top of the line and even prototype devices for capturing, editing and producing video.

"My first instinct was because Seibel ordered it. But that was wrong."

"How do you know it's wrong?" Wyrick knitted his fingers together and brought his two index fingers to his lips. Lance had seen Wyrick do this many times and cataloged it under "deep concentration."

"This is not Seibel. He wouldn't have you watch someone for two years. Hell, two months would be too long."

Wyrick didn't reply. He was waiting for Lance to move through the various scenarios racing through his mind.

Lance had been leaning against the wall. He stepped away and ran his fingers through coal-black hair. Wyrick couldn't help but look at the tattoos covering a good part of each upper arm. "If I had to venture a guess, I would say that you, Frank Wyrick, are much more than meets the eye. I would say that you have been keeping something, something very big from Papa for some time."

"Go on." Wyrick knew a good bit about Lance's mental processes, having captured a fair amount on video and audiotapes six years ago and during his CIA orientation and training. He knew Lance was just getting started.

"I could go into a good many details about what I am thinking and where I'm headed. But I need to know when was the last time you saw Braden?"

"You mean doing his morning tai chi?"

"No, and it's called qigong. When was the last time you saw him in person?"

Wyrick's procerus muscle tugged his eyebrows together. "Two weeks ago in D.C."

Preacher leaned back against the wall. "And was there any advance intelligence about me coming back?"

"Nothing. I heard something about Saint Petersburg week before last. Fuchs is over there tracking you now. Evidently, not very well." Wyrick put his laced fingers and hands behind his head.

"What do you know about my mission?" Preacher put his head against the wall as he asked.

"Not much."

"How much were you involved after New York?"

Wyrick looked at Lance for a few seconds. The hesitation was its own answer. "None. My work took me all around the country. I was never operational with you."

"So you don't know where they had me, where they kept me afterward?"

"No."

Preacher stepped from the wall and turned to lean against the desk on which all of Wyrick's video equipment sat. "I figured it out."

"What?"

"All of it, well, most of it." Preacher smiled and ran his hands through his hair again.

"Meaning?" Wyrick sat motionless. He was like a bird or squirrel with a coiled cobra just feet from him. He knew his life was tenuous in this and the next few moments.

"Meaning Seibel did an excellent job building up his usual wall of confusion, but wasn't able to keep it all wrapped up."

"I'm not following." Wyrick only moved his lips, his breath shallow. There was a gun in the drawer on the right, but he'd never get to it before the cobra struck.

"He broke everything, told my family I was dead, convinced me she is dead and had Braden give me my mission. But that wasn't the reason. It is never that simple with him and his damn layers." Preacher bent to rest his hands on his knees. "He had me working on something I had no idea about. But now," he gestured to the frozen image of Braden doing qigong on the monitor. "I think I have it figured out."

"What is it?" Wyrick asked.

Lance Priest had a decision to make. He owed nothing to Frank Wyrick. It was actually the other way around. Wyrick owed him big time. He didn't need to share anything more with him. He simply could not trust the man. He had no idea if Wyrick would call Seibel the moment Lance left him.

So, what to do? He could leave right now without telling Wyrick any more. He could tell the surveillance expert a few lies and leave it at that. Or he could just kill him and be done with it.

Frank Wyrick didn't want to die. He'd faced death several times and always escaped. But in all his years of doing this lousy work for Seibel, he'd never been this close. And he knew it. Sitting here in his little video domain, death stood right in front of him. He could see death in the artificial black iris of Preacher's eyes. This man that he had first investigated as a pre-pubescent alleged murderer, had become an agent of death. Murder was on his skin, in his words. Wyrick held some of the blame for who Lance had become. He was a part of the death this Black Angel carried with him.

Frank Wyrick decided to stay alive.

"I know about the list. And I know about Braden." Wyrick said the words he hoped might make it through to whatever remained of the original Lance.

"What about Braden?" Lance tilted his head.

"Your suspicions about him." Wyrick added.

"And what are my suspicions?" Preacher kept it under control, even though the pull of heroin and pulsing adrenaline and the image of Marta tugged at him to move, to run.

Wyrick sat forward, slowly, and put his elbows on his thighs to run his hands over the stubble on his balding head.

"So what does this have to do with my suspicions?" Preacher needed this conversation over quickly so he could get moving, anywhere. "The next thing you are going to tell me is you have secret information of this type on Seibel."

Preacher's statement put Wyrick back in his chair. His eyes wide open.

"Come on, I'm crazy and going through withdrawals. I'm not stupid." Preacher's matter-of-fact tone was eerie.

"You figured all this out right now?"

"No. I had time over the last year."

Chapter 29

He had been with her all day in an abandoned warehouse in Kiev; just lying around talking. She helped him work through the story, the angles. It just didn't make any sense, none of it. All of it.

Such a waste. Needless.

"Go back, what did he say?" Marta, the ghost of Marta past, asked as she lay beside him stroking his head.

"Braden?"

"Yes, Stuart." She was endlessly patient with him when she came to him through the point of a needle in his vein.

"I can't remember every word. Something is in the way. And Sedaka just won't stop singing." Preacher turned to look in Marta's eyes. This day, they were her eyes from Yap, the tiny island where they spent three weeks after escaping from the hospital in Hawaii. He looked into her ghost eyes and got lost.

"Lance, Preacher, what did Stuart say?" She asked.

He jerked and shook his head. "Sorry, sorry honey. I was thinking of Yap, and..."

"Yes. A time I'll never forget either. But focus, what did he say exactly?" She was always the stronger of the two; even now, as a ghost. Preacher reached out and caressed her cheek. It wasn't there.

"Sorry. Braden came in to my room and sat beside the bed. He asked me how I was doing. How my eyes felt."

"The surgery to change their color. Did that hurt?" Marta frowned. It made Preacher laugh. She knew full well it hurt. She knew everything he did.

"It hurt like hell. It was weeks before I got the bandages off."

"What did Braden say after the small talk?" She got him back on track.

Preacher shook his head slowly trying to recall through the thick mist and haze of the drugs they had given him. "He waited a whole 10 minutes and then he broke the news that you were gone. You were dead." Preacher looked down, his eyes watering. He'd never felt pain like that before or since.

"Baby, don't." Marta's ghost put her hands around his shoulders and her cheek to his. A tear ran down his skin, through her ghostly skin. "I'm not gone. I'm here."

Preacher dropped his head to the pillow. Her spirit could not console him when he recalled the pain of learning of her death.

"Lance. Lance." She was no longer lying beside him. She stood a few feet from the bed. "Lance, what were his words? Think."

He brought his head up from the pillow to look at her transparent beauty standing there in shorts and t-shirt. He sat up and spun his feet off the bed to the floor. "Okay. He said you never came to. You slipped away later that night, after I left you."

"After you were shot with tranquilizers and taken away. You did not leave me."

"Yes. Can you friggin' believe they shot me with tranks? That's crazy." He ran his hands through his hair.

"Please Preacher, what were Stuart's exact words? Please." She was pushing him, prodding.

"He said," Preacher looked up at her. "He said 'some wounds are too serious. She was too far gone. Lance, I'm so sorry.'" Preacher rubbed his face and began to shake his head again.

"Stop." She ordered.

He obeyed and looked again into her eyes.

"Do you recall hearing those words somewhere else, from someone else?" Marta asked, a tiny smile on her beautiful ghostly face.

"No."

"Yes you do. Think." Her patience was beginning to wane.

"Where? When? I don't remember."

"Someone else said those words."

And that was it. Marta's spirit, or at least Preacher's manifestation of her ghost, had done it again. She was so much better at figuring things out. He smiled at the irony of needing a figment of his life's love to help him decipher the jumbles of his brain. "Seibel. Right after the Empire State Building, he called and told me you were gone. He used those exact words."

Marta smiled her brilliant and unique smile that was only for Lance. "Yes. And that begs the question."

"Why would he use those exact words? How would he know them?" Preacher stood. He wanted to hug her, but he knew how that would go. His arms, seeking only her touch, her body, would find no purchase. He could only hug the air in this dilapidated room with a filthy bed, broken mirror on the wall and exposed single light bulb. "It is a message."

"Ah-hah." Ghost Marta nodded her head.

The Black Angel nodded.

"Plenty of time to figure things out." Preacher nodded to Wyrick. "But I think you are about to tell me something I don't know."

Frank Wyrick did indeed know a few things Preacher did not. In fact, he knew things no one on this planet besides Geoffrey Seibel knew. And the reason he knew them was because he is a spy. More so than any of the people he had been assigned to spy on over nearly three decades, Frank Wyrick had been a secret agent. He gathered intel on Seibel that others would find truly, truly amazing. And Wyrick kept it secret. Never told anyone. "What do you want to know?"

"The list." Preacher nodded.

"Where did it come from?" Wyrick asked.

The question caught Preacher off guard. He was interested in the process Seibel used in compiling the nine names on the list. Where it came from was not one of the questions he had. "Came from? It came from Seibel."

"No it didn't. He got it from someone else."

Preacher was stunned by the information. "You're wrong. No one else but him could put together a list of longtime deep-cover operatives like that. No one else in the CIA has that kind of institutional knowledge."

"You're right there." Wyrick nodded.

Preacher's procerus worked overtime crinkling up his forehead and pulling his eyebrows together. In ultra-rapid succession, he ran through six-plus years of information he'd gathered and cataloged on Geoffrey Seibel, super spy. Leaning on the desk in front of Wyrick, Preacher processed millions and millions of bits of data. He was looking for something he had missed. Wyrick just sat and watched. He knew the basics of what was going on in Lance's head. He also thought that maybe the immediate danger had passed. He might just live through this.

"Not Seibel?" Preacher asked.

"Nope."

"Not Fuchs or Braden or you?"

"No." Wyrick shook his head.

"Smelinski?"

"That's what I thought originally. It made sense that he had discovered these moles in KGB operations and provided the information through some veiled back channel to Seibel. He had the resources and the means to pull together the list and strategically share it with Seibel."

"But?" Preacher cut in.

"But, it wasn't him. None of the lists came from him."

Now, Wyrick could have stopped with 'it wasn't him' and Preacher would have had a few follow-up questions. But the addition of 'none of the lists' was something of a little thunderbolt. And Wyrick knew it.

The shock sent Lance reeling through years and faces and pages and computer screens and satellite images and dreams and Marta and sound and light and emptiness. He settled on one thing when the tornado/tidal wave of cataloged cranial data ended. It was Fuchs. But not the Fuchs Preacher knew and loved. It was another. A younger man.

"I'm version 2.0 aren't I? I'm the second edition, the sequel. I am working a second list." Preacher looked up at Wyrick. The graying, African American surveillance expert just shook his head. It perplexed Preacher. He was sure he had it figured out.

"You are third generation Black Angel."

Chapter 30

He needed the strain, the lung-crush. He pushed on, a solitary figure moving through a broken Philadelphia neighborhood on cracked streets past block after block of beaten-down row houses. Pushing, increasing output, lifting rubber soles off the road and gently slapping them back down. He was a hydraulic machine with a hate-filled steam engine driving pistons and spinning gears.

Wyrick turned out to be the key. Damn.

He pushed on mile after mile. How far had he gone now? It had been 22 minutes and 34 seconds since he exploded out of Wyrick's office, down a hallway, out into the night and then south. He could run all the way if needed, but that would take a few days.

Damn.

Damn.

Damn.

Damn.

He cursed out a four-beat rhythm along with the slap of his soles. How the hell could he have missed all this? Hell, how could he or anyone have ever figured it out? This simply couldn't be true. The word 'impossible' kept banging around his head. "Impossible," he huffed out loud as he crossed an intersection with a shuttered factory on the right and a boarded up convenience store on the left. He knew from the cross streets that I-95 was only two miles ahead. He would need wheeled transportation for that portion of this journey.

He closed his eyes as he barreled forward. But instead of replaying the conversation with Wyrick, he went back to last night.

After three days in the New York area tracking down leads that languished over the past year, Preacher traveled to Philadelphia. And late last evening, he stood outside of a back yard. He had to wait for a neighbor to let their Bassett Hound, with his good ears, sharp nose and deep bark, back inside the house. Once the old fella was inside, Preacher scaled the six-foot wood fence and dropped silently into the yard.

He stood silent and motionless breathing in his surroundings, absorbing the darkness. He had become night over the last year. He embraced everything night had to offer, from stealth to secret to death. Wrapped in caressing darkness, he had but one goal. He needed to enter this quiet home on this peaceful street and satisfy curiosity.

Being here, implementing this one-night project was Marta's idea. If he was not committed to total immobility, Preacher would have shaken his head. Of course Marta didn't come up with this idea.

He concentrated on the job at hand. Months of training and years of experience showed him how to enter a home without detection. He stayed next to the fence and slithered up to the house. He'd learned long ago the value of a small, powerful flashlight and pulled it out to examine the telephone box next to the power meter on the side of the house. He saw the basics, no additional cables coming out and running the length of the house feeding an alarm system. If there was an alarm, it was not connected to a service provider and local authorities.

He moved back around to the rear of the house, to the patio with French doors and windows. He tried the doors. Locked. He stepped to the first window. It too was locked. Good. He was glad this family practiced basic security.

But locks are not real deterrents for dedicated invaders. He pulled out his knife and began cutting away the rubber seal around a pane of glass in the window furthest to the left from the French double doors. After the rubber seal was removed, he stuck the knife in the seam of the aluminum windows and pried the two pieces apart at the bottom right. He did the same at the top right so that when done, he was able to bend the metal and use the knife to pry the panes of glass out. He then slid the sheets of glass out and leaned them against the wall.

He stepped through the open window into a sunroom. He then moved from this room into a living room, which flowed into a formal dining room and kitchen. He skirted the kitchen to make his way down a long hallway. Everything was on one level in the house.

He passed a bathroom on the left and a bedroom on the right. Peeking in, he saw two children asleep on each level of a bunk bed. Peter and Louis, or "Lou." Up ahead on the left, Preacher stuck his head into the girl's room. Brittany. She was older; pre-teen. Boy band posters on the walls.

That left the master bedroom at the end of the hall.

He paused outside the room to listen and then stepped in. A woman slept alone on the left side of the bed. Her name was Allie. The man, her husband was not here. Although, it looked like the right side of the bed had been slept in. He looked around. A few articles of clothing were draped over the bed and on a side chair. But he wasn't here.

He stepped back to the doorway and turned to take in the room again. He glanced at the woman in bed. Preacher had never met her, but knew her favorite restaurant, the make and year of car she drove, where she shopped. He also knew what she looked like. Allie Braden was Asian American.

He opened his eyes on the darkened South Philly street. If he'd only known about the basement in Braden's house. He'd seen the door five years earlier the first time he invaded the house on a whim one Saturday evening with the Bradens out of town. And again last night, he had mistakenly assumed that a closet was behind that door. Wyrick showed him on videotape that indeed a basement and secret room lay at the bottom of a set of stairs.

If only he'd known about that last night. He would have stepped down there and confronted Stuart Braden. But there wasn't time now. Preacher needed to get to Washington, now. He stopped running, stepped onto the sidewalk and rested his hands on his knees as he sucked in oxygen. He told Wyrick to keep a lid on it and not talk to anyone tonight. That shouldn't be too much of a problem. It was almost 2:00 a.m.

Preacher looked around and saw what he needed. He walked over to a dimly lit tavern parking lot. Several fellow night-dwellers milled about. Two stood beside a beat-up Monte Carlo.

It was probably brown originally, but rust was now the vehicle's dominant color.

He pulled the hood of his sweats top up over his head and stepped right up next to one of the two African-American men.

"Guys. I need a car. I need your car." He used a thick Russian accent.

"What? No way man." The less inebriated of the two replied. It was presumably his car.

"$2,000 cash. Give me the keys; I give you the money."

"Get out of here fool." The other dude waved his arm in a whirling, over-dramatic drunken arc.

"One-time offer. Take the cash." Preacher pulled the bills out of his pocket, counted off 20 $100s and stuck them into the outstretched hand of the guy leaning against the car.

"Damn." The guy said as he accepted the cash and reached into his pocket for the keys.

"You got a lot more than 2K there man. You need to pay D-Jack $3,000. Yep, three grand is the price of this ride." The second drunk was emboldened by the flash of cash.

Preacher had masses of adrenaline coursing through him from his 40-minute run from Wyrick's office. Times like these, with withdrawal howling like an inner wolf, made him cranky and impatient.

He reached out and took the other guy's hand and squeezed it. "Brother," the Russian accent thicker and menacing. "Two thousand is more than fair and D-Jack has accepted the offer. If you want to get in and come with me out to the swamps, we can negotiate further. My friends will enjoy meeting you. Come on." Preacher pulled the guy to the car as he accepted the keys from D-Jack, who started counting the bills.

The grip he had on the dude's hand was sending shockwaves up through the guy's arm. He tried to pull back, but Preacher pulled him in close. In the dark, his black eyes were holes. "Please, come with me." His smile drooled with evil intent.

"No, no man. You go on. I think 2k is good, right D-Jack?" The guy was pulling back for all he was worth now. His friend was busy kissing the bills.

Preacher let go of his hand and pushed him back from the car. "Good. You gentlemen have a nice evening." He got into the filthy car and drove out of the parking lot heading west a quarter of a mile to enter the onramp onto I-95 South.

It was all coming together as he drove south with the windows down. If he had half of it right, then this was one whopper of a tale. His wizardry at spinning lies paled in comparison to this epic saga. He was living; had been living it for the previous year. But this Greek tragedy, Shakespearian three-act marvel and Tolstoy 1,000-page treatise was not a creature of the present. This story was a relic of the past. This was all about the puppet master, the wizard, the one and only Geoffrey Seibel.

Chapter 31

The past caught up with the master in the morning.

Geoffrey Seibel, master of his own empire, king of his personal, worldwide fiefdom, high priest in the order of the cloak and dagger, awoke to his last day as such. Neither he, nor his current wife asleep beside him, knew what the day held.

He rose well before the sun as usual. Waking up in his bed had been a rare luxury for the past week. He started a pot of coffee, stepped out the front door onto the walk and then down the long driveway to retrieve the Washington Post and New York Times.

Something was wrong.

The Times weighed too much for a Wednesday. He raised the cylindrical shape and rotated it. He couldn't see in, but it just felt too solid. He instinctively looked around into the gathering dawn. No one was out. Everything still.

He was bending to put the Times back down on the ground when he saw the piece of paper sticking out of the Post in his right hand. After setting the Times down, he slipped the band off the Post and the piece of paper fell into his hand.

Geoffrey Siebel was done.

It happens like this to men of his caliber. Growing old and rocking on the front porch was never a possibility. He expected to die long before he reached retirement. It was only fitting for a killer, a destroyer. He expected nothing more.

Instead of death this crisp, cool morning, Siebel received something colder, something significantly crueler. Geoffrey Siebel was relegated to CIA history, his world dismantled in seconds. The note contained only a few sloppily scribbled sentences. The words forced America's premier spymaster to suck in air and exhale slowly. It read:

"I am the Black Angel. Wife 3 did not die last night. Daughters 2 and 3 off at college will wake from their sleep. Number 1 did not meet her maker along with your two grandchildren on a hillside in Carmel, Indiana late last evening. I spared them.

"Fall to hell. Watch them rise to heaven. Death meets us all. It never forgets a face.

"It will come back for you, tomorrow. Today you die a different death.

"You put faith and trust in three. Two have reciprocated. One has guided you for 25 years. He has done so on behalf of another master.

"This life is over. Join me."

Siebel picked up the New York Times and removed the rubber band to unroll it. He found a worn paper sack. Inside, he found a plastic bag with rocks and powder, a spoon, two syringes, cigarette filters and a lighter. He ran back in the house. He was inside for 17 minutes. Leaving, he knew he might never return. He left wife three sleeping peacefully.

Chapter 32

Looking through the filthy windshield of his $2,000 Monte Carlo three hours earlier, Lance Priest, not the Black Angel, reached a brilliant conclusion. He was driving south on I-95, just north of Baltimore. He pulled over and "borrowed" a cell phone from a car in the parking lot of roadside diner.

The pull, the tug of gravity he had been battling while driving the past two hours proved too strong. Preacher dialed a number he memorized a couple of years ago and left a brief message. He had left several painful messages over the past year, mostly when completely stoned or strung out.

He then used data imparted by Wyrick to call information and track down a number in West Virginia. He placed the call, told a few beautiful lies to the human who answered the phone, and then a couple more lies and an offer of money for services rendered. He then let magic take its course as he continued south past downtown Baltimore and Chesapeake Bay. He stayed on 95 until he reached 495 north of Washington, D.C. He went west, toward McLean, Virginia.

Chapter 33

Marta Sidorova left a deeply troubled and violent childhood behind when Seibel and crew rescued her at 16 from a life in institutions and prisons. Being deposited on the side of the road near an orphanage in Russia was a new beginning. The successive years of violence and death and manipulation were exciting but unfulfilling, until she found herself face-to-face with a young man with that certain something in his eyes.

She was born anew in that moment and can barely recall the pain from him shooting her, twice. As always, she instinctively rubbed the scar on the palm and back of her left hand where his bullet passed through.

She had tried, without success, to explain her plight to Braden after Lance was lost in the World Trade Center bombing. Braden was kind and considerate and always patient with her. It seemed that he genuinely cared. She knew part of that compassion was directed at Lance and the big hole his absence left in their lives.

A knock interrupted the book Marta was reading. She looked at the clock and then the door. It was nearly 3:00 a.m. She got up to look through the peephole in the door. It was Pete, the maintenance man.

"Yes?" She called through the door.

"Miss Parsons, I have a delivery for you," the man answered.

This didn't fit. She tensed and felt something she hadn't in months. She recognized it right away – adrenaline. "What is it?"

"I have a message for you ma'am," he answered.

"Who's it from?"

"Ma'am, I know this is strange. I don't know who it's from. I got a call a few minutes ago from a man who described you and had me write down the message and deliver it to you now and I get $200. I'm sorry, that's all I know ma'am." The man's accent turned ma'am into three syllables. "I can leave it right here on your doorstep."

"No, that's okay." She opened the door a few inches and he stood back at a respectable distance. Another response flashed through that hadn't in over a year. She looked at the human standing in front of her and analyzed the best method to kill him. Shocking how quickly it came back. She reached out her hand and took the note.

"Thank you." She whispered.

"No problem ma'am. He said to deliver it tonight. That it was very important. Sorry if I disturbed you." Pete backed up as he said it.

"Thank you again." She smiled and closed the door.

Marta looked at the piece of folded paper and turned it over in her hands. She limped over to her sofa and sat, just in case something troubling was inside.

After taking a deep breath, she unfolded the piece of paper. It simply read: "check your messages." Her forehead crinkled as she reread it a dozen times.

What messages?

The answer shocked her. Why hadn't she thought of it before?

And then it was clear. Self-preservation had prevailed.

It was self-preservation, no matter how weak or feeble, that prevented her from thinking of it before now.

She needed a telephone.

That was a challenge out here in her cottage, but by no means impossible. She rose and walked across the room to the front door and pressed the intercom button. It was a direct connection to a central nursing station inside the hospital. Pressing the button was something she had never done before.

A minute later, Marta took her finger from the intercom and opened the door. She limped out onto her porch, down the ramp and up the walk toward the main building. At this time of night, no one was out. She didn't encounter a guard as she traversed the 200 yards from the back gardens where her cottage sat. The place was still a prison. Call it a hospital and have guards walk around in nurse's uniforms. It was still a prison for people with mental health problems.

She came to the building's rear entrance and found it locked, as expected. She pushed an intercom button. The same nurse came on. "Yes?"

"I really need to use a phone. Please let me in." Marta was the voice of courteousness.

"Ma'am, I'm sorry. Like I said a few minutes ago, you will have to wait until morning. Please, you need to go back to your quarters." The nurse put a little more emphasis on the please this time.

Marta pressed the button again. "I don't think I am being unreasonable. I have not made this request before, but this is something of an emergency. I must insist that I be allowed to use a phone." Her request was met by silence.

Less than a minute later, she saw activity through the glass door. Two people were approaching. Lights flicked on and she could see a woman, most likely the nurse. A man in uniform walked beside her. A guard. They approached the glass door and stood on the other side without opening it.

The guard spoke this time through the glass. "Miss Parsons, now please, you need to wait until morning to use a phone. Those are the rules. Please go back to your residence."

Marta continued to smile. She took two steps back from the door, left her hands at her sides. She was non-threatening. Her retreat did as she'd hoped. The guard opened the door so he wouldn't have to shout and disturb others. He took a half step out. "You understand the rules Miss Parsons, don't you?"

She looked him up and down. She'd seen him hundreds of times from a distance, spoken with him in passing maybe three times. "I understand the rules. But I hope you understand that emergencies happen and rules need to be bent for times like these. Please."

He looked back at the nurse standing behind him and then moved further out the door to expand his presence in front of Marta. He was creating a somewhat menacing human wall. "I understand you feel you need to use the phone. But I am going to have to ask you to wait until the morning. We can tell the morning crew when they arrive and you will be the very first to use the phone. I promise." He slid his foot another few inches out the door. He was now holding the door open behind him.

She did not like having to do it, but she changed tactics in a quarter second as she leaned forward just an inch.

"You will allow me to use a phone now, within the next two minutes." Her voice was hard, deeper. A Russian accent crept in. The smile was gone as she spoke to the guard only, leaving the nurse out of it. "Your name is William Taft Hicks. You weigh 194 pounds, are 43 years old, left-handed, asthmatic with a limp from a knee injury, most likely football in high school. You have no weapon and no means of defending yourself from one who knows hundreds of ways to kill you. You are not fast enough to take two steps back and pull the door closed to protect our good nurse before I move from my current position and break your nose, fracture your sternum and collapse your esophagus. When you have crumpled to the ground, your wallet and identification will be easily accessible. Your address, family members and other pertinent facts will be obtained and evaluated for exposition and involvement." She smiled slightly.

"I have no desire to harm either of you or your families. I understand the challenges inherent when you chose to make your living in a place such as this. Encountering individuals who have killed many is a fact of life for you. But enough; you have only seconds to disregard protocol and permit a model patient access to a telephone. Quickly now, don't delay or deliberate."

Her words worked. She was pleased that she did not have to resort to actual violence. The guard and nurse accompanied her, a few paces behind, in through the door, down the hall to the community room and the telephone on the wall.

She smiled at them and nodded. They got the message and stepped back to the doorway to give her privacy. "Thank you."

Marta picked up the receiver and hesitated. She dialed a number she hadn't since, that day. *Since New York.* The adrenaline of her little show with the guard was already wearing off and trepidation was taking over. Her hand shook as she pressed the buttons in a sequence that started with a toll-free number and progressed through a secure, password-protected system to eventually reach a voicemail box. It was one of the accounts she and Preacher had established after moving operations to the US while tracking Anwar the terrorist bomber. Neither of them trusted cell phones.

She heard the familiar female voicemail prompt. The electronic voice was a comfort to her.

"You have five new and four saved messages." The pleasant voice gave her the option to listen to the new messages or access the saved audio files. Marta assumed the new messages were from that day when she was incapacitated after nearly being killed by bullets and a horrific explosion. She smiled as she pushed the number 2 to access the saved messages. She knew the one she wanted to hear.

A moment later, her smile broadened and tears flowed as she heard Lance's voice, well not his exactly. It was him doing Bart Radish a car salesman, Marta's favorite character, among the hundreds he could assume. "Ma'am, I'm afraid I have some bad news," Bart spoke very slowly in a deep Texas drawl. "Your friend, a fool by the name Rance or Vance or whatever, forgot to tell you something very important last night. That damn fool up and left you without telling you he likes you. He really likes you ma'am. I believe the fella might even love you. He's just such an im-bi-sell," he drew out the word into three excruciatingly long syllables. "I hope you'll find it in your sweet, loving, kind and generous heart to forgive the fool."

Marta laughed. She actually laughed for the first time in what felt a whole lot like forever. Bart finished his message, "And ma'am, if you don't mind me saying, I got to tell you, you are one fine filly. I mean one fine specimen of a woman. I hope that fool you let come around tells you that the next time he sees you. Bye now."

She bent over and then fell back against the wall to slide down to the floor. She had been right to keep these reminders from coming into her mind. She needed time to pass before she could expose herself to this. She felt like a fool who'd just won the lottery. Marta had discovered a treasure trove of recordings that she could keep forever. She took a deep breath and dove into the next message.

After listening to the four in history, she debated hanging up and keeping the five new messages for another time. She didn't really want to hear his voice mails as he looked for her, wondering where she went that night, why she hadn't returned his calls. These messages would hurt. His voice would bring that horrible day back to her.

She pulled her legs up and wrapped her arm around them to rest her chin on her knees. The attraction, the allure of his voice was too much. She did not have the strength to wait. The nice electronic voicemail lady asked again if she would like to listen to new messages or saved recordings.

She took a deep breath, pressed 1 for new messages and was reborn in the next moment.

Chapter 34

"How'd I do boss?"

He shouted to Seibel who was getting out of his car.

"About like I expected." Seibel called back to him and began to walk his way, weaving through the trees.

Lance was sitting against a towering oak tree 22 miles southwest of Washington, D.C. It was a place at which they had met several times before. The trees provided shade, but more importantly, obstruction for anyone looking down from a plane or satellite.

"You just had to do it." Lance looked up at Seibel and shook his head. "Couldn't help yourself, could you?"

"Some problems call for extreme measures." Seibel looked down at him without emotion.

"Where do you go now?" Lance leaned his head back against the tree. He looked as tired as he was.

"I'm going somewhere?"

"Either you leave or you get locked up. If you're lucky. You're done." Preacher looked away, then up at the waving leaves. "The CIA can't allow the guy who let a 25-year mole under the covers stick around. Congress and the public can't hear about this one."

Seibel plopped down and leaned back against an oak. "Who knows?"

"Beside me?"

"Yes."

"Wyrick, if he's figured it all out."

"How did you?" It was a simple question that carried mountains of complication, obfuscation and misdirection. Seibel had dumped the entire thing on his young protégé's head. It could have very well killed him. "Well, who is it?"

"Which one do you think?" Lance smiled.

"I don't care for games right now Preacher."

"Oh, I'm sorry. No time for games. Only time to put me in the middle of your chess board and spin me like a top." Lance could always give Seibel as good as he got.

"Do I really need to explain it all to you?" Seibel leaned his head back and looked up at the undersides of the waving, shimmering leaves. They whispered as the breeze ignited their dance.

"No. And that's how I figured it out; how she figured it out." Their eyes locked. Nothing more need be said, but of course, more was said.

"I'm sorry." Seibel raised his hands, palms up. He knew the apology did, and meant, little. "How is she?"

"I don't know. I haven't seen her."

"But she figured it out. You said..."

Lance chuckled and rolled his head. Seibel recognized the move well. He had seen Fuchs do it hundreds of times.

But instead of exploding to his feet and bursting to and through Geoffrey Seibel, Lance did something worse. He slowly unbuttoned the left sleeve of his shirt and folded the sleeve up above his elbow. In doing so, he exposed a bruised and blackened forearm marked and marred by dozens, hundreds of track marks. "She did. She figured it out when she came to me."

Seibel couldn't help himself. He stared at the damage, the addiction. He knew about it from the field reports and from Ludkovich. But seeing it made it too real. "Damn."

"That's my line." Preacher smiled. "Why heroin?"

"What do you mean?"

"Why did he choose heroin? Why not cocaine or amphetamines?"

"No one chose heroin for you. You did it yourself. I suppose you were influenced by some of the medication they used on you before and after the eye surgery, but no one stuck a syringe full of heroin into your arm."

Lance had to think back, but his memory of that time a year ago was fuzzy, cloudy.

"Jesus. You can't remember much from then can you?" Siebel shook his head.

Preacher tried to go back. But he couldn't see it clearly, not at all. He was sure addiction was forced on him.

Seibel raised his eyebrows. His frontalis muscle contracted, pulling up the eyebrows, creating horizontal lines. It gave him away. Preacher rose to his feet with gun drawn. He looked in all directions at once. Lance shot up through the trees to the clouds. Preacher returned his vision to Seibel. Nothing. The guy had nothing. No alarm in his eyes. Checked out. Resigned.

"Spill it. Just tell me." He looked down to see what Seibel was looking at. It was the gun pointed at Seibel's head. "Enough with the facade and maneuvering. Your plan worked. I did your bidding once again and found out who your mole is. Braden."

Seibel raised his eyes from the gun. "You're sure?"

"Positive. So, now you're done. You won't ever be trusted or set foot inside Langley again. Not after allowing a deep-cover operative into your operations. Next chapter, Papa."

They eyed each other for a few moments.

"So just tell me where the list, the lists, come from." Preacher hadn't moved the gun. It was still pointed between Seibel's eyes.

"Where do you think?" A grin on Seibel's mouth. It was a Socratic response, as usual. A question for a question.

It hit him. The answer.

"You don't know." Preacher lowered the gun and stepped a few paces to the left. He scanned all horizons, still not comfortable being out of doors in the light of day. "You received a list, three lists over 30 years, with names of turned operatives and you never think to ask where they came from?"

It was Seibel's turn to laugh. "Who was I supposed to ask?" Always a question as an answer with Papa.

"How about the first name on the first list you received? Start with the beginning."

"You think I didn't do that? I interrogated the first four on that list. None knew anything about the list or how their name came to be on it. None knew how their treachery, their actions were discovered." Seibel shook his head. He was lost in the past, seeing faces decades old.

"So, you just accepted the list, worked it and eliminated those cross-overs. Doesn't sound like you." Preacher kept the gun in hand. He was still uneasy.

"Nope. Completely out of character for me. But the lists are like that. They make people do strange things. They make me do strange things." Seibel lowered his head and reached to pick a piece of grass. "1959." He answered Preacher's next question before it was asked.

"That long ago? Where?"

"Moscow." He looked up. "There was a second sheet of paper detailing a legend, a ghost that haunts the night."

"Yah, that guy. I did a little research into him too." Preacher smiled at his secret. "Did you know legend has it that the Black Angel was born in the smoke rising from piles of burning bodies during the plague."

"The Black Death." Seibel nodded.

"Exactly. The Black Angel rose from the flames and smoke and flew away into the night to wreak havoc on the evil, the unjust." Preacher raised his eyebrows a couple of times. "Pretty cool, heh?"

Seibel could only look at him and shake his head. In six years, Lance, or Preacher, had become everything the CIA master had envisioned. It worked. And that reality smacked him in the face. Truth be told, it wasn't always Seibel's vision of perfection that Lance embodied. It was his friend, another protégé, a trusted confidant who believed Lance Priest would become the CIA's greatest weapon.

Braden.

Stuart Braden, an exceptionally brilliant young psychologist sought out Seibel and his growing legend in the early 70s to run some ideas by him. The second Black Angel list showed up a few months later. Seibel had been fooled, snookered, duped by a real pro. He missed the coincidence in timing. It was beyond impressive. A KGB plant made his way deep inside.

Preacher stood there watching Seibel basically fold in on himself. This was really something. The indomitable Geoffrey Seibel was lost, falling apart.

But Preacher is at his heart, a mean, brutal human being. He wanted Seibel to suffer for what he'd done. Losing his CIA fiefdom and having to live after such loss was a fate worse than death for someone like Seibel. Preacher had to stifle a grin.

"You owe your career, your legend to a list given to you 35 years ago. It made you, didn't it? Made you who you are. And then you received another list that you turned over to Fuchs. And finally, me."

Seibel could only nod. It was a simple admission.

This was a brilliant friggin' plan. It worked to perfection. But who was behind it all?

"At least you're alive dude." Preacher's words pulled Seibel from his little mental whirlpool.

"How does it feel?" Nothing gets past Papa.

"Being dead?"

"Yes. Being cut loose from the bonds that tie us to others, to rules, to reality."

Preacher had been fighting the shaking, the trembling since Seibel arrived. Like usual, it started in his right pinky. Chills, sweating, itching, sneezing and akathisia, or profound restlessness, would come soon. He clenched his fist and turned back to Seibel. "Yes, it's pure freedom. Even better, I know my mother and brother and the rest of my family are comforted knowing that I am in a better place."

"It had to be this way."

"Had to? Why? Because Braden said so?"

"You know why. You had to be released from everything that held you back. Everything."

"No other way. No other possible way do get this done." Preacher took a step toward Seibel. His fist still clenched. The gun in his left hand now. "I needed to be dead. She needed to be gone. My mother needed to be told her son died. You're right, there was simply no other way to do this. No other way for you to find your mole."

"It has to be this way. Always has been."

Ah-hah. Preacher was right. There was pattern behind this madness. "That's why."

Seibel's procerus tugged at his eyebrows and nostrils. "Why what?"

"That's why you and Fuchs are orphans. That's why you have no histories." Preacher nodded. He also glanced up at Lance 400 feet in the air.

Seibel saw the glance. "Is he up there?" He gestured to the sky. "Your other set of eyes?"

"He's up there. And he says its time to go. We've got what we need."

"That's it? You don't have anything. Nothing complete." Seibel raised his hands.

"I guess I do have one question."

"Just one? Go ahead."

"Do you want me to kill you now?"

Seibel's hands dropped slowly to his sides. You could tell he was thinking about the question, the offer. In a matter of minutes, Seibel had been brought down, ruined. He was no longer the master.

But the code, the signal in the action was immediately apparent. The dropped hands were a signal to a shooter. But Lance knew a secret Seibel didn't.

Preacher dropped to his left and dove forward. He swung his right foot up, striking Seibel's shoulder, knocking the older man back into the tree. Seibel was strong and recovered immediately. He threw a chopping left hand and caught Lance on the right side of his head as he spun back around. The blow caused Lance to switch from a swinging right backhand to using his left, which still held the gun.

He brought the handgun up with the barrel pointed directly at Seibel's midsection, but he didn't pull the trigger. Instead, he rammed the weapon into the older fighter's exposed ribs. It was an incredibly painful blow. It caused Seibel to bend over. He was unable to pull his own handgun because of the position he was now in, so instead, he burst forward, driving Lance back three steps toward a tree trunk.

Preacher felt the move and went limp, falling to the ground so Seibel could not hurl him into the tree. And because he sagged to the ground, he was able to reach and pull Seibel's collar on the back of his jacket, to begin a judo throw. But Seibel was no amateur and felt Lance's tug, so he pushed off his toes to speed up the roll Lance had started. The effect of the two combined moves was Seibel flying forward and twisting away from the tree trunk as Lance fell to the ground and rolled to use the laws of physics to toss Seibel away.

When they released each other and rolled to their feet, they stood for a fraction of a second facing each other, crouched and ready to explode.

Seibel glanced down at the gun in Preacher's hand. Preacher smiled and used the momentary distraction, to jump at Seibel with his right knee bent and rising. The 16th of a second it took Seibel to react and look from the gun to the approaching knee had more to do with age than skill. Seibel was three decades Lance's senior. Nerves and tendons and muscles simply did not react as quickly as they did when he was the original Black Angel in the late 50s.

Seibel brought his left forearm down to block the approaching knee, but in doing so, he committed an error. He left his head exposed.

Lance waited for Seibel to move his eyes up from the knee to his own to complete the real move. It was an elbow. As

Seibel's left elbow made contact with Preacher's right knee, the younger man's right elbow swung up and around in a concise concentric arc. It made contact with the master's left temple.

It was a lightning fast, ferocious blow.

Lance Priest watched Seibel's eyes as his elbow made contact with the older human's cranium. He watched in microscopically slow-motion as Seibel's head was forced to the left and up. The concussive pressure of the strike caused a violent collision within the CIA spymaster's frontal lobe as his brain smashed up against skull. Consciousness was lost before Seibel's head completed its journey backward. He was out on his feet as his body began a slow drop to the grass and leaves covering the dirt below.

"Wake up. Quickly Geoffrey, I need to go." Preacher slapped Seibel's face again. The old guy had been out for more than ten minutes.

In that time, Lance had made three calls, relieved Seibel of his firearm and rifled through his former boss's wallet.

"Tell me Seibel, do you want me to be kind and generous and fire a hot piece of lead up through your submaxillary triangle, through your brain and out the top of your skull?" Preacher pressed the barrel of his gun into the flesh between Seibel's chin and Adam's apple. "Now. Or do you want me to make the decision for you?"

"Do it." The beginnings of tear started in Seibel's right eye. He was ready to end this. He was beaten. Done.

"Hah! Right." Preacher stood up. Lance Priest is a mean, vengeful, evil, unpredictable sonovabitch. And as much as he wanted to bring about an unmerciful end to Seibel's life, he had no intention of making it easy for the old bastard to go quietly into that gentle night. So he shot the guy in the leg; shot him clean through the right knee.

The CIA living legend reached down and gripped his ruined knee with both hands as blood began to flow from the wound. But Seibel didn't scream. He only bit his lip and looked up at Lance as he sat up and inched back to lean against a tree.

Seibel was still groggy from being knocked out and the pain he was experiencing was only slightly better than when he was shot in the chest almost three decades earlier. "So, I guess you got to Wyrick?"

Preacher bent to a knee so he could be only inches from Seibel's face. "I did. He and I had a nice chat last night and he showed me some interesting video of the mysterious Mr. Braden. And yes, I told him that when he received your call this morning he should agree to whatever you ask, but of course, do nothing." Preacher smiled. Ever the chameleon, it was Seibel's own smile he had perfected after seeing it hundreds of times.

"You're a real prick Preacher." Seibel leaned his head onto Preacher's shoulder.

"Thanks boss. That's the best compliment you could ever give me."

"Get it over with." Seibel bent his wounded knee and cringed in pain.

"We'll be in touch. I'm taking your car and your phone, but check your messages. You're not done yet. Good night sweet prince." Preacher nudged his shoulder up and swung his right elbow around again to make violent connection with Seibel's left temple. It was another knockout blow. And it was a generous act, considering the violent imagery rocketing through Black Angel's messed up head.

Lance rose and stood there for a few moments looking at his unconscious mentor, his former master. And as he had done a number of times, he thought about what Marta would do. It used to piss him off that thinking of her got in the way of his work. He smiled. If he did right now what Marta would do, Seibel would have another couple holes in him.

He bent and tore part of Seibel's shirt and tied it around his leg to slow the bleeding and tied another piece around the damaged knee. Preacher then ran over to his former boss's Mercedes and hopped in. He needed to travel 231 miles northwest to West Virginia, quick-like.

Chronic use of heroin leads to physical dependence, a state in which the body has adapted to the presence of the drug. If a dependent user reduces or stops use of the drug abruptly, he or she may experience severe symptoms of withdrawal. These symptoms—which can begin as early as a few hours after the last drug administration—can include restlessness, muscle and bone pain, insomnia, diarrhea and vomiting, cold flashes with goose bumps ("cold turkey"), and kicking movements ("kicking the habit"). Users also experience severe craving for the drug during withdrawal, which can precipitate continued abuse and/or relapse. Major withdrawal symptoms peak between 48 and 72 hours after the last dose of the drug and typically subside after about 1 week.

Chapter 35

Clarksburg, West Virginia April 17...

Stuart Braden would ordinarily fly to the North Central West Virginia Airport. It was only an hour or so, much better than sitting in a car for nearly six hours to get from just outside Philadelphia to Clarksburg, WV.

But this morning, he didn't have time to arrange a flight. He needed to get to Marta as quickly as possible. She sounded horrible, horribly desperate when he was woken up by her phone call just before 4:00 a.m.

At 10:15 a.m., Dr. Braden checked in at the front desk of the undisclosed medical facility. The guard at the desk knew him from his weekly visits over the past year. After signing in and getting a visitor's badge, Braden walked quickly from the desk, through the building, out a rear door and along a sidewalk to a bungalow situated pleasantly amid other quaint little cottages.

The psychologist knocked on the door and took a step back.

Now, when people knock or ring a doorbell they sometimes take a step backwards, maybe step off the porch to the walkway. It is common courtesy and provides ample room for the front door to open.

But Stuart Braden's step backward was something different. The way his right foot fell back further than the left provided adequate spacing for an explosive forward movement. And the way Braden's right hand drifted back behind him was another subtle positioning move. The hand was inches from a slight, almost imperceptible bulge under his suit jacket.

Most humans wouldn't have perceived these understated movements as anything other than the respectful actions of a guest. Lance Priest is not like most humans. He stepped from behind the corner of a bungalow next to the one Braden stood in front of.

The space between he and Braden was approximately 80 yards of open landscaping with grass, bushes, a few trees and a small pond. Not a large area, but big enough that Lance and Marta needed to separate a few minutes earlier to cover it properly. Letting go of her hand stung.

Braden continued to stare straight ahead at the door. After 10 seconds, Marta and Lance were in position.

"Privet-stvuyu moi drug," Preacher called out greetings to Braden in Russian.

Braden didn't immediately turn around, but his head lowered. Preacher could almost see the processing going on inside the mole's head. Braden lifted his head and spoke straight ahead, not turning to Preacher. "That's the thing. We don't know how to speak Russian. It protects us."

An amazing admission. A confession.

And again, the tone, cadence and delivery Braden used would be perceived by most people as that of a pleasant conversational exchange. Lance knew what was next. That's why he and Marta held guns. He had given Seibel's Walther 9mm to Marta 12 minutes ago, just a few minutes after greeting, hugging and smothering her with kisses that would have never ended if life and death didn't get in the way.

He glanced over at her now. She returned the glance with a nod. He had to fight to keep control and not run to her. Gravity pulled.

"This is one incredible story Stu. It's one of those tales very few people will ever hear, just amazing. I'm super impressed."

Braden turned around slowly. His right hand still just beside his hip. He moved his eyes from Lance to Marta and smiled. No surprise in his look. "Damn. Now, this is something. Look at you two. No, this is an incredible story." A smile broke on Braden's face. "Two of the world's most dangerous killers rising from the grave, reunited."

Lance took a few more steps to the right. "You must be pleased since you wrote the script."

"So I assume you've spoken with Seibel. I wonder if you killed him?"

"I shot him."

Braden chuckled. "Of course. But left him alive. You probably put a bullet through his knee. Must have hurt like hell."

"He told me what I needed. His plan is slightly less convoluted than yours." Preacher stopped. He was in position. Small talk over.

Marta butted in. "Stu, I think I have a good idea, but was I your creation as well?" Marta's question did two things. It raised a very interesting point and it drew Braden's attention away from Lance for a moment. Preacher was ready to move.

But Braden had things covered.

"Don't move. Drop your weapons." It was a voice from behind them. Without looking, Lance knew it was the security guard. Braden had probably simply asked the guard to follow him and stay back a few hundred feet. Smart move.

Time collapsed, like an accordion. It folded neatly as Lance took in everything from above. As Preacher turned, he saw that a second security guard stood 60 feet behind Marta. He also held a gun.

He glanced at Marta. It was a fleeting moment, an instant shared. It was acknowledgement that she already had her plan worked out. In the same moment, she was diving to the left where a small rise created a barrier between her and the guard over her shoulder.

Another glance showed Braden pulling the gun from his hip. Preacher was in motion well before thinking about his first move. He knew the physiology at work as muscles contracted, toes flexed, arms raised, shoulder twisted as he dove behind an oak tree. Never make yourself an easy target.

"Drop your gun Dr. Braden." The first guard moved his aim from a diving, rolling Preacher to Braden. Now the guards had to think about this new element. They hadn't expected the good doctor Braden to pull a weapon. The guard's words were sadly his last. Stuart Braden adjusted his aim while sliding to the right and put a bullet through the man's forehead. An expert shot from 75 feet. Braden continued his dive to the right. He ducked, dropped to a knee while spinning and brought his aim to the other guard who had taken three steps forward and moved his aim from Marta to Braden.

This poor man, like the first guard, was pierced in his chest by a hurtling piece of lead. A second shot from Braden's gun entered and exploded out the back of the guard's neck. He collapsed and died on the spot. By the time Lance finished his roll and came back to his feet with gun ready to fire, Braden had ducked behind the corner of Marta's small home.

Marta rose to her feet and angled to the left to provide an expanded view of the rear of the structure and the heavy woods beyond. Preacher darted to his right and then stepped over to the bungalow next to Marta's and peeked around the corner. No sign of Braden as he scanned the line of heavy woods about 60 feet to the south of the homes. A high barbed wire fence stood another 100 feet or so to the south. Damn.

Preacher wanted to stay on Braden. But the immense force of gravity won. Marta, his Marta, no figment, no dream, stood less than 100 feet away. He needed to touch and hold her more than he needed to kill Stuart Braden. He turned from the house and ran back around the front of the structure where he could see Marta. She was pressed against the wall of the small cottage on the other side of hers' with her gun aimed to the south.

Their eyes locked; this time for more than a fleeting second. He could have stayed here, walked slowly to her, bringing her closer to him with every step. But the world and time worked against them. Sirens wailed in the distance. They needed to leave; no time to try to explain this to authorities.

Marta darted to the east. Lance was on her tail in seconds. He noticed the slight limp as she ran. The damage done by the explosion a year ago was permanent.

They reached a small building with a 10-foot fence on either side. Marta gestured to the building's roof. They scaled the fence quickly and climbed onto the roof. They ran across to the other side of the building, jumped onto the roof of a van and then to the ground. They didn't have time to run the quarter mile to Seibel's stashed Mercedes, so Preacher pulled his gun and stepped in front of a Toyota Corolla entering the side lot.

It was a pleasant, respectful car-jacking. Preacher even pulled a wad of bills and tossed some cash at the guy as he and Marta hopped in, Marta behind the wheel. Off they went in the opposite direction as two police cars converged on the facility. There would be a police net; an all-points bulletin issued for Braden, a woman resembling Marta and another male resembling Lance. Sunglasses and a ball cap kept most of his face hidden. The stolen Toyota would be reported and relayed to law enforcement within minutes as well.

"The airport." Lance whispered. Marta nodded.

Alas, there was no time to reach out and touch her face and run fingers through her hair, to kiss her neck. So he just watched her, watched her do her thing as she pushed the vehicle to its max and turned expertly into corners on hilly West Virginia back roads. Her eyes were in constant motion, but kept making their way back to him. The frantic, hurried and desperate situation couldn't keep the smile from her face. She reached out a hand to Lance as they came into a brief straightaway. He took it and brought the back of her hand to his cheek.

And then they were at their destination. She had maneuvered through the outskirts of Clarksburg and Bridgeport, West Virginia to circle around to the tiny regional airport. She had to release his hand to grab the wheel with both of hers as the vehicle picked up speed around a turn and then left the road to blast through the chain link fence surrounding the airport property. Marta kept the Toyota next to the fence as they raced to the north, toward several hangars.

They reached the buildings and circled around behind them to hide the vehicle between two structures. They exited the Toyota and entered a hangar with its big doors open. Inside, they split up and made their way to the rear of the building where three men sat smoking and shooting the breeze.

Lance rushed the three of them and quickly threw them to the floor beside the table they were sitting around. He hadn't pulled his gun out. No need.

He used a thick Eastern European accent, "Gentlemen, there is a white Cessna 172 just outside the hangar with tail number N61848. Whose is it please?"

One of the three turned his head and looked up at Preacher. A quick tap on his forehead with the sole of Lance's shoe turned the man's face back to the floor.

"It's mine." The guy in the middle with dyed black hair, dyed beard and dyed eyebrows answered.

"Let's go." Preacher picked the guy up by his jacket and pushed him toward the door. While Preacher escorted the man to the open hangar doors, Marta stepped over to the other two gentlemen. Unlike Lance, she had a gun in her hand.

The pilot reached his plane and decided to make a stand. But even with all the dyed hair, thick jacket and pressed black jeans, Preacher could see the physiological process. The planted right foot inside its boot, the tensing of the flexor hallucis longus in the pilot's calf, which in turn, flexes the big toe. The abbreviated tension in the right shoulder was an immediate precursor to the man's right arm bending, becoming rigid and then being brought back rapidly to make connection with his kidnapper's skull.

Problem with this move was that the pilot was a human, with basic human anatomy and standard human mental processes at work. Lance simply stepped to the right and watched the flailing of the man's arm, followed by the rest of his body as he put his all into the aggressive move. As the pilot righted himself and stood back up, Lance stepped in close, close enough to kiss the gent. Then he did the scariest thing of all. He raised the sunglasses and showed the poor guy the two black orbs, sunken cheeks and vampire-like pallor.

"Your name please," the accent even thicker.

The pilot shook his head involuntarily and then whispered," Pete. Pete Buckner. The man's accent was deep West Virginia.

"Pete, get in the plane. We can file our flight plan from the air. You will not be hurt if you do as you are told. You will be compensated for your time and inconvenience." Preacher leaned in closer and put his lips to Pete's left ear. "Your wife, your grown children and grandchildren will be glad to see you this evening and in the days and years to come. Do nothing more than fly the plane and think of their faces for the next several hours." A perfect threat. Death implied.

Black Angel had hitched rides with pilots like Pete all over Russia and Eastern Europe this past year. Small planes landing in remote airports were perfect for undetected transportation across borders. Cash made it a profitable venture for the pilots.

Pete got in and started the Cessna's engine. Lance stepped around and opened the passenger door and looked back at the hangar doors. Right on cue, Marta came walking out. He knew the physiological processes going on inside his body as well. He knew his heart didn't just skip a beat when he saw her. But it felt like it. He watched her walk over to the plane and up to him.

A year of loneliness and night and empty hours and dozens of killings and the list and needles and that damn Neil Sedaka album on repeat in his head simply melted away as she melted into him. She collapsed into his crushing arms and his enveloping kiss. They merged right there on the tarmac of a tiny airport in the hills of West Virginia with a Cessna's whirling propeller blowing away all other sound. The air rushing by them was cleansing, purifying. They could barely breath but found a way to keep their lips and hands and arms and legs locked.

Pete watched it all from his pilot's seat and wondered just what the holy hell was going on here.

Chapter 36

Flying blind? Anything but.

Mobile cell phone coverage in April 1994 was still in its infancy in many, many places. But it was pretty darn good in metro Washington, D.C. In the 35 minutes that Lance had cell phone coverage after shooting, knocking out and stealing Seibel's car, he made several calls. He jotted down number after number as he told lie after lie to obtain information. One conversation he had was with Allie Braden, Stuart's wife.

Preacher called the Braden home under the guise of a fellow psychologist who went to school with Stuart. He lived on the West Coast and was traveling along the Eastern Seaboard at present and looked up Stu and his parents. He had so enjoyed spending a few weekends traveling back home with Stu to hang out at his parents' place.

"Did they have the house in Mount Pleasant that far back?" Allie asked as the lovely conversation transpired.

"Yep. Beautiful home. Love that yard and access to the water." Lance replied to her question. A brief whirlwind of Mount Pleasants memorized in his cranial atlas gave him a mental picture of the suburb of Charleston, South Carolina. "Just loved visiting that place."

"Oh, I know. The kids love spending a couple of weeks there each summer," Allie added.

Preacher threw another Hail Mary, "I can't quite remember Mr. Braden's first name." He waited.

"Roger."

"That's right, Roger. Great guy and a surprisingly good cook." Preacher recalled a tidbit about Braden's dad being an excellent chef during a session several years earlier.

He hung up from that call and dialed Wyrick's cell number to get him to stir things up and contact resources in both the CIA and FBI. He told Wyrick to convince the FBI to place the Braden's Philadelphia home under serious surveillance and be ready at a moment's notice to move in and take Allie and her three children into protection.

Next, Preacher called information in Charleston, South Carolina and had a delightful lie-filled confab with an operator who related completely to a southern boy who wanted to escape to the Carolina's after too much time up north where the folks just don't get it. The operator located both the number and address for one Roger and Linda Braden in Mount Pleasant on Raintree Drive. Lance had only peripheral knowledge of Charleston and it's roadways and couldn't see the house on his mental map.

The 562 aerial miles from Clarksburg to Charleston took the Cessna just under four hours. During that time, Lance and Marta worked through dozens of variations of the plan he had hatched the night before when he learned just about everything from Wyrick. And even though four hours is a long time, especially crammed into the tiny back seat of a Cessna, it was not nearly long enough for either of them.

Intermittently, one or the other would just stop talking and kiss the other. It was involuntary. Marta had to do a little more work though. She could see in the first moments after Lance knocked on her back window hours earlier that he was struggling. His addiction was rifling through him. Marta tried to hold his hand and keep him from scratching himself raw.

She also couldn't stop herself from staring into his black, lifeless eyes. They were definitely freaky.

When the plane landed at Mount Pleasant regional airfield, Preacher handed Pete a wad of bills and wished him well. Marta hugged him and bade him thanks and farewell.

Twenty-two minutes later, they were dropped off by a taxi at the top of the neighborhood where the Bradens lived. They had their plan worked out to the tiniest detail and split up. Marta walked on the sidewalk. Preacher took a route through a common green space surrounding the posh residences.

Most of the houses in Charleston are raised, built up at least six or eight feet off the ground. This is because of flooding and hurricanes. And many of the nicer, newer homes had their garages in this large crawl space. The Braden's home was very nice, very charming. The garage door was open and their Volvo was running as Marta stepped onto the driveway. A man, obviously Mr. Braden, hurriedly came out of the door, down the steps and tossed a bag in the back seat. Mrs. Braden was already waiting in the passenger seat.

As the Volvo backed out, Mr. Braden looked in the rear view mirror and saw Marta standing in the drive. He turned around and looked at her. Mrs. Braden didn't look up. Mr. Braden, Roger, stopped the car and stepped out. "Can I help you?" he asked quickly, in a rush to leave.

"I'd like to speak with you for a minute," Marta replied and took a couple of steps forward.

Meanwhile, Lance moved up, out of the thick overgrowth behind the house. He stepped onto the driveway and up next to the car. He had been watching Mrs. Braden, Linda, for over a minute now and didn't like the way she kept her head down, not looking up.

Thirteen seconds later, he got his answer as she raised a gun to her mouth. He was nine feet away with a closed car door between them. So he shouted, "Hey!" Linda Braden glanced at him, but didn't move her head. She simply continued the action she started a moment earlier, placed the gun's barrel in her open mouth and pulled the trigger. The exploded round fired up through her brain and skull and then through the roof of the Volvo. Damn.

Both Lance and Marta watched Roger Braden. He turned to the car. Ran to the passenger side and yanked the door open. He cradled his wife's body as it slouched lifelessly into his arms. Blood was everywhere. It was a horrible scene with a frantic man who had just lost his wife of five decades. But Preacher and Marta had no time for mourning someone they never met. Lance stepped around and pulled the keys from the ignition as Marta reached in and grabbed the woman's purse.

He opened the trunk to find it stuffed with bags and a few pieces of memorabilia. Marta dumped the purse on the concrete and examined its contents. In the wallet, she found photos of Stuart and his family. The only items that interested her were a phone and pager. She grabbed them up and put them in her jacket pocket. Preacher closed the trunk and they looked at each other.

Lance walked around to the moaning, screaming, crying husband cradling his deceased wife's bloody head to his chest. "Mr. Braden, we don't have much time." He bent and grabbed the man on both sides of his head. "Roger, you were leaving. Where were you going in such a hurry?"

The blank look on the man's face was a mixture of pain, agony and despair. Lance could see the processes at work under the man's skin. The muscles tugging, nerves firing, blood flowing. He looked into the elder Braden's eyes. They were wild, as expected. Lance flicked the recent widow's left ear to pull him out of his tailspin. It worked. "Where were you going?"

"We, we were heading north. To see our son."

"Your wife, did she receive a phone call earlier? Quickly, now." Preacher squeezed the man's head between his hands tighter and brought his attention back from Marta standing several feet behind. "Did she get a call from Stuart?"

"Yes. She got a call about two hours ago."

"Did you speak with him?"

"No. No, he only spoke to Linda for a few moments. She said we needed to leave." Braden shook his head, trying to free it from Preacher's grasp.

"Did the call come to the home or to her cell phone?"

"Her cell. It hardly ever rings."

"Thank you Roger. We are truly sorry for your loss." Lance released the grieving man's head and stood. Then he spun back to him. "I'm sorry Mr. Braden, how long have you been married?"

"Forty nine years next August." He whimpered.

Lance and Marta moved quickly down the driveway and to the next street over where they stole a car sitting in a driveway with keys in the ignition.

As they drove away, Marta turned to him and asked, "Why did you want to know how long the Braden's were married?"

He turned to her from the window. "Just trying to figure this out." He held the dead woman's cell phone and pager in his hands. "It was obvious from his bone structure, skin tone and hair that Mr. Braden is not the good doctor's father. Not the male biological donor, at least."

"You think she was more than just his mother? More than a nurturing influence in his life?" Marta could see Lance processing. She loved to watch him work through problems. She loved to watch him anytime. His being alive and just arms' length away had her on edge. But she could also see the struggle. His addiction was tearing at him, pulling at the seams.

"She was his biological mother. And I think she was his operator, his programmer, his mentor."

"You're saying that she raised him to be a spy."

"That's exactly what I'm saying. I think her background is the key." He looked out the window. "When we talk to him in a little while on her cell phone, we will only have the one chance. He is more than likely only hours from leaving the country."

Marta just shook her head. She whispered in Russian, "Damn, he was good. How did he do it?"

Lance turned back to her. "He blew you and me away. Way better, way deeper than we ever got. He fooled Seibel for 25 years. He fooled everyone."

Marta watched him for another mile then spoke. "Please don't be offended honey, but are you Lance or Preacher right now?" She smiled as she asked.

He cracked up and leaned over to her to kiss her cheek. She would have none of that and turned her lips to meet his. It made driving difficult. He pulled away after they swerved off the road a second time. "I'm both, but neither really. They're both in here. But I'm not really myself, haven't been for some time."

"Then who are you?" Marta, always direct.

He smiled again. "I'm the Black Angel."

She thought about that for a few seconds. Her beautiful procerus tugged at her beautiful eyebrows. She was the most beautiful thing he'd ever seen. Ever.

"Well then, nice to meet you Mr. Angel." She nodded. "I assume with a name like that you are not the sweet kind of angel. You're not here to spread pixie dust and watch over all the children."

He nodded. "No. I'm here to kill."

Chapter 37

Decision time.

They lay in bed in the nearest motel they could find after stashing the stolen sedan and purchasing two pre-paid cell phones. The new phones sat next to the late Mrs. Braden's cell phone and pager on the bedside table.

What now? They didn't have to do anything. They owed nothing to anyone. Walking away was a viable option. A great friggin' option.

But there was this little thing that ran through Lance Priest and Marta Sidorova. Like a nerve impulse running through a spine, vengeance pervaded them. It was a necessity. Lance didn't give a flip about how deep Stuart Braden had made his way into the subversive environs of the CIA. Marta cared even less that Braden had snookered Seibel and others for decades. That was their problem. A wife and three children left behind, a dead mother and a broken and mourning father were of no concern. Happens every day.

But vengeance and payback, that was another matter.

Her head lay on his chest. She had perused his body extensively after they made love, twice. The tattoos were freaky; freakier than the black eyes and the changed face. Her Lance, her Preacher, had been transformed during the year he was dead. She smiled and then laughed.

"What is it my love?" His eyes were closed. He was drifting with his life's love in his arms.

"I was just thinking about being dead. About losing you."

"And that made you laugh?"

"No, not the losing. The trickery, the conspiracy. It was brilliant." She drew circles around tattoos on his chest.

"The fact I fell for it ticks me off." He grinned.

"And what does it all have in common? What is the common thread?"

"Seibel of course. But I'm sure you're referring to our friend, the murdering and missing Mr. Braden."

"Yes, that Mr. Braden."

"So, what are we going to do about him?"

And the answer for them both was obvious and unspoken. They did owe something to someone. It was death. And it was owed to Braden.

They kissed and held each other tight and she moved over him and gazed down on her Black Angel. Time and vengeance and lies faded as they looked in each other's eyes. Right on cue, one of the phones on the table rang. It was Mrs. Braden's.

Time to lie.

Chapter 38

At 37,000-feet over the nighttime Atlantic Ocean, there is only black. Small pockmarks of white light fill the sky. Sometimes a bright and brilliant moon reflects the sun's rays and illuminates a trail of a billion sparkles on the surface.

Surreal is probably the word to describe the miles-high scene on the Gulfstream Lance rode in. Seated in the fourth row, there was no one in front or beside him. But right across the skinny aisle sat someone he knew, or at least thought he knew. Stuart Braden was drinking a cola. Lance had finished his coffee with extra cream and sugar. The fact they were both on this trans-Atlantic flight from Washington, D.C. to Paris was more than coincidence.

When Lance stepped onto the jet just minutes before it took off, their eyes locked. Neither pulled a weapon. Three other military passengers were aboard. Neither spoke to the other for the first hour of the flight. With their drinks gone and the other passengers sleeping, they each leaned across the aisle.

"You look pretty sharp in that uniform Major." Lance nodded to the Army Major uniform Braden wore.

"And you as well, Captain." Braden replied.

"Surprised to see me?"

"Never surprised by you Preacher." Braden smiled. He was different. The facade gone. His every word was tinged with what could only be described as superiority.

"You're hoping that I don't do anything crazy up here."

"You won't. You know I am prepared for that." Braden replied.

Lance looked around to make sure everyone was asleep. Before turning back to Braden, he punched him in the nose. He hardly ever hit people with a balled fist, but it just felt right. Braden took the blow and sat back in his seat to grab his napkin and dab his nose. Lance waited.

Half a minute later Braden leaned back over. "I deserved that and probably much worse."

"Much worse."

"I always knew you would be the one. You'd figure it out someday." Braden dabbed his bloody nose again.

"I figured out part of it. She did the rest."

Braden nodded in affirmation. "When did you learn she was alive?"

"About two weeks ago. Lance told me."

That got some squinched eyebrows out of Braden. "Lance told you?"

"He showed me. When I was in the Neva River." It sounded crazy.

"Tell me more about these visions Lance, I mean Preacher."

"You mean Black Angel. Sorry, no more sessions doctor. Your time is up."

"Not yet, not yet. There are many variants in play in this scenario." Braden looked around and leaned closer. "And of course, nothing is as it seems my friend."

"So, Meadows radios Paris and a full contingent of local law enforcement and CIA operatives is there to meet us."

"Won't work. First, we are not going to Paris. Change of plans. And second, you are wanted as badly if not more than I. You are a suspect in dozens of murders across Europe. I just happen to know the names, the identities of those killed." Braden tossed the blood-soaked napkin aside.

"And your female accomplice is a suspect in even more killings. And, to top it all off, you are dead and any action to bring you back from the great beyond will undoubtedly result in harm coming to your still-grieving family."

"Beautiful. Threats to my family before we even get started." Lance shook his head.

"Why wait? You know that I have nothing to lose, so why not go there? Everything is in play."

"And what about your family? Your wife and children?"

"Props, facade."

"That's nice. You're a real cold prick."

"A lecture from an assassin? Such high morals." Braden smirked.

"Still a game to you. Seibel co-opted, Marta and I shredded for a year, those two unlucky guards at the hospital. You are proving yourself to be quite the bad dude, Stu."

"Oh yes, you have such remorse for loss of life. So let's cut to the chase, the bottom line." Braden laced his fingers together and rested his forearms on his thighs. It was a position, a move Lance had seen countless times before. It was a Seibel move.

"Before we do, a couple of questions?" Preacher interrupted.

"I'll answer those I care to."

"When did your Mom tell you why you were born?"

The question threw the deep-cover, bulletproof spy for a loop. "Interesting question," he stalled.

"When did she tell you that you were born to be a spy, a traitor to your country?"

"What did she tell you?" Braden asked.

"Not all that much. Then she pulled a gun and I had to put one through her head. Sorry."

"I expected as much. But I assumed Marta had done it. More her style."

"Nope. So when did you learn?"

"Next question."

Chapter 39

Lisbon, Portugal April 19...

Braden had a two-minute head start. That was how long it took for Lance to get everyone else off and hundreds of feet from the Gulfstream to be sure they wouldn't go up if indeed there was a bomb in Braden's briefcase left aboard.

Lt. Meadows was not pleased with the excitement, but he and his co-pilot complied. Meadows was already peeved about changing his flight plan from Paris to Lisbon. Just before Lance left, he turned to the pilot

"I don't know how much longer you can sit on the sidelines Meadows. I guess that's two favors now." And Preacher turned away.

He burst across the tarmac to a Cessna rolling forward toward the runway. He ran in front of the small plane, causing the pilot to slam on his brakes. Preacher stepped around the propeller, opened the passenger door and jumped in.

Portuguese is one of those screwy languages that intermingles pieces of other languages but still stands alone. Lance knew several phrases but that's about it. "Vamos agora," is one of them. The pilot only looked at him, so Preacher pulled out his gun and repeated, "Agora." *Now.*

The pilot, a man in his mid-forties with a thick beard, obeyed and got the plane rolling forward. It picked up speed and taxied onto the runway. The pilot increased power to push the plane up to takeoff speed.

"Do you speak English?" Preacher asked after putting the other headset on.

"A little, not much." The pilot replied over the roar.

"How about Spanish?"

"A little more."

"Okay, then do as I say." Preacher said in Spanish. "Turn back south and take it to 500 feet."

"Too low." The pilot replied.

"We're going lower."

And lower they went. Preacher scanned the roads below, looking for the car he had watched Braden get into minutes earlier. He regretted not subduing or killing the psychologist on the jet, but the guy had things covered with his "bomb in the briefcase" and simple remote trigger he held in his hand.

Whatever. He'd get him, just a matter of time. Maybe minutes. He spotted the red Fiat below. It was moving south, toward the main highway which criss-crosses Lisbon from east to west. "There. That car," he pointed to the vehicle. "Take us down."

As the plane descended, Preacher opened the briefcase he brought with him. He pulled out and put on a pair of leather gloves and kneaded his hands together to warm the leather. The pilot looked at this strange man in the U.S. Army uniform. Preacher glanced over at the pilot and smiled.

"Do you know what I am?" He asked the man in Spanish.

"No."

"I'm a spy, a killer. And I am here to kill another spy and maybe save the world. You are going to help me. Take me down to that car."

The pilot did as told. Lance knew how this was going to work. Because the window didn't roll down on this Cessna model, he would need to open the door to take his shot. Cool.

The Fiat Braden had stolen was near the highway. Things might get interesting at higher speeds. Lance looked back at his pilot and nodded. He took the headset off and opened the passenger side door. The wind rushing in at 70 miles per hour required him to step into the doorframe to brace himself. The pilot brought the Cessna down to below 100 feet and increased airspeed to catch up with Braden below.

Finally, the plane was even with the vehicle. Preacher reached his hand back and signaled the pilot to take it lower. He obeyed and the brought the plane down to 60 feet. Perfect.

Now, hitting a moving vehicle on the ground from a moving vehicle in the air with 80 mph winds buffeting the open door would have been categorically impossible for Lance Priest several years ago. Maybe even just a year ago. But now, after the list and loss and black eyes and tattoos and heroin addiction, it really all came down to a pair of leather gloves. Pitiful, yes. But sometimes that's just the way life works. Humans are seriously flawed creatures.

Preacher gripped his Sig Sauer 9mm in his leather gloves and took aim at Stuart Braden driving on the Auto-Estrada da Costa do Estoril Highway below. His first shot was aimed at Braden's head. It hit the window, but he couldn't be sure it hit his target. He adjusted aim to shoot at the front driver-side tire and then the rear. He hit with more than half of the ten shots he fired. Not bad.

Braden's stolen Fiat lost control, swerved across three lanes and slid down an embankment. Cool, no one else hurt.

"Get me down, now." He turned and yelled at the pilot. He pointed to a field a quarter mile away. "There, now." The pilot brought the plane around immediately and reduced speed as the plane bounced down in the field. The backend of the Cessna shimmied like crazy across the rough ground. Lance had his briefcase back in his lap and pulled out a dozen bills and tossed them at the pilot as he jumped out. He hightailed it across the field toward the highway and Braden's disabled vehicle.

It took him about two minutes to get to within 100 feet of Braden's car. He approached from the rear with his gun drawn. Braden wasn't there. Preacher looked in all directions and guessed the most likely escape route. About 200 meters away was an intersection. And Braden was there with gun aimed at a vehicle. "Stop, Braden drop it." Preacher shouted.

He didn't. Braden stepped around the vehicle he had stopped. He pulled the driver out, slid in and floored it. Lance was 100 meters away. He stopped and fired off the remaining shots in his Sig. Five struck the vehicle. But on it went.

He ran into the same intersection and pointed his pistol at an approaching Peugeot. The driver held up his hands and got out when Lance yanked the door open. "Muy obrigado." Preacher thanked the man and slapped him on the shoulder. He was in the car and rocketing after Braden seconds later.

Back onto the highway, he opened his briefcase and pulled out a new clip for the Sig and then he grabbed the cell phone he'd brought from the U.S. He and Marta paid extra for phones that work on both sides of the pond. He dialed the memorized number while changing lanes and accelerating to 100 mph.

"Hello darling," he said and smiled when Marta answered.

"And hello to you my darling. How is your day?"

"Spectacular, thrilling even. Lisbon is lovely in the spring."

"It is." Marta agreed.

"How was your flight?"

"Fine, thank you. But I'm sure it wasn't as interesting as yours." The smile on Marta's lips came through the airwaves. It brought an involuntary smile to Lance's lips.

"Interesting is a word."

"But then you commandeered a plane. I can see it in the field right now."

"Good, then you're just a few miles behind me and Mr. Leadfoot up ahead." Lance swerved around a semi-truck and accelerated onto the shoulder, pushing the car well past 120.

"I think I can see you up there. Your bad driving is unmistakable." Marta giggled.

"Thank you."

Turns out, both Lance and Braden ending up on that flight from D.C. to Lisbon was anything but coincidence. Anything but.

Preacher got right to work using his new cell phone in the minutes after hanging up Braden's deceased mother's cell phone. Sitting naked on that motel bed with his living dream sitting naked beside him, Lance told no less than 400 lies in 33 minutes. They ranged from little white ones to colossal whoppers. And all were designed to cast a net and then tighten a lasso around a fleeing Stuart Braden.

Lance called Allie again and asked if she had heard from Stu since this morning. She said she hadn't and it was a weak lie. He then asked her the color of the two cars posted out in front of her house. He wished her health and safety and asked her to think of her children first before doing anything.

Preacher called the Mount Pleasant police department as an FBI field agent and asked that they do a full-court press on the suicide at the Braden residence. He then called the CIA and told them a little story about spies and generations and the Bradens.

The Black Angel called Wyrick again and asked if he'd heard from Seibel. He said he hadn't and it sounded like the truth. He dictated four assignments to Wyrick and gave him his new cell number to call back when they were completed.

Lance called a pager number, left his new number and got a call back in six minutes from Lt. Stan Meadows. He asked him when his next flight was leaving and was told of the Paris flight.

Lastly, young Mr. Priest placed calls to three international numbers he had memorized the year before. In succession, answering at the other end of the line were Fuchs, Tarwanah and Jamaani. In brief conversations with each, Preacher got them moving from their current positions on the globe toward Paris where the flight was supposed to land.

Marta made one call from the motel room. She called a number only she knew. At 1:47 a.m. in Moscow, a sleepy Gregor Smelinski answered his bedside phone and put his feet to the floor. The KGB Cold War legend's breath was cut short when he heard her voice after nearly three years. He always knew he'd hear from her again. He just assumed it would be from behind and in the last moments of his life.

Marta then stepped onto a private jet arranged by Wyrick that took off 21 minutes after the Gulfstream. She was right on their tail.

Chapter 40

Speeds were well into the 100+ range as the little parade pushed through a gentle pass and into an open area in advance of moving into central Lisbon. This was mega dangerous. Crazy even. Probably not the best plan they could have put in place.

But truth be told, and it isn't often told by Preacher, simply stopping Braden did not encapsulate the entirety of Lance and Marta's plan. They were each so completely blown away by the realization that Stuart Braden was a deep-cover double agent that they simply had to learn more. And following, tracking, hounding him to the ends of the earth seemed as good as any other idea.

Up ahead, Braden's second stolen car exited the highway into a business district. Glancing over to the right, Lance could see the coast and the bay. It was lovely. Marta pulled up beside him and barreled past onto the exit ramp. She had an instinct, an innate ability to push vehicles to their limit but never lose control.

Seconds later, she was on Braden's bumper. That's when things got interesting. Suddenly, another vehicle, a van, slowed down beside Marta's car and the side cargo door slid open. Lance laughed at the bad action movie scene, pitiful. He slammed on the gas pedal and slingshot forward, striking the van's rear bumper. It shimmied and slid to the right. Marta spotted the action, lifted her gun and fired seven shots through her rear passenger window into the van while keeping her eyes on Braden's car.

Preacher couldn't help but be impressed by her. She was, is, a marvel. A whirlwind, a tornado of violence and death. As the van drifted to the right into an embankment, Lance accelerated into the rear of the vehicle again to push it further up the hill where it skidded, teetered and spilled over. He laughed watching his rearview mirror as the van rolled over several times down the embankment. But a second glance in the mirror showed two other vehicles, another van and a Porsche, flying up from behind.

He tapped on the horn and Marta glanced in her rearview and spotted them as well. Suddenly, Braden hurled his car to the left and sideswiped two parked sedans. Tourists screamed and dove to the sidewalk. The two following vehicles came around the turn on Lance's tail. Just who the hell were these guys?

One way to find out. He slammed on the brakes and slung the car sideways to block the road. Just before the van made impact, he put two bullets into the driver's forehead and ducked. The collision was violent, but before his vehicle was done spinning, Preacher opened the passenger door, rolled out and came back to his feet. From the corner of his eye, he watched the Porsche come to a screeching stop and spin around. But his focus was on the van.

When the first head appeared in the passenger window, he put a bullet through it. The splatter covered a good part of the driver's window and windshield. He took six steps to place him at a three-quarter angle off the passenger side rear bumper. With a clear mind, now 15 days without the lubricant of heroin, a delightful little thing happened. He looked at the street view in front of him and from above simultaneously. It was something of a reward for keeping a needle out of his vein.

"Thank you," his whispered to Lance, to himself. He saw the flash of a barrel and dove to his left as one of the rear windows of the van blew out. It was a machine gun. He rolled forward, under the van and waited. The driver-side cargo door slid open and a boot stepped out, followed by a second boot. Preacher rolled to the other side, stepped forward to the front of the van and then to the right.

The guy who'd stepped out was facing the rear. He'd do.

Preacher rushed forward and put a bullet through the back of each of the guy's knees and rammed an elbow into the fella's neck, slamming the poor dude to the ground as Preacher dove into the van and put four more bullets into the man who'd fired the machine gun out the rear.

He quickly jumped back out to the street. The Porsche spun tires and accelerated right at him. There was a driver and passenger inside. It was maybe 140 feet, so the Porsche couldn't get going all that fast, maybe 30 or 35 mph. It should take four seconds. So he concentrated on the passenger for the next two seconds. His aim would be challenged since he was running. But he still launched three shots before leaving his feet to jump. When his right foot hit the hood of the vehicle, he shot one more time down through the windshield at the driver.

He lifted his left leg up like he was back in Tulsa running the hurdles. The roof of the sports car clipped his right foot as he was raising it. And, just like embarrassingly tripping over a hurdle during a race back in high school, he proceeded to do a forward roll, ducking his head and taking most of the force on his left shoulder and back. His momentum completed the roll. He came back to his feet and spun back around toward the Porsche. But it hadn't gone far.

The vehicle slammed into the van. The collision forced the Porsche to fishtail to the right exposing the driver's side window to Preacher as he approached. No need to put another bullet in the driver. The one fired while hurdling the car had gone right between the guy's eyebrows. A perfect friggin' shot.

"Holy shit," Preacher laughed and looked around at the few pedestrians on the street. "Cut; that's a wrap." He chuckled as he turned and ran back to the van. Marta always gave him hell about lousy American action movies with impossible stunts. She would have loved this one.

He made it back to the guy he had shot and cold-cocked. He rolled him over, lifted the man to a sitting position and then hoisted him over his shoulder to carry him back to his battered stolen car that was still running. With the driver's side smashed by the van and Porsche, he opened the passenger door to toss the guy in the back seat and climbed in.

He found his cell phone on the floor and dialed while punching the gas.

Marta knew time was short; something neither she nor Lance could figure out was going on here. Stuart Braden running, fleeing the scene of his decades of crime and recent double homicide, was understandable. Threatening all the lives onboard the plane that jetted him across the Atlantic was out of character. But a rolling cavalcade of guns and more guns and, crap- Marta ripped the steering wheel to the right. On the overpass ahead, a guy had an automatic rifle aimed at her.

What the hell?

She fishtailed to the left and floored it. Her car shot forward into the left rear bumper of Braden's car as a dozen or so bullets strafed the hood, windshield and roof of her Mercedes. Enough. She veered left and then right to clip Braden's rear again and set his car spinning. She slammed the brakes and pin-wheeled around.

Marta opened her door and rolled out, just like Lance had done a minute earlier. Her first shots were aimed at the shooter on the overpass. Two shots struck the man in the chest. She stepped forward and unloaded ten more shots into Braden's car, blowing holes in the passenger window and windshield.

But just as she lifted her Sig to change the clip, Braden popped up and fired a barrage as Marta dove back behind her car. She skittered around the rear of the Mercedes and rolled into a prone firing position, taking aim at the space under Braden's car. But he wasn't there. She saw his shoulder duck around the corner of a building and then saw another head come out from behind that same corner. Another shooter appeared.

Just then, Preacher came flying around the corner and spotted the guy. The shooter was busy taking aim at Marta and didn't look up until the microsecond before Lance's stolen car hit the curb, took to the air and literally imbedded the man into the wall. It was going to take a crowbar to pry some of the guy's parts from the bricks.

Lance looked to the right and saw Braden duck into a building and another armed man step out of the door. Looks like they had tracked the rabbit to its hole. Pretty darn exciting stuff. He put the car in reverse and backed away from the seriously crushed dude in the wall. He spun the wheel and shot over toward Marta who was getting back into her car. He drove past her and nodded a smile. She smiled back. She was glorious; a glorious destructive, murderous wonder. He shook his head and looked in the back seat. His passenger with ruined knees started to stir.

He found an alley a few blocks over and stuck the car in it. Marta pulled up a second later. Lance stepped out and opened back door to grab and lift the guy he'd captured. He tossed the man onto the bricks and stepped aside. Marta was quicker at these things than him. She bent a knee into the man's chest and jammed her thumbnail into the poor fella's left eye and pried it in and up. The pain was apparently worse than the holes blown in the backs of his knees because he screamed until Marta brought a knee to his throat.

"Français?" Marta whispered.

"Oui." The poor fella uttered. Lance looked at the man's shoes. They were too fashionable. French guy.

"You are a contractor, not official. I can tell." Marta said. "You didn't plan to die today, I can tell that also. Do you want to tell me what I need to know or do you want me pull it out of you and kill off the rest?"

"No, I'll tell you."

"Good. How many men in the building?"

"Eight, maybe ten."

"Where is the cargo going after this holding location?"

"We are to hold him and await instructions, after eliminating you."

"Where did the job come from?"

"I got a call in Paris yesterday. I don't know where it came from."

"Say your name, parents' address and phone number. You are ours now. You are lucky to leave this day with your life, but your time, your heart, your soul are no longer your own. The price you pay for taking a job sometimes."

The man looked from Marta to the Black Angel and knew he had no other option. He recited the information and Lance kicked him in the head to knock him out. They stood and faced each other. Once again, they had options. They were not required to be here or to force their way into the building around the corner. She stepped to him and put her forehead to his neck. She reached her right hand down to his left and squeezed. He cringed and she brought the hand up to look at it. Three fingers were already swelling, broken.

"Car wreck." He smiled. She examined the swollen fingers.

"These three are broken."

"Yep. Ready?"

"One moment." Marta took out her phone and dialed. She kissed him while it rang. A voice answered. "All set?"

Frank Wyrick answered her question from 3,584 miles to the West. "Everyone has converged on your position. Foxy, Jordan 1 and Jordan 2 are on the south side of the structure. That was a hell of a car chase." Wyrick sat next to a satellite monitor technician in an ultra secret facility outside Silver Springs, Maryland. He was looking at a large monitor that featured live satellite imagery from a bird flying over southern Europe about 190 miles up. The picture was freakishly clear.

"Yes, it was fun. Counterparts?" Marta was cheating a little with the satellites, but she didn't have Lance's screwed up vision from on high.

"Four hostiles on the rooftop at the corners. Several more have stepped out and are fanning out your way."

"Vehicles?"

"Nothing. You took them out from what I can see. Also, there is an underground parking structure just north of the building, about 150 yards from your location. I saw a couple of vehicles take the ramp down about five minutes ago." Wyrick replied.

"Thank you."

Wyrick added. "You don't have to go in there."

"Try to stop us." Marta hung up and turned to Lance. "Now we're ready. And your friends are here."

"Foxy made it to the party?"

"And the Jordanians."

"Damn, this will be like a reunion. A bloody, messy, reunion. Just like the ones my family used to have. Huge body counts at those things."

"Before you died." She smiled.

"Buzz kill. You have to be all reality-based and remind me that I'm a ghost."

She put a finger to his lips. "Not a ghost. An angel."

Chapter 41

"So, how old were you when you were handed your list?"

Preacher and Fuchs stood next to each other at the corner of a funky visual arts school just across Avenue Dom Carlos from the building Braden was holed up inside.

Fuchs only looked at him, no response.

"Okay then, tell me this. Did you die in Vietnam?" Preacher asked his mentor. It sounded like a crazy question. But crazy just about sums up all things related to Seibel.

"Yes."

"That's what I thought. But I don't understand why I, why Lance, didn't die in Iraq. Why didn't he just do all this then?"

Fuchs looked in all directions. He was the consummate stealth operative. "First, you have to know I was opposed to all of this from the start. But my vote doesn't count. Second, I have wondered about the timing for the last year. My best guess is that he needed more time to build a case, build a wall of confusion so he could uncover his leak. Braden."

"Can you friggin' believe this? How long have you known Braden?"

"Twenty-three years. He was just a young gun, a brilliant psychologist who Seibel just happened to stumble upon."

Lance's procerus did some tugging.

"What? What is it?" Fuchs asked. He'd seen Preacher's mind working like this.

"It's him." Lance stepped away and looked up to the top of the weird triangle-shaped art institute building. "It's all him, Braden."

"All?"

"You, Marta, Me. We are all his projects, experiments. I knew it. I friggin' knew it."

"I don't follow."

"Siebel ran it all, but they weren't his ideas. He was influenced by a brilliant young rocket scientist of a psychologist and his ideas, his theories." Preacher smiled and shook his head. "He was so good, he hid in plain sight. All the time, for decades."

"I don't see it." Fuchs shook his head.

"And to top it all off, when Papa started looking for his mole and killing off ol' Lance Priest, Braden had him looking to Russia, ghosts in the KGB."

"Wait," Fuchs was catching up. "You're saying Braden is not KGB, not a KGB plant."

"That's exactly what I'm saying."

"Who then?" Fuchs leaned in to hear Lance tell his secret.

But Preacher just shook his head and raised his eyebrows a few times. "Let's go ask him."

Lisbon, Portugal is famous for many things. The Belem Tower, the Jeronimos Monastery, a world-class seaport. People come from all over the world to see the sites. Not many people came to Lisbon this morning for an epic car chase and gun battle. But a few lucky people did.

"Confirmed. No change on the rooftop. Four additional sentries just off the corners. No discernable pattern in vehicle traffic." Wyrick's report via satellite phone to Fuchs wrapped up a series of verbal reports from the members of an elite team stationed at the perimeter of a square-shaped set of buildings on Ave. 24 Julho. Fuchs relayed the information over the radio headsets Tarwanah and Jamaani brought to the party. No one knew what to expect inside the building. The information shared by the chap with ruined knees put the number at eight. But there were that many in view right now. So that was obviously wrong.

Tarwanah reported ready at the southwest corner.

Jamaani was prepared at the southeast corner.

Fuchs was on the roof of the art institute just to the east.

Marta was positioned to the northeast in her car.

Lance covered the northwest. But that darn underground parking garage just 80 meters from his current location was beckoning him. He wished it were nighttime, midnight instead of nearing midday. And he wished these damn tourists weren't around. Innocent people were going to die.

All was set. Marta's diversion would start things off. The rest would then move in. Fuchs would take out the men on the rooftop before hightailing it over to join the action.

Marta had operational control. She was just a second from issuing the go order when another voice came over their radios. It was the voice of God.

"Latest intel has noted a large vessel docked a half mile from current position with up to 30 operatives visible. This party is about to grow in size. Time is of the essence." Seibel's voice should have shocked everyone. But surprises and changes of plan and misdirection are part of the game.

"Source?" Marta replied.

"Russian satellite watching the coast." Seibel was matter of fact. Where he was at present was another matter. But he was close.

"Confirmed." Wyrick reported to Fuchs over the sat phone. "Sorry, I wasn't looking to the water. That vessel came in 30 minutes ago."

Fuchs relayed Wyrick's confirmation to the crew.

"Abort?" Marta asked the open radios, but her question was for Lance only. She couldn't give a shit about the others and hoped Seibel would meet his end within minutes.

The next words were sung not spoken. Lance sang a line from one of his favorites from the Doobie Brothers. Everyone cracked up.

Marta tamed her laughter and spoke, "Go."

Risking such valuable resources to catch a single spy was excessive. It was stupid, foolish really. But every member of this deadly little team had a reason for being here and completing this job. And almost all of it centered on loyalty. As silly as it sounds, these fools were loyal to something bigger than themselves. Bigger than their bond.

Braden was a mole. A traitor.

And he worked for someone. And that someone wanted to jeopardize the safety of America and what it stands for. This was more than hand over your heart stuff. This was core, central, pivotal. Essential.

Braden had to be caught or killed. He could not slink away into the cracks and whatever hole he came from.

Marta's go signal caused the squeezing of fingers on triggers. The running of feet across open spaces, dives and rolls and bullets and blood. The sentries positioned around the building were the first to go down. Next were the poor guys on the roofline. They were easy targets for a deadly marksman like Fuchs. He took them all out in a counter clockwise fashion with his silenced rifle.

People screamed. Tires squealed. Cars crashed.

Tarwanah reached the building first and signaled Jamaani to make the initial entry into a store that faced the ocean. They needed to enter and move quickly out the back into a central courtyard.

Marta was behind the wheel of a stolen Mercedes and proceeded to take out her sentry by spreading him across the grill of the sedan. She plowed the car onto the sidewalk and into the doorway Braden had entered an hour earlier. She was out of the vehicle and firing into the destroyed doorway in seconds. She had to trust that Fuchs would do his job and take out the guys on the rooftop so they couldn't fire down at her.

She dove into the building. The hall was clear. She rose to a knee and looked back out the ruined doorway in time to see Lance deviating from the plan and running to the down ramp of the underground parking structure.

"Honey, that's the wrong way." Marta whispered in Russian.

"Sorry my dear. Too irresistible. You've got that covered and Fuchs will be to you in 30."

"I'll be there in 20." Fuchs corrected as he ran.

Marta waited just inside the door until Fuchs stepped in. They proceeded down the hallway to an open area and then another hall. It was something of an ancient labyrinth inside.

The buildings had been constructed 250 years ago and eventually all been connected. Made a big hollow square.

They came to a stairwell and a gunman opened fire on them from above. He was up on the second floor landing occupying the higher position. He had them pinned down pretty good. But the guy had made a fatal mistake by standing beside a window facing into the inner courtyard. He didn't see the gun take aim or hear the bullet fired until it pierced the back of his neck and exploded out the front. Jamaani was a hell of a shot, especially from 60 feet.

Fuchs wanted to go up, but Marta didn't like it. She could feel the deception in the placement of shooter there. It was facade and meant to lure them up.

"We need to go down."

Her words into the open radio mic caught Lance's attention out in the subterranean parking structure. "Down. Go down," he agreed with Marta.

He was in the underground garage and moving toward the doorway of the building in which the action was taking place, but stopped and looked around. Wyrick reported that no vehicles had come out of the parking garage's exit ramp on the west side of the building in the last hour. So that meant it was likely that Braden was still inside the building. Unless.

Preacher looked in all the directions in the low-lit parking level. The entry to the structure Marta and gang were now in was just ahead. But wouldn't it be natural for other buildings on the block to have underground entrances from the garage. A quick scan answered his question. Yes. There were four other doors and hallways at the sides of the parking level. Damn.

"Guys, I'm afraid it was all for show. All those sentries were there to keep us watching the building. There are underground tunnels and connections to at least four other buildings down here. My gut tells me he took one of them."

Every member of the team knew the value of Lance's gut.

"My guess is he was waiting for us to move on the building and plans to move out now."

He heard it, the air movement, the rustle of fabric, the nearly silent exhale of breath. He only had time to move his head an inch to the left. It was enough to escape full force of the blow. But the strike did knock the radio headset from his head. He spun to the right and ducked.

When he came back up, Braden stood in front of him.

"An excellent plan, don't you think?" Braden asked with hands raised ready to attack or defend. He stepped around Lance and crushed the headset into the concrete.

"But just more of the facade." Lance replied.

"Yes. And look at it all, how it has all worked out. Here we are. Here you are."

Lance looked around again. Four men came out of four doorways he had spotted just seconds earlier. Another stepped around a pillar to stand in front of the ramp he had run down minutes earlier. "This is all for me?"

"Thank you for figuring it out. Saves me the time of explaining it. Now, we don't have much time. We need to leave. Quickly." And before he finished saying the word, Preacher was struck by three tranquilizer darts.

"Leave?" he asked after pulling two darts out of his shoulder.

"Yes, you are coming with me." Braden stepped closer. He was within four feet, emboldened by the chemical agents now coursing through Preacher's body. Braden smiled and nodded. Lance marveled again at the transformation.

He closed his eyes and shot 100,000 feet into the air and then to Moscow, then Sarajevo, then Saint Petersburg and the U.S. before settling back in Lisbon. The trip, which reviewed thousands of faces and hundreds of locations, took a whole three seconds. The Black Angel opened his eyes. "Cat and mouse and cheese all in one." Lance laughed. "The list was yours and Ludkovich and Saint Petersburg were traps set by you. They were supposed to take me there."

"Damn Lance. It took a little time, but you eventually figured everything out."

"You guys gave Seibel the list. And then you changed the names on it before handing it to me. Did you also give him the list Fuchs worked in 73?

"Yes."

"And I know who provided him the first list in 59."

Braden smiled. "Go on."

"Mama Braden."

"Excellent. They are going to love you in Moscow."

"Nope," Lance shook his head and chuckled. He also started to get dizzy. "Not Moscow."

"Don't tell me you figured it all out." Braden nearly laughed.

Lance's chuckle turned into laughter and then full belly laughs. "Almost." And then Lance stopped laughing. "Go." He hit the deck as Marta, Fuchs, Tarwanah and Jamaani fired dozens of shots, taking out the men pointing weapons at Lance from the perimeter. They had come downstairs a minute earlier and silently stepped out of two doors coming from the buildings above.

Braden hadn't moved. He stood in place, pulled out a cell phone and held it in his hand, but said nothing.

Preacher stood back up shook his head. "You've still got another card to play." Marta and Fuchs came walking up. Tarwanah and Jamaani stayed at the perimeter.

"Insurance." Braden whispered. He was shaken by the recent developments. "Others will die if this open line is hung up or if I give the word."

Lance looked to Marta and then Fuchs. "People die every day. I put a bullet through your skull and you don't issue any more orders. Game's over."

Marta stepped around to the side of Braden so she could see his face. "Your friends back in Moscow won't be able to help you after that," she said.

Braden looked at Marta and raised his eyebrows, his frontalis muscle doing the work.

"Not Moscow," Lance said. "That's how good this is. He had Seibel looking for his mole and his connections for the past year and years before in Moscow and Europe."

"Where then?" Marta asked.

"Beijing." Lance looked at Braden as he said it. Preacher had indeed figured it out.

"You're good Preacher." Braden nodded.

"China?" Marta's beautiful procerus tugged away under her beautiful skin.

"Freaky, huh?" Lance grinned. "This guy is not a 25-year double agent planted in the CIA. He is a life-long mole put in service by his mother, a 50-year mole."

"How?" It was Fuchs asking this time.

"Commitment, dedication, cunning." Lance looked from Braden to them. "I hope Seibel is hearing this."

"I am." A voice in the four remaining headsets.

"I saw it in her eyes." Lance returned his gaze to Braden. The world was spinning about him. "In that moment before she pulled the trigger and ended her career as a deep-cover mole."

Braden's head tilted minutely. "What did you see?"

"I saw what I've been feeling around you, in your presence for years. I can only say that I saw her foreign, her Asian, sensibility. I saw someone else underneath her skin."

"Like I said, you're good."

"And in the last two days, Wyrick has been doing research into travel and passports and CIA employment and other interrelated patterns." Lance pulled a cell phone out of his pocket. "I've got an open line as well."

He raised the phone and spoke into it, "How many again Frank?"

"Four." Wyrick replied from 3,500 miles away.

"Four so far. Wyrick found and authorities have taken into custody four Chinese operatives. Deep, deep-cover operatives." Lance took a step forward. "I hope your friends can hear that. Like I said, game's up." He turned to Marta. "Did that son of bitch hear that? I did what he asked."

"I heard." Seibel's disembodied voice replied in the other team member's ears.

"Be sure to tell him I'm done." Lance shook his head a little as he spoke.

"We're both done." Marta added.

"Very good." Braden had seen and heard enough. "Shall I say the words and end lives here and in Tulsa and Boise and Buffalo? Or should I walk out of here now and we continue this conversation another time?"

Lance turned to Fuchs. "Boise. I knew it was either Idaho or Montana." He turned to Marta. "I told you, didn't I?"

Marta smiled and walked right past Braden until she stood in front of Lance. "Yes. You nailed it. What do I owe you again?" And she kissed him. She raised up on her toes and kissed her living angel. Braden and danger and whatever chaos lay ahead in the next few minutes melted away. She didn't care, literally didn't care in the least about Braden and what he'd done and the mishmash of strange forces that intermingled to bring them all here to this parking garage in Lisbon.

She pulled away from their kiss. Lance didn't like that. "No lies now, how long have you known that I was alive?" She asked.

He snuck one more kiss from her lips before answering. "I just learned for certain from Wyrick three nights ago."

"But?"

"But, he told me two weeks ago."

"He?" She asked.

"Lance told him," Braden butted into their lover's chat. She turned to Braden and he continued. "Evidently, Lance came to him when he was in the Neva River in Saint Petersburg two weeks ago."

She turned back to Preacher. "In the Neva? On a boat?" She looked cross.

"No. In a car, an SUV really." He raised his eyebrows.

"Underwater?"

Fuchs butted in this time. "Craziest damn thing those people had ever seen. He evidently started out on foot, took out a seven-man KGB hit squad and then led a car chase that wrapped around the entire city before he took a plunge into the Neva." Fuchs was shaking his head. Tarwanah and Jamaani, standing to the sides, couldn't help but chuckle at the story.

Braden even got in on the action. He couldn't keep from laughing at the ridiculousness of the tale. More than 3,500 miles to the east, Wyrick sat there watching his monitor with tears in his eyes from the story. "Crazy son of a..." he whispered to the satellite tech sitting beside him.

"Jesus," Seibel muttered from somewhere.

The only one not laughing at the story was Marta. "So what did he say?"

"Who, Lance?" Preacher wiped the smile off his face and answered.

"Yes. Lance. What did your ghost say to you when you were underwater in the friggin' Neva River?" Marta was insistent. Her tone silenced everyone else's laughter.

"It was cold and dark down there. The vehicle was rolling, cartwheeling along, bouncing on the bottom and all of the sudden Lance appeared. He had been staying away because of... you. He told me to close my eyes and just look. He showed me a picture and then it started moving.

"It was you, and then Braden was at your door and he handed you a package and newspaper. You set them on the table and then stepped outside. I wanted to follow you. This was a great vision he was showing me. It was the clearest image I'd had of you in a year, but Lance wouldn't go. He made me stay in the house and look down at the newspaper, the date on the paper."

"Two weeks ago." Marta whispered.

"Yes." He smiled at her.

She turned to Braden. "You brought me a packet of cases to read and evaluate. You also brought me the newspaper that day."

"I did." Braden looked from Marta to Lance and then the others. "Is he here now? Is he looking at us, watching us now?" Braden looked back to Preacher.

But Preacher was gone. The Black Angel had taken his place.

"Yes. He's right over there looking down on you and your lies. It's your sternocleidomastoideus muscle on the right side of your neck connecting your skull to your sternum. That's your lie tick. It gives you away."

"How so?"

Black Angel squeezed Marta's hand and stepped forward to within two feet of Braden. "That beautiful little muscle, the prettiest in the human body, gives you away Stu." He closed his eyes. "I am looking at a dozen scenes right now from my eyes and from Lance's above. In each, I can see the muscle tensing, jittering ever so slightly. For instance, I can see you sitting next to that bed I was strapped to after New York. It was doing fine, but just before you started telling me the horrible news about Marta, it started quivering unsteadily."

He stepped even closer, just a foot separated he and Braden. The psychologist brought the phone up between the two of them. "I only need to hang up and innocent people die."

Black Angel snatched the phone from his hand and brought it to his ear. He didn't know much Mandarin Chinese, but enough to get the job done. "Your secret is no secret anymore. Good luck, good-bye." He pressed the button and severed the line.

"Your sternocleidomastoideus Stu. There are no teams in Tulsa, Boise and Buffalo. You're not going to kill mine or Fuchs' or Marta's families. It was a weak bluff; not your game. Your deception lies in building a facade over years. You are not a good spontaneous liar."

Braden's gig was up, but there was still that smile on his face. Wyrick, from across an ocean was the first one to see why. But, unfortunately, what he was seeing had about a seven-second delay from earth to space and back to the monitor he was watching.

"Three vehicles moving rapidly toward your location..." By the time his words came through Preacher's cell phone, the lead vehicle was already barreling down the parking garage ramp.

Preacher knew he shouldn't glance that way because of the smile on Braden's face. That sideways glance was all the deep-cover mole needed to pull a knife and slash Preacher's throat. Stuart Braden was fast. Preacher made a mistake coming so close. He made it easy.

But there are a few universal laws on planet Earth. Gravity, rising and falling tides, night following day, following night. But included on this list of unshakable universal truths is a little cause and effect gem known to a few unfortunate humans as the "don't pull a knife on Lance Priest" rule.

Evidently, Stuart Braden didn't know this law.

In the split-second before the roaring engines of three SUVs burst into the underground parking garage, Black Angel moved his upper body to the right maybe three-quarters of an inch. This motion caused the razor-sharp blade in Braden's right hand to slice through Preacher's gorgeous sternocleidomastoideus, but not deeper into a somewhat vital little vessel referred to by medical professionals as the carotid artery. Preacher knew that the carotid artery lying under skin and muscle on the left side of his neck supplied his deadly, dangerous brain with oxygenated blood. But no time for anatomy lessons.

Cause and effect. Universal law.

Preacher is as lightning fast as any human. And it was more than likely a year of doing heroin that kept the tranquilizer chemicals from subduing him a few minutes earlier.

As the blade sliced through muscle in his neck and a black SUV shot toward him, Preacher applied pressure to the ball of his right foot, threw his right arm and hand upward, pointed his middle and forefinger and surgically jammed said fingers into Stuart Braden's left eye socket. He closed the fingers around the round object inside and put pressure on the ball of his left foot to throw his body and Stuart Braden's left eyeball down and backward in the microsecond before the left front bumper of the black SUV struck him.

He continued to roll away to the left, glancing to see Marta diving just ahead of him. After the lead SUV, came a second and third. They went in three different directions. Automatic weapons blasted from open windows in each vehicle. Chaos.

He and Marta continued their rolling and skidding behind two vehicles parked close by. The SUVs came to screeching halts and in between hundreds of bullets fired, the screaming of a certain psychologist could be heard. Preacher tossed the gooey round thing in his hand to the ground and nodded to Marta. They rose up enough to fire their weapons in unison into two of the three vehicles. They could see that Tarwanah and Jamaani were doing the same from the other side of the garage.

In the next second, the lead SUV peeled its tires and shot back up the ramp with Braden inside. The second vehicle did the same. Lance and Marta adjusted their aim and put several bullets into the spinning tires. They exploded, but the vehicle still made it up the ramp and back to street level. The third didn't make it.

The driver had made a mistake by not hitting Fuchs. The lethal operative, had simply hopped behind a pillar and then stepped back out and blasted the driver, passenger and poor guys in the back seat. Four dead.

As the sound of revving engines and squealing tires faded and the echoes of gunshots ended, the team gathered at the third vehicle and saw the same thing. The dead men inside were Asian. Best guess, Chinese.

"The driver and rear shooter in the first vehicle were Asian." Preacher said.

"Those in the second vehicle were Chinese as well." Tarwanah added.

They looked at each other as Marta ripped her shirt and applied it to Lance's neck. "We need to evac now."

Lance felt a sensation he hadn't in two weeks. It was like the sweet aroma and spreading pleasure he only found in a needle or a burning rock. This was something different. Good old-fashioned blood loss. And like his demon heroin, Marta was with him. Only, that Marta didn't cuss and scream and issue order after order. But his Marta was just as beautiful, even more so. Because his Marta was here. She was real.

Fade to black. *Catch your breath.*

Chapter 42

This was an honest to god spy caper. It was a triple-layer cake like his grandma used to bake. But instead of flour and butter and sugar and a hidden layer of German chocolate frosting, this one had Lance dead, Marta dead, the Russian mob, the KGB, deception, the list, more deception and a deep, deep, deep Chinese mole. Dang.

Lance was fine with all of it. It was part of this screwy holdover Cold War. But what he didn't care for, couldn't understand, was the ability of a person to create a life, with a loving wife and children, and just leave it behind.

"No mission is worth that," he whispered. "No country."

"Some dedication has no limit." Marta answered and caressed his forehead. He was with her ghost again. Her spirit fingers ran through his hair. He needed nothing more than this. It could all go away.

"If I could have kept my grip; I had him..."

The light slap to his left cheek, followed by a not so gentle poke in his chest was not the caress of an angel. At least the ghost didn't smack him in the neck, where a serious bandage covered a serious wound. He opened his eyes and smiled. She was with him, hovering beside the hospital bed.

"Stop that," he said.

Another slap.

"Hey."

"He forced your hand. Hell Lance, your hand is broken."

That was not the gentle, soothing, nurturing voice of his angel. He squinted. The light was too bright in here. He focused on his ghost Marta. She smiled and everything was okay. And then his eyes drifted to the rest of it.

Everything was okay, except for the bandages and the I.V. and complete lack of heroin in his system and the pain in his neck and broken fingers on his left hand and the trembling in his right pinky finger and the light of day burning through the open blinds and the bruising around ghost Marta's right eye and the shaking now starting in his right shoulder and the muted television up on the wall with news anchors smiling and the words on screen in Portuguese and the full-body quaking now rifling through his body and...

She took his hand. His ghost angel took and held his right hand and raised it up to her lips and kissed it. The violent shaking and searing, aching, relentless pain eased.

She spoke in Russian, "I love you."

He could only see her eyes and the lovely wrinkles created at the corners of her eyes by the constriction of the orbicularis oculi muscles under her lovely skin. She was real.

But then she turned her face away, to the door. "Don't go." He whispered.

A woman entered and smiled, stuck a needle into his I.V. line and the shaking was subdued to a general tremble.

Marta leaned in close and he breathed her in. But instead of bliss, he felt anger, betrayal. Not with her, with Braden. He smiled at that.

Getting angry with Braden for being duplicitous was like getting pissed at the devil for being evil. He moved his head. His neck, with its deep three-inch gash now stitched up, screamed. But it just felt too good placing his forehead against her cheek. There was warmth.

He drifted.

Seibel was waiting for him. Although they'd never officially met in person, each knew the other's face like that of a spouse. Nearly four decades of competing with each other does that. Smelinski walked into the mountaintop cafe and stomped his boots to loosen the snow. He spotted Seibel and walked over.

The Russian intelligence legend sat down across the small table from the now deposed CIA living legend. They didn't speak. The innkeeper, a paunchy man with a long beard walked over and placed a cup of coffee in front of Smelinski. His tablemate had evidently already ordered for him. The man refilled Seibel's cup and left.

"Black, like you prefer." Seibel smiled.

"Yes. Thank you." Smelinski took a small sip and then a swallow.

"Have you been here before?" Seibel asked.

"Once. In 1981, I believe it was," Smelinski was warm enough now to take his coat off and put it over the fourth chair at the table. Seibel's lay over the other one.

"Thanks for coming, for meeting me." Seibel took a swig of his black coffee. Neither man needed cream or sugar. Each had served in the Army, where coffee black was mandatory. Tea was taken the same way by Smelinski.

"My pleasure. I was pleased to receive the invitation. So much change taking place. So much uncertainty nowadays."

"Indeed. Change is the only constant. Makes one long for the days when the lines were much cleaner. You were bad. I was good." Seibel smirked.

"Something like that." The Russian smiled back. "I suppose we should get right to the point of this meeting."

Seibel sat forward and leaned in. "Agreed. I could cloak it in phrases and codes, but I think I'll just be direct."

"Please."

"What year did you receive your first list?" Seibel brought his cup of coffee to his lips in both hands.

Smelinski was expecting a great many things from this conversation with his nemesis – his former nemesis. But any mention of the list was forbidden by the simple instructions. Smelinski had shared his knowledge of the lists with two other humans. Seibel could only know about them if he was behind them; something Smelinski had always suspected.

"I understand your hesitation Gregor. And I certainly understand that you have always suspected I planted them with you to rid myself and my country of turncoats, double agents." Seibel put the empty cup down. "But you will have to believe me when I tell you I am not behind the lists. I was given my first list in 1959 in Moscow."

Smelinski was not prepared for this. Of all the topics to discuss, the ultra-secret lists that had been supplied to him over the years were not on his radar. Not even close.

"I received the second one in 1972. And the third list was left in my coat pocket in Amsterdam two years ago." Seibel's openness and honesty was disarming.

"The first came in 1960. The second showed up in 1971. And the third was on a bedside table one morning when I woke up in Prague three years ago." Smelinski matched Seibel's honesty with his own.

"Where do you think they came from?"

Smelinski finished the coffee in his cup. "From you."

"Not me. Not from America."

"Who then?"

The cafe owner came back with the coffee pot and refilled their cups. Seibel thanked him with a nod.

"I learned the source three weeks ago. I understand you received an unexpected phone call about the same time."

Smelinski knew that Marta would come up during the meeting. "I did. Most unexpected, but then again, not. She has always been so full of surprises."

"Yes, I know." They smiled in mutual admiration. "She was partially responsible for uncovering the source."

"Which is amazing, since she was dead." Smelinski's eyebrows rose.

"I assumed you had heard that. I wonder, did you believe it for a moment?"

"Not a moment. This little planet we are on would have fallen out of orbit or skipped a few spins if she was no longer among the living."

"Interesting observation." Seibel felt the same to an extent. "You have likely heard the very recent news that I have been somewhat discredited."

"I heard."

"A longtime associate turned out to be a mole."

"I heard that as well. But what I can't understand is for whom did this mole dig so deeply into your operations?"

"My assumption three years ago when bits and pieces started emerging was that the mole was yours." Seibel replied.

"I certainly have resources in CIA operations, as do you in the FSB. But, unfortunately I cannot lay claim to this one. Sorry."

"I know. That is what I learned three weeks ago." Seibel waited.

"Go ahead. Please tell me." Smelinski didn't want to wait.

"Would you humor me by at least taking a guess?"

Smelinski did not play games well, but was willing to grant a small request to his longtime enemy. "I would have to assume it to be a mutual counterpart. So Germany makes the most sense."

"I agree. That makes the most sense. France, Italy, even England were on my radar. But alas, they were not even close."

"Please, tell me."

"It is your neighbors to the east."

Smelinski's procerus muscle crunched up his eyebrows. He was genuinely surprised by the news. "You are certain?"

"Positive."

"I'm sorry, was the mole, this psychologist Braden, of Asian ethnicity? I've not seen a photo of him."

"No, not at all. Fair haired, blue eyes. All-American type."

Smelinski was still processing. "And how long do you think he was working for the Chinese?"

"All along. More than 23 years in the CIA."

"You believe he was working for them when he started? So long?"

"Is it so different than those we have placed in each other's operations?" Seibel shook his head as he said this.

Smelinski shook his head as well. "No, no I guess it isn't. Sleeper agents, a necessary expense."

"Yes, but here's the best part. He was not planted in our operations by the Chinese when he was 25 or in the U.S. when he was a teenager. He was born into this world as a spy. His mother was the plant. She was the original mole."

Smelinski rubbed his chin. If this was true, it was diabolical and ingenious. "The mother? You are sure?"

"As far as we can tell, but I am not actively involved in the investigation because of my connection to the culprit." Seibel sat back in his chair and looked out the window at the beautiful snow falling outside.

"Your authorities have the mother though, correct?" Smelinski implored.

"No, we don't have her. She swallowed a bullet right in front of Marta."

Smelinski sat back as well. The interesting session and outcome he was expecting from this first-ever direct meeting with Seibel had been turned on its head. But he knew what had to be done. "We need to start looking in Russia for mothers and their children as well. We are undoubtedly in the same situation as you. We were invaded decades ago and didn't even know a secret Cold War had been declared."

Seibel turned back from the window. "They are winning this war."

The two icons of espionage sat in silence for a few minutes. The innkeeper refilled their cups. Smelinski was the first to speak. "I had one other item I wanted to discuss with you."

"I know," Seibel took a sip of his coffee.

"Prizrak, that killer you sent."

"Yes. I knew you'd want to talk about him." Seibel nodded.

"He was your third Black Angel."

"Yes."

"He was amazing. Did you know he sat right in front of me? Talked with me?"

"Yes. I heard that." Seibel replied.

"He killed everyone else in that room. And then he killed several brutal murderers in a prison courtyard. That young man is possibly the most efficient asset I have ever encountered or even heard of."

"He is that, and much more. He will change the world before he is done."

Smelinski smiled as he asked the question. "I have to know, why didn't he kill me?"

Seibel crossed his damaged leg painfully and leaned in close. "Gregor, I can only assume that he didn't kill you because he wants to give that pleasure to Marta."

Subcommittees are everywhere on Capitol Hill. In the U.S. Senate, one particular subcommittee is more elite than others. This particular body, a sub-unit of the powerful Select Committee on Intelligence, oversees funding for the Special Activities Division of the Central Intelligence Agency. And SAD means black ops.

The current chair of the subcommittee had listened for 39 minutes to report after report from a CIA mid-level manager tasked with obtaining funding for covert operations. This was the super secret of super secret stuff coordinated by CIA spooks. The subcommittee leader, a senator from a western state, who loved nothing more than getting back to his ranch and riding his horses across open land, had heard enough.

"Sir, this is I believe the third time you have come before this subcommittee with these issues. Each time, we have listened openly and been receptive to the concerns of our operatives in the field. But once again I, and the other two members of this committee, have grave concerns about where this is leading."

The Senator looked to his fellow Senators to the left and right and received affirmative nods. "Our position, and the position of the U.S. Senate and therefore the funding authority for intelligence operations, has not changed. We will not authorize any, and I do mean any, covert activity within Mainland China that could negatively impact our carefully cultivated, and extremely delicate relationships with business interests in that country.

"Listen very clearly. We will not get involved in operations that could lead to the Chinese government taking measures to restrict commerce with U.S. business interests. Am I making myself clear sir?"

The CIA representative closed a file folder and nodded. "Yes Senator. Crystal clear." He understood. Let nothing get in the way of trade and commerce and cheap labor and profits.

The teacher addressed his students with casual informality. The standard American sarcasm was evident in his morning greeting. Glad to be here, but not really.

The assembled students, with a variety of hair and eye colors, were your standard Caucasian bunch. There was not much ethnic mix in this classroom. Just one black student. It was your average suburban school setting. An environment in which many, many young Americans grow up.

The topic of today's session was U.S. history. Your basic boring. But the students were enthralled. The instructor was into this stuff. He worked in stories, personal recollections, humor and several anecdotes. The students listened, laughed when appropriate and asked questions when prompted. No one was rude. No one stepped out of line.

There were several reasons for the well-behaved nature of those in this classroom. The students came from good, stable homes. The community was dedicated to high achievement and excellence. And honor was much more than a personal trait; it pervaded every aspect of every student's life.

Oh, and there was the fact that this classroom was not in a suburban American community. It was not even in America. If one were to stand on top of the building or even shoot up miles into the sky above the structure, the only country you would see for thousands of miles in each direction was China.

"So, did Abraham Lincoln know how important, how historic, his Gettysburg Address would be for future generations?" The teacher asked. Several hands popped up. He nodded at a girl near the back on the left.

"I believe President Lincoln knew his speech would be recorded and shared throughout the mainland," the girl, a petite thing with blue eyes and freckles answered.

"Very good Annette. But please remember, in America, they don't refer to the contiguous 48 states as the mainland unless one is from Hawaii or Alaska. It is just 'the land' or the country." He smiled and spoke in a very encouraging tone.

His students enjoyed his lessons and found it easy to speak with their teacher before and after school. He was a pleasant, friendly fellow, even with that patch over his left eye.

The man of Middle Eastern descent stepped off the plane and walked up the jetway to the main concourse of the Mactan-Cebu International Airport in Cebu City, Philippines. He walked casually out of the facility and disappeared into the congested metropolitan area.

He left a present behind on the plane, a gift for Allah.

He had boarded Philippine Airlines Flight 43 in Manila hours earlier. The plane was bound for Narita Airport in Tokyo. It didn't quite make it. The bomb, stashed underneath seat 26K of the Boeing 747, exploded when the plane was over Okinawa, Japan. The passenger in the seat, a Japanese businessman, was killed instantly.

Despite a hole blown in the cabin floor, the pilots maintained control of the plane and made an emergency landing. As far as terrorist bombs go, it appeared to be a failure. Only one killed.

But Ramzi Yousef was quite pleased with the results. He was certain that Anwar, his teacher in the ways of the bomb, would have been satisfied with the operation.

The bombing proved his methods were sound. He moved forward with his plans. The first phase involved killing the Pope during his visit to the Philippines in early 1995. Phase two required significantly more detail as he and other true believers placed much more powerful bombs on a dozen airliners bound for the United States.

The Great Satan would feel Allah's wrath and pay dearly for their support of Israel and other infidel regimes.

Epilogue

"Retirement" wasn't the right word. One can't just retire from working at 27, or 30.

But retirement worked better than "resignation" or "separation" or just plain "quit." And that's just what he'd done, just what they had done together. Lance and Marta quit. They left spying behind.

One look at the body of work of these two supremely gifted individuals and it becomes evident that some people are never truly released from duty. Ever.

But, extended vacations and leaves of absence are granted. And in the case of these two, no one wanted to be the one to call upon them anytime soon. With Geoffrey Seibel gone, their privacy was respected. They were dead, after all.

Days drifted into weeks and then months after they returned to their mountain retreat purchased two years earlier by a wad of cash Marta carried around. Lance tried a beard. It was patchy and wimpy and the source of a good many jokes by Marta. She tried her hand at gardening and was ecstatic when her tiny garden produced its first tomato.

The lost year apart faded. They had each other every night, and more importantly, every morning. They found themselves touching all the time. Whether a hand within a hand during a walk beside the stream or a foot flat against his calf under the covers on a chilly night or the back of a couple of fingers caressing an arm sitting beside each other in front of a fire. Touching was a constant.

Another was exercise. They were each the equivalent of Italian sports cars that require excessive speed, excessive output. They climbed, jogged and ran up and down mountainsides. The result of months of physical activity was two humans in seriously dangerous shape. They didn't talk shop around the cabin. But between breaths on their hikes and runs, they discussed business; unfinished business and a world that would stay away for the time being, but not forever.

Because of this uncertain future with danger the only thing guaranteed, they incorporated practice into their workouts. One day featured ju jitsu. The next focused on firing weapons at moving targets while running. The following day allowed them to hone their skills at tracking one another across rough terrain. To say they were scary and dangerous was the proverbial understatement. Deadly was the only moniker that fit. And each found the other's lethal skills a complete turn on.

The only downtime was the week it took Lance to recover from the surgery to have the semi-permanent black contacts removed. Marta was thrilled to have his hazel eyes back.

Time around the cabin was often spent speaking other languages. Their conversations would start in Russian, progress to German, Arabic, Turkish and French. But a good part of many days was spent listening to "how to learn Mandarin Chinese" tapes and reciting back the words and phrases. After some time, they carried on conversations over days on end in

Chinese. Lance couldn't help but crack up at his beautiful Marta making some of the sounds the language required. He would purposely lead her to recite these phrases and try like hell not to laugh. Funny stuff.

Also in the category of understatements was the word *love*.

It was simply inadequate.

Lance's feelings for her had moved into universal law classification. She was an addiction that made heroin seem a joke. To Marta, her Lance was nothing less than gravity. Famous loves have been cherished throughout history. The great and timeless affairs detailed by classic novelists were cool and a little quaint. This thing, this love, was something else, something more.

It was the wind in the pines. The sun on the meadow. The snow falling, blanketing all.

Each knew this was dangerous. This thing between them had already been used against them. It changed the playing field, the purpose and meaning of life. Lance and Marta were no longer citizens of the United States or even the world. They belonged to their own nation, their own world, a separate universe. Deep? Yes.

But how else to describe it? Anyone, everyone they knew or had ever met would use this against them. No doubts, no question.

So what to do?

Play it safe? Stay close, keep things under complete control? Never let a guard down for a fraction of a moment? Nope.

Humans have to pee. Marta chose to urinate this particular time behind the trunk of a blue spruce pine tree just 200 yards or so from the summit of their favorite mountaintop. Lance waited for her up at the top looking down on a pristine valley below, with millions of snow-covered pines. She stepped out from behind the tree and slowly, very slowly, walked up the hill toward him. She was holding something in her hand and looking at it intently as she progressed.

It took her almost five minutes to reach him. When she did, her face was completely blank. No detectable emotion present. She had practiced this exercise with him many times. She learned that relaxing and tensing different muscles in her face and neck brought on the blank slate. She even learned the names of the facial muscles in Chinese.

She stood there emotionless, her hands behind her back. A blank slate for him to try to decipher.

Lance smiled at her. He looked her up and down and admired her for the umpteenth time today and the four-billionth time since he first saw her. "Ready?" He asked.

"Ready." She replied in monotone.

"I'll say, no."

She remained a blank slate. "Negative?"

"Yes. Negative."

She switched to Russian, her most comfortable tongue. "You are such a wonderful liar."

He answered her in Russian, "It's who I am."

"And that's why I love you." She replied and took the final step to him. She rested her forehead on his shoulder. "Congratulations sir. Your many, many skills will serve you well as a father."

He grabbed her and hugged her and lifted and spun her there on that mountaintop. He picked her up into his arms and cradled her tight. They were not playing it safe. They were doing the complete opposite.

She lifted her head from his shoulder and he kissed her.

"Congratulations to you, Mrs. Angel," he whispered.

ABOUT THE AUTHOR

So, here is where you read interesting information about Christopher Metcalf. The basics – he's married to the beautiful Diana. They have five incredibly bright and good-looking kids. Most of the family lives in Oklahoma. You can learn more about the author or contact Chris by visiting his website: www.christophermetcalf.com.

Chris really appreciates your time and hopes you enjoyed reading *The Perfect Angel*. If you haven't read it, *The Perfect Candidate* is the first book in the Lance Priest series. *The Perfect Weapon* was the second installment. The fourth book in the series – *The Perfect Union* – will be published in 2013. Envision a demented romance novel.

I've been asked – "why heroin?" I wanted to change Lance, to make him see the world differently; to take away his natural advantages. Lance turned it into something else. He does that.

Heroin drug facts courtesy the National Institute on Drug Abuse: www.drugabuse.gov/publications/drugfacts/heroin.

THE PERFECT UNION

COMING SOON

Wind gusts shook snow from the branches of tall pines. The hunter stopped and watched the wind, its direction and pattern. It swirled in a counter-clockwise or sometimes a backwards-spinning wheel pattern when it rolled into this valley from over the ridge. The wind also caressed and spread branches below intermittently.

Like a stop-frame moving collage, pine trees populating the valley swayed and shimmied. And as they did, they provided brief microseconds during which an experienced hunter and tracker can see almost the entire way to the valley floor. It required controlling heaving lungs, steadying spent arms and legs and total concentration through a mounted scope.

The killer lay prone on a blanket of fine powder to compress the mixture and create a firm bed from which to spy the terrain and any noticeable movement below. This exercise was designed more to seek and find than to kill. The fleeting half-moment during which prey can sometimes be spotted did not provide an avenue for the perfect shot. But this method can confirm a hunter's intuition. And sometimes one gets lucky.

A curling breeze blew through, lifting branches, sifting a fine mist of snow onto branches below. Slowly, gently, the killer panned the rifle from right to left. The scope mounted atop the rifle magnified the sloping hill and the trees and...

The blow was like a hammer dropping from a shelf overhead. It did not kill, but it hurt like hello and goodnight. Damn.

The killer was correct. The prey was indeed on the hillside below. But sometimes in life and death, the advantage is not found at higher ground. The dead killer adjusted his aim and brought the scope a little further to the left until he spotted his killer on the hillside below.

She was smiling. And he was happy once again that he was dead.

He brought his gloved hand up to the hat on his head and wiped it. It was covered in yellow goo. Because it was in the 20s today, the paintball was almost frozen. That made it heavier as it traveled through the air and when it struck his head.

Of course Marta had to hit him on the noggin. No matter how many times they played this game, she hated being the prey. He looked again into the scope and watched the love and light and reason for his life get up from her excellent position beside the base of a tall pine. She expertly capped her paintball rifle, slipped the strap over her shoulder and slung the weapon onto her back as she began her ascent. Smiling all the way.

The Lance of old might have been a total jerk at this particular moment and put a messy little paint goo spot on one of her knees. He hated to lose.

But alas, losing to Marta was just part of the equation. He learned in the moments and minutes and years after their strange introduction in Baghdad just as bombs started falling from the sky as Dessert Storm started, that she was simply better than him. She had more talent, more skill. She was even more ruthless, more heartless when it came to dispatching others.

But just as she possessed greater skills than he in the ways of killing, she also possessed greater reserves of love. She might rave about his unique, unmatched talents at lying and seeing the details others miss, but it was all really just love. She made him love. Forced Lance to feel. Obligated him to be a human being.

"I'm sorry about your hat, baby." Marta raised her eyebrows as she called up to him.

He noticed she didn't say she was sorry about his head.

"That's okay hon. It's just laundry. But truth be told," and it wasn't often told by Lance Priest, CIA killer, spy, liar. "I kinda like the yellow splotch. Looks like a cool logo."

Marta Sidorova, former-deep cover CIA/KGB super agent, reached her prey. He took her bare hand and pulled her close. Their frozen lips found heat when they met.